# YOU DRIVE ME *crazy*

USA Today bestselling author
## JULIANA STONE

# PROLOGUE
## Thanksgiving Week

It was a true fact the moment Arlene Moody pressed her foot against the gas pedal of her beat-up Chevy Malibu and sped out of the grocery store parking lot, she set in motion a series of events that would forever change the lives of two people. The two people in question, Wyatt Blackwell and Regan Thorne, weren't exactly friends.

Case in point.

On that day, less than forty-eight hours after a Thanksgiving meal that had led to a near-perfect turkey coma, Regan had done everything in her power to avoid running into hometown hero Wyatt. She knew he was being presented an award and that the ceremony was to take place downtown. With that in mind, she'd purposefully taken the long way to the hospital and avoided any chance of running into the one man in Crystal Lake she disliked more than any other. She'd even managed, however briefly, not to think about him. Not even in passing. It was her day off, and her only plan was to catch up on paperwork. She would hole up in her office for the afternoon before heading home under the cover of darkness to curl up with her three-legged dog, Bella, and watch *Love Actually*.

Not exactly an exciting night for a woman of twenty-nine, but with limited options in a town the size of Crystal Lake, it was all she had.

Of course, this was before Arlene had tossed an extra-large carton of eggs onto the passenger seat and driven off humming an old Hank William's song. As she'd sung along to "Jambalaya" and approached the main intersection downtown, she'd taken the corner a little too fast, and the eggs had gone flying. Instinctively, she'd reached for them, but unfortunately, as Arlene tried to rescue her eggs, she'd taken her eyes off the road and plowed into the back end of Wyatt Blackwell's truck.

Less than twenty minutes later, both Arlene and Wyatt were taken to the hospital. They'd both protested, heartily, according to several witnesses, but the EMT who'd attended the scene insisted.

As Regan put up her feet and read over notes from a case she was working on, she got paged to cover Dr. McEachern's shift in the ER. He'd just assessed two patients involved in a traffic accident but had been called up to Maternity because his young wife of three years had been admitted four weeks early and was about to give birth to their first child.

Regan tossed her notes aside, picked up her tablet, and headed down to the ER. It was the moment both Regan's and Wyatt's lives changed. Ironically, neither one of them knew it at the time or sensed what was coming.

But for these particular individuals, that was probably a good thing.

# CHAPTER ONE

He heard her voice before he saw her—low and raspy, with a hint of softness that curved around her words like warm water. It was a voice that belonged in the dark, riding the waves of late-night radio—not here under the harsh glare of the ER lights. Wyatt shoved his cell phone back into his jeans and listened intently. There was something familiar about the voice, and he frowned from his perch on the gurney, chewing on his lower lip as he tried to place it.

He didn't realize he was holding his breath until the curtain was drawn back and he glanced up with a start.

"We'll have you out of here in no time, Wyatt. I'm just waiting for the doctor to sign off on your release."

The nurse, Lisa Booker, bustled into the small area as if she owned the place, sporting a big smile that crinkled the corners of her soft brown eyes. Her platinum hair shone, a loose ponytail swaying as she moved toward him. Wyatt had known the woman all his life, and while surprised she was still working, he'd been happy to see a familiar face.

"Thanks, Mrs. Booker."

Her eyebrows shot up at that. "Mrs. Booker?" She shuddered. "I have been married for nearly thirty years, and when someone calls me Mrs. Booker, I look over my shoulder expecting to see my mother-in-law. Now, she was a lovely woman, God rest her soul, but we're nothing alike." She winked. "Lisa will do."

"Okay." Wyatt laughed, glad he couldn't remember that far back. "I was just trying to be polite."

"Oh, shush now. Polite is for strangers. I recall wiping your butt when you were nothing more than an imp."

That was something he didn't need to know. "How's Arlene doing?" The woman had been brought to the ER with him and was on the other side of the curtain.

"She just had a wee bit of abdominal discomfort, so the doctor has ordered her upstairs for some more tests. We just want to make sure there's no internal bleeding."

Concerned, Wyatt sat a little straighter. "Shoot. I hope it's nothing serious. She seemed okay."

"And I'm sure she will be." Lisa offered a smile. "Don't you worry about a thing." Her eyes softened. "I hear your dad is doing much better."

"He's home. So that's something." Wyatt kept his voice neutral. He hated talking about his father. Hated acting like everything was fine between them, especially when it had been bad for so long, he couldn't remember any of the good. He supposed at one time, back when his mother was still alive, there'd been memories worth remembering. But damn if he could recall them at the moment.

"The Blackwells are known for their strong constitution, and I suppose your daddy is no different."

Wyatt snuck a peek around Lisa, searching for the owner of the voice that was now a low murmur coming from the next door. But the curtain remained in place, and all he could see was a pair of black running shoes and jean-clad legs.

"You boys made quite a stir coming home for Thanksgiving. I can't remember the last time all the Blackwell men were in Crystal Lake."

"Uh-huh." Pink laces on the black running shoes brought a slight smile to his face. And was that a… The feet in question turned slightly. Damn right it was. A small pink Hello Kitty was fastened to one of the laces on each shoe. The fact that he knew what Hello Kitty was must say something. But what that something was, Wyatt didn't care to dwell on.

"And how wonderful that your brother Hudson is back to stay."

"Yeah. It's all good." *Hello Kitty*. It tugged at something inside him. Some memory he couldn't seem to shake loose.

"Nash told me that he and Rebecca are back together."

The black runners moved again, and the curtain shook a bit. "Yep. They seemed to have worked things out."

"You know my boy is back to stay as well." Lisa stepped directly in front of him, blocking his view of the black runners and Hello Kitty. "Nash bought The Coach House, and while I don't think a bar is a good investment, he seems happy, and, well, I'm just glad he's home."

If only Lisa would move a bit, maybe he could—

"Wyatt?"

"Yeah?" The curtain was fluttering big-time, and he could see that it was slowly being pulled back.

"Are you listening to me?"

"Sure am."

In truth, he had no idea what the hell Lisa was going on about. Something Nash. Something Coach House. It was all Greek to him. He was focused, eyes and ears tuned to the curtain as it was tugged all the way back. But the shoes had moved on, and Arlene offered him a wan smile from her bed as an orderly rolled her bed away.

Shit. Where'd she go?

Wyatt glanced to the end of his bed and spied the Hello Kitty runners on the other side of his curtain. He sat up straighter. *Okay.* Now he was getting somewhere. Anticipation curled in his gut as the curtain slowly moved aside.

Long legs. Denim. The kind of denim that was worn. The kind of denim that was meant for nicely rounded hips, and though he couldn't see her backside, he was going to assume her butt fit the hips. Wide brown leather belt. Black T-shirt. Willie Nelson gracing the front of said T-shirt. Not exactly what he expected a doctor to be sporting, but he wasn't complaining, because, well, damn, she filled it out the way a guy liked. His eyes moved upward.

Her head was bent, long dark hair waving over her shoulders and obscuring most of her features, save for a mouth that matched the sexy-as-hell voice to a T. Of course, it did.

"All right, Mr. Black…" The words trailed off, and Wyatt watched closely. She bit her bottom lip and was silent for a few moments, one finger trailing over the tablet in her hands.

The silence stretched on for so long that it became uncomfortable. There was weight to it. Wyatt had always been a guy to trust his instincts, and he knew something was up. He kind of had a feeling that something wasn't exactly a good thing. He frowned. What if he'd been concussed? That wouldn't be good. Not so close on the heels of his last one.

Concerned, he shot a look over to Lisa, but the nurse stood quietly, hands shoved into the pockets of her pink-and-blue scrubs, head cocked to the side in expectation as she waited for the doctor to speak.

Doctor Hello Kitty cleared her throat, and Wyatt was about to say something when her head jerked up and he was nailed by the greenest eyes he'd ever seen. Eyes that punched a hole straight through his gut.

Gold flecks. Thick dark lashes. And an expression he couldn't quite read.

Those eyes narrowed, just for a second, and then she turned to Nurse Booker. "Thanks, Lisa. I'll take it from here." Gone from her voice was the smoke and sex. This woman was all business.

Lisa answered with a smile. "Perfect timing. I'm heading for break." She winked at Wyatt. "Give my best to your father." She slid past the doc and closed the curtain behind her.

Wyatt stared at the woman who was now almost directly in front of him. Her face was averted once more, and he angled his head for a better look. She was damn familiar. That voice. Those eyes.

"You can button your shirt."

"Excuse me?" His eyebrow shot up.

She gave a curt nod but didn't make eye contact. "Your shirt. Tests are done. We don't need the peep show." She pursed her lips, eyes on her tablet, a small frown marring her forehead.

He glanced down. His shirt hung open, still undone from when the previous doctor had given a listen to his heart and lungs. His head felt a little thick, and maybe he was concussed, because he felt more than a little confused. He was definitely missing something. Doctor Hello Kitty didn't like him one bit. That kind of irritated him.

"Do I know you?" he asked, slowly buttoning his shirt, eyes on her once more.

"You've got to be kidding me." Her head whipped around, and this time there was no mistaking the dislike. It was black. Hot. Full. Her cheeks flushed, and disbelief hung between them.

And then it clicked. Nice and simple like, as if it had been there all along. For several moments, he stared at her in silence, sorting through the pictures that flooded his mind.

Prom.

Balloons. Blue, purple, and white.

Pale pink dress. Keg party.

Mud splatter along the skirt and a tear along the neckline.

Smudged makeup.

Tear tracks down her cheeks.

*"I hate you."* Her words echoed in his head. Angry. Hurt. So damned hurt that even now, they made his throat tighten uncomfortably.

His stomach turned over like a stone, heavy with guilt and a bunch of other stuff he hadn't thought about in years. She looked different. And yet the same. He was an idiot not to know who she was.

"Regan?"

Her chin lifted. "It's Doctor Thorne to you."

Shit. She wasn't going to make this easy. The girl could definitely hold a grudge. And while he'd been a dick that night, the fact it had happened over ten years ago should count for something. Hell, he wasn't a self-absorbed eighteen-year-old who only cared about himself anymore. The kind of kid who would ask a girl to prom on a dare and end up with another girl at the after-party. He was an adult, and so was Regan. Things didn't have to be like this. And though he was pretty sure some of the women in his life would dispute that claim, at the moment he decided to do what he did best. Charm his way out of a sticky situation and make her see he wasn't the same guy.

"Doctor." He offered up a killer smile, though it did nothing to penetrate the frost in her eyes. "I'm impressed."

"Are you?" She glanced back at the tablet and swiped her finger across it.

"If I remember right, you were the smartest girl in school."

"For such a smart girl, I didn't always make the right choices, now did I?" The dig was unmistakable, her tone dismissive, but Wyatt wasn't the sort to give up. Character flaw? Maybe.

"Captain of the debate team," he said, smile still in place.

She pursed her lips. "Yes."

"Student president."

She nodded but didn't look up. "That too."

"You ran the Helping Hand program."

She set the tablet down onto the table beside the bed, dislike still in her eyes. "I did." She shrugged. "I'm surprised you remember that."

*Okay.* This was encouraging. "I signed up to help out with the food drive."

"You signed up to get into Lana Larson's pants."

"True." A slow smile curved his mouth as the memories returned. "But I didn't have a chance, now did I? Not with you ordering me around like a drill sergeant. Christ, I barely had time to scratch my—"

"Let's not do this." Her mouth was firm, those green eyes of hers hard.

"Do what?" He slowly slid from the bed and stood, forcing Regan to look up at him.

"This." She gestured wildly. "Whatever it is. I'm not interested in walking down memory lane with you." She took a step back.

"Not in the least."

There was silence for a few moments as the two of them stared at each other. And curiously, Wyatt felt something stir inside him. Something wicked. His eyes fell to her mouth. To the generous curve of that sexy-as-hell bottom lip. To the pink tongue he could just see.

Suddenly, he was thinking things he had no right to think. Mainly, how would she taste if he dipped his head and kissed her?

"Regan," he said slowly. "Let's grab a coffee or something so I can apologize properly for being such an asshole on prom night."

"Coffee?" She looked surprised as hell, and that was a good thing. Meant he'd knocked her off balance.

"Yeah. Coffee."

"You actually think coffee will make things okay?"

He searched her face, saw the confusion, and he got it. She hated him and had every right to. But still, if he could make things right, then he could leave Crystal Lake without a guilty conscience. Maybe that was selfish of him, but at the moment, he was going with it.

Just then, the curtain was yanked back, and Daisy Miller, the pretty EMT who'd brought him into the emergency room, appeared. Her blonde hair was no longer slicked back into a bun but hung loose, and her wide blue eyes smiled up at him. Uniform gone, she looked at him expectantly.

"You ready?" she asked.

"Um…" Maybe he *was* concussed, because in that moment, Wyatt had no idea what Daisy was talking about.

"You're clear to go." Regan picked up the tablet from the table and took a step back. "Cognitive tests were normal, and your bloodwork is good."

"Regan." He sure as hell didn't want to leave things like this.

But he was dismissed. She nodded to Daisy and, without another word, stepped past them. Wyatt watched Regan Thorne leave the emergency room, his eyes moving over her as she pushed her way through the double doors.

The Hello Kittys attached to her running shoes lit up when she walked. They were the last things he saw. It was that one image he'd think about many times over the next few months, because, as it turned out, life was about to throw him a curveball he hadn't seen coming.

A curveball that would give Wyatt Blackwell lots of time to think.

# CHAPTER TWO
## Eight weeks later...

Winter in Michigan meant one thing—snow, and lots of it. This particular January was no different from most Regan remembered, and she shook off a bunch of the fluffy white stuff as she slammed the door behind her and tossed thick pink mittens and a bunch of mail onto the hall table. It was Friday, just past seven, and the only thing on her mind was a glass of red wine and maybe a few episodes of *The Gilmore Girls*.

She flipped on the lights and glanced around her home, feeling that same bit of satisfaction she did every single night. Open concept, the bungalow had been built to her specifications and paid for with her money. There was something to be said for being independent.

Bella came running from the bedroom, her three legs not slowing her down at all. Regan doffed her boots and shrugged out of her coat before scratching the little gray-and-white terrier behind the ears. She turned on the television and headed for her bedroom to grab the pink-and-white pajama bottoms she'd left on the floor and the large Michigan U sweatshirt that most likely lay beside it. The damn thing nearly came to her knees, but it was comfy and familiar, and to Regan, that was all that mattered.

After topping up Bella's food and water, she wandered over to her cupboards. She didn't need to look inside them to know they were mostly bare, but she did manage to find a box of Lucky Charms with just enough of the sugary goodness to fill a small bowl. After picking out the green marshmallows, she poured all that was left in her milk carton and leaned against the counter. She gazed out the window into the dark. It was snowing again, but only lightly, and as she watched, large feathery flakes floated to the ground. She'd had a full day at work, and this was the first Friday she'd had off in a month.

She eyed the answering machine that blinked at her from the tiny desk tucked away in the corner of her kitchen. No doubt there were several messages from her girlfriends or her sister-in-law, Violet, wanting her to join the real world before she became a spinster. Her forehead furrowed. Was spinster still a thing? Wasn't it acceptable in this day and age for a successful woman to live on her own without the companionship of a man?

Regan finished the Lucky Charms and tipped her head back so she could get the last bit of milk as well. Once done, she rinsed her bowl in the sink and let the silence of her home wash over her. Usually after the chaos of the hospital or her practice, she relished the quiet. But tonight…ah tonight, she thought with a sigh as she let loose the knot of hair at her nape, tonight she was restless.

Just then her cell phone rang, and she grabbed it from the counter without thinking.

"Regan. It's your mom."

Crap. Regan winced and swore under her breath.

"What was that?" Her mother's tone was sharp.

"Nothing," she managed to stammer. Dammit, she was so not in the mood. She loved her mother, *of course she loved her mother*, but she had to take a moment and collect her thoughts. Katherine Thorne was a force of nature. She loved fiercely and was a no-holds-barred kind of person. She was a smart, tenacious, sometimes overbearing (sometimes devious) in-your-face woman, so Regan needed to be on her toes.

She rubbed her temples, eyes once more on the blinking

answering machine. "Why are you calling my cell?"

"Because I knew if I called the house phone, you would let it go to the answering machine."

True. So, damn true.

"Mom. Really."

"Regan, at least have the decency to admit I'm right."

She smiled at that. "Okay. You're right."

"I know I'm right. Which is why I called your cell."

Regan rolled her eyes, glad her mother couldn't see through the phone. "So what's up?"

"Are you meeting Violet and the girls in town tonight?"

"Um…" She searched for an excuse—any excuse that would do—but she had nothing. "No?" she answered, stretching the one-syllable word into at least two.

There was a pause. "Regan. When is the last time you went out and had some fun?"

"Mom." She gazed across the large open space to her television. "Do we really have to do this now? It's been a long day."

"We'll do whatever I damn well want us to do. I'm your mother, and I'm worried about you."

Oh. God. The speech was coming. How many times had they been down this road? How many times had she listened to her mother go off on the sad state of her personal life? Lips pursed, she shook her head and briefly considered tossing her cell. But A) that was childish. And B) her mother would probably drive over. So C) she might as well get into it.

"Why?" she asked abruptly, eyes once more on the snowflakes outside her window.

"Why am I worried about you? Do you want me to recite the list? Because I can."

"No, Mom. I don't want you to recite the list." The list hadn't changed in about five years, and she could pretty much recite it word for word.

"You spend too much time alone and you should be going out with your friends tonight. I know there's a function in town and all the girls are going."

The function was a prequel to the high school reunion next weekend, and Regan had no desire whatsoever to revisit that past. At least not tonight.

"Well, maybe none of them worked sixty hours this week." Petulance rang in her voice, and even Regan made a face at how pathetic she sounded.

"Did *you* work sixty hours this week? Let's not pretend you're working at Seattle Grace."

"Seattle Grace doesn't exist, Mom."

"What?"

"Seattle Grace. It's from *Grey's Anatomy*, and it doesn't exist in the real world. Actually, it doesn't exist on the show anymore. It's called something else now."

"Don't be smart with me, Regan. You know what I mean. You work normal hours at the family practice, and you cover the odd shift at the hospital. You don't work sixty hours."

She sighed. Her mother had her there. "You're right. I think I only clocked maybe fifty."

"It's not about the hours."

"Then what's it about?" Regan snapped.

"It's about the fact that you work hard and you're successful, and I couldn't be more proud of you for everything you've accomplished. But Regan, you do nothing for fun. Nothing for yourself. When's the last time you went out on a date?"

"I don't know." Regan bit her lip and seriously reconsidered plan A and tossing her phone. "A few months ago?"

"With who?" Her mother made no effort to hide her disbelief. As it turned out, her mother had every right to be a nonbeliever.

"Look, there's no one in town who interests me." She snorted. "Actually, there's no one in town to date."

"Ethan Burke is back. He took over his father's veterinary practice."

"His voice is nasally."

"What?"

"His voice. It's high-pitched or something."

"Sean McAdams is a good-looking man. A lot of women my

age comment on his looks."

Okay. Ew. The man was a pig. "Mom, he's thirty years younger than you guys."

"Doesn't mean we don't look."

"Sean might be good-looking, but he's a meathead. All he cares about is beer and football."

"Well, sometimes a man who doesn't have a lot going on between the ears is a good thing."

"Good for what?" she asked, eyebrows raised.

"What do you think," her mother replied dryly.

"Oh God, Mom. I'm so not discussing sex with you."

"David Smith."

"David Smith?" Incredulous, Regan had to take a moment. "His skin."

"His skin?"

"It's so soft. Have you seen it? His cheeks are smoother than mine. It's like he never made it to puberty. I don't even think he can grow facial hair."

"Regan." There was that tone. The annoyed one.

"I'm serious. What woman would date a man with nicer skin than hers?"

"Jarret Cavendish."

"Nope."

"Nash Booker."

"Mom. No." She closed her eyes and prayed for an intervention.

"He's a bad boy. I thought all girls were into bad boys."

Sure. Bad boys were hot. But the thing about bad boys? It was too easy to get burned. Regan should know. She'd been burned once, and it had hurt like hell.

"Look, honey. All I'm saying is that you need to put yourself out there. Don't you want a husband and a family?"

You can do this. Count to three.

One.

Two.

Three.

"Regan?"

She exhaled. "Yes, Mom, of course I want a family. But Jesus, don't hang me out to dry just yet. There's still time."

"It's not just the dating thing. You don't live. You don't do anything for fun." Her mother went on as if she hadn't heard a thing. "I bet you came home from work with takeout."

"Nope. Wrong."

"Then you ate cereal for dinner."

Damn. Her mother was good. Regan's eyes moved to the bowl drying on the counter.

"You're wearing those ratty pink-and-white Hello Kitty pajamas that I threw in the garbage when you were sixteen, and I still can't believe you dug through everything to get them back."

"Got me there."

"The Michigan U sweatshirt?"

"Yep."

"And what do you have planned for the night?"

"A bottle of wine and Netflix." She knew she sounded defensive, but whatever. She was done with this. Time to say good night and see you at Sunday dinner.

"I don't think so."

"Excuse me?"

"Carly is on her way over, and she's not taking no for an answer."

"Carly?" Carly Davis, her oldest and best friend lived in California and had done so ever since graduation from Michigan U, when she'd taken a job for a public relations firm.

"If you checked your answering machine once in a while or your personal email, you'd know she was home. She stopped by here looking for you. Apparently, you haven't sent her your new address. She had no idea you'd bought your own place."

The doorbell rang, slicing through the silence, and Regan jumped. Guilt rolled over her because her mother was right, well, almost right. She'd been avoiding Carly's messages and emails for months now, and the crazy thing was? She had no idea why.

"Regan?"

"I have to go, Mom. Someone's at the door."

"Good. That would be Carly." *Click.*

Defeated, she stared at her cell phone for several moments, wincing when the doorbell rang out again and this time eliciting a reaction from Bella. Cheeks hot, Regan clamped down on the urge to hide. Cowardly, yes, but that was the way she was rolling tonight, and if it were anyone other than Carly, she'd do it too. She'd find a dark corner and wait it out. But it *was* Carly, and her friend would break in if she had to.

With a sigh, Regan headed for the door and yanked it open. Cold air seeped inside, and a few snowflakes rode the breeze until they landed on her face. A tall, cool, poised blonde stared back at her, with warm brown eyes and a wide smile Regan didn't deserve. A lump formed in her throat, and she had to work at it in order to speak.

"Hey," Regan said softly, feeling her heart squeeze a little as she gazed at her oldest friend. The girl who'd been there through everything.

Carly looked as put together as always. Her long blonde hair hung down her shoulders in expertly curled waves. Dressed in a brown leather jacket with fur trim, dark denim, and knee-high leather boots, the red, blue, and white scarf woven carelessly around her neck was a blast of color that created the perfect foil to her outfit.

Carly's eyes widened a bit, and she looked Regan over slowly, her gaze running from the top of her head all the way to the bottom of her toes. When her eyes finally made their way back up and met Regan's, she winked and breezed past her into the house.

"Sweetie, your mom was right. Those Hello Kittys have got to go."

# CHAPTER THREE

Wyatt sat back in the dark corner he'd claimed nearly half an hour earlier, and gazed out at the boisterous crowd. He was nursing the same beer Jarret had bought him a few minutes after they'd arrived, and for the life of him, Wyatt wondered how in hell he'd let Cavendish talk him into coming.

A scowl touched his face, and he let out a long breath as he thought longingly of the quiet cottage he'd given up to come here and hang with a bunch of people he hadn't seen in years. He was done explaining his situation. Done talking about himself. Done listening to half-baked advice from a bunch of folks who didn't know shit about NASCAR or the crash that had brought him home.

How many of them had been involved in a wreck that saw one of his colleagues die? Didn't matter that the crash wasn't Wyatt's fault. Didn't matter that he was in the wrong place at the wrong time. What mattered was that he'd been there. He'd watched a friend die and walked away with a couple of bruises and a sore collarbone.

So yeah. So he was done listening to their bullshit. He was done avoiding questions.

Screw it. He was just freaking done. Fresh anger hit Wyatt in the gut, and he pushed the beer away and got to his feet.

"Where you going?" Jarret appeared, a wide smile on his face, and with a bunch of guys Wyatt hadn't seen in at least ten years.

"I'm heading out." He nodded to the men.

"Not gonna happen." Jarret set down two jugs of beer, and Nash Booker elbowed his way through with a tray of mugs, as well as one more jug of draft. A buddy of his older brother Hudson, Nash had been one hell of a quarterback back in day and had played college ball in Texas. He wasn't the kind of guy Wyatt had ever figured to own a bar, but hey, if he was happy…

"Good to see you out, Wyatt. You staying at Hudson's place?" Nash's dark eyes were curious as they gazed at him. His brother had bought a resort up in the mountains, one Wyatt's family used to frequent when they were younger and his mother had still been alive. It had been closed for years, but the plan was to get it up and running for the summer season.

Wyatt nodded. "In one of the cottages."

"I didn't realize Hudson had started updating them."

"He hasn't." Truth was, the cottage he was holed up in needed a shit-ton of work. But hell if he'd stay with his father.

Nash held his gaze a heartbeat longer, eyes narrowed, before he took a step back. "I've got to get back behind the bar. It's crazy in here tonight with all the alumni in town for the hockey game." He flashed a smile to the other men. "You all coming back for all the shenanigans next weekend?"

"Hell yeah." Robbie Bane was half in the bag, his full head of ginger curls bobbing as he reached for the nearest mug. "Wouldn't be anywhere else."

The rest of the men piled in, each of them slapping Wyatt on the shoulder or pumping his hand in a shake. Each of them murmured some kind of condolence about the crash, and all of them wondered when he was going to get back to racing.

Wyatt was vague in his answers, mostly because he had no idea.

"You better sit your ass down," Jarret warned.

Knowing he wouldn't be able to leave without the boys making a stink, Wyatt slid back into the booth, though he shook his head when Jarret would have poured him another mug of beer. He was content to continue to nurse the still half-full one he already had and listen to the conversation.

In less than ten minutes, he learned the fate of each and every one of them. Robbie Bane, the jovial ginger, had married straight out of college, the only girl he'd ever dated, and his wife, Beth, was expecting twins. She'd stayed behind in Louisiana and sent him north for two weeks with her blessing.

"Says she needs to nest in peace," Robbie said with a shrug. "Not that I'm complaining. She's been so damn emotional lately. I can't walk or talk without her crying."

Sean McAdams had never left Crystal Lake and was currently unemployed having recently been laid off from his last job. He'd moved back in with his parents, and though it was a blow to his ego, he was enjoying the home-cooked meals and the fact that his laundry was done and folded neatly on his bed. He wasn't interested in dating, but rather preferred random hookups. According to Sean, "They're hot, man."

Then there was Calvin Andrews. The guy was a bona fide chick magnet. Always had been. His coloring was inherited from his African-American mother, while his light blue eyes were a direct gift from his Nordic father. It made for a combination the ladies seemed to love. With a big laugh and stories for every occasion, he'd been one of the guys Wyatt missed most when he'd left town. Now a marketing genius living and working in Chicago, Calvin was recently divorced and not particularly interested in a serious relationship.

Jarret was another one of those guys who'd stayed in Crystal Lake and taken over his father's business. Specializing in custom homes, the company was flourishing with all the dollars pouring into the area and the new developments across the lake. Still single, he was looking for that perfect girl but losing hope he was going to find her in this small town.

"What about you, Blackwell?"

Startled, Wyatt glanced up at Calvin. "What about me?"

"You got a lady or you still playing the field?"

The guys looked at him expectantly, and he shrugged, clearing his throat. "I'm not with anyone, if that's what you mean."

Sean elbowed him and guffawed like a damn donkey. "That's not what we mean. Buddy, you've had the opportunity to get your hands on some grade-A pussy. We want details. In particular, the goods on what's her name, the Hadley twin you've been banging?" Sean's eyes widened as he thought hard, and then a big smile spread across his face. "Marissa. Yeah. That's the one."

Wyatt shot the man a look. Pussy? Since when did grown men use words like that? Hell, he'd never spoken that way when he was a teenager, and if he had, his father would have kicked his ass all over Crystal Lake and back.

"You've been with Marissa Hadley?" Calvin looked shocked and impressed all at once.

Uncomfortable with the attention, Wyatt gave a half shrug.

"Yeah," Sean answered for him, slapping him on the back once more. "The Victoria's Secret one. Not the other one."

"Way to go, bro," Calvin murmured with a wink. "That's something."

Wyatt supposed most guys would think that. But in fact, being with Marissa was about as far from "something" as you could get. Constantly worried about her looks and waistline and carbs, the woman ate less than a bird, smoked two packs of Marlboros a day, and spent more time looking in the mirror than the evil queen in *Snow White*.

He wasn't exactly sure what they had, because other than sex (and it wasn't all that good), they didn't do much else. He'd accompanied her to some parties, and she'd shown up when he was in Daytona or at his place in Miami Beach.

Truth was, he hadn't talked to her since she'd visited him in the hospital after the crash, and Wyatt hadn't realized that fact until now. So there you have it. Not much substance.

"Hey, isn't that Carly Davis?" Jarret's head was cranked at an unnatural angle as he tried to see over the crowd.

Wyatt sat up a little straighter. Carly Davis. Now that was a blast from the past. His buddy Jarret had had a huge crush on the girl all through high school, but she'd dated Dan Hutchens right up to graduation. She'd been best friends with—

"Who's with her?" Calvin was looking now and gave a low whistle. "She looks familiar. Is that…"

"Regan Thorne." Wyatt spied her right away. They were near the bar, and she was smiling up at Nash, who leaned close to hear whatever it was she was saying. The two looked pretty damn cozy, and Wyatt's jaw tightened as he studied them. He was irritated. Now why the hell hadn't she smiled at him like that?

"Really?" Calvin shot a glance at Wyatt. "That doesn't look like the Regan I remember."

"No shit." That was from Sean. "She left for college a four-eyed geek with a little too much junk in the trunk, and came back a total babe." He sat back and shook his head. "I've been trying to get in her pants ever since she came home, but so far, no go."

Annoyed, Wyatt dragged his gaze from Regan. "Do you actually listen to the shit that comes out of your mouth? Or do you just let that thing ramble on, hoping the limited brain power you've been blessed with makes you sound half-human."

Sean just smiled and rolled his eyes. "Calm down, buddy. I'm not saying anything you guys aren't thinking. Besides, I'm don't mean anything bad by it. I'm giving the chick a compliment."

Wyatt thought back to the woman he'd encountered in the ER. Somehow, he was gonna guess she wouldn't take too kindly to Sean's compliment.

"She still live in Crystal Lake?" Calvin asked.

"Sure does," Jarret replied. "She took over Doc Hogan's practice and works at the hospital too."

"I thought of changing doctors. Wouldn't mind her hands on me." Sean was practically licking his lips.

Disgusted with the locker-room talk coming from the grown man sitting across from him, Wyatt got to his feet without another word and pushed through the crowd. He wasn't exactly sure what he was doing, but he was a guy who trusted his instincts, and at the moment, his instincts were all up in Regan Thorne's business.

Carly and Regan had cocktails in hand and were making their

way through the throng of people at the bar. They were headed in his direction, and Regan's smile froze as her gaze slammed into his. The transformation wasn't subtle in the least, and the woman made no effort to hide her dislike. A lesser man's balls might have shriveled up right then and there. Luckily, Wyatt didn't have to worry about that. His balls were just fine. He had this.

Regan's eyes narrowed.

Wyatt's smile widened.

"Wyatt Blackwell." Carly took a sip from her cocktail, tone nonchalant, though Wyatt didn't miss the look she shot at her girlfriend. "I didn't know you were back in town."

"Good to see you, Carly." He turned slightly. "Regan."

She nodded but didn't reply, though he noticed the pulse at the base of her throat. It was beating a mile a minute.

"Are you here for alumni weekend?" Carly waved at someone behind him.

"Just a coincidence. I, ah, took a few weeks off from the track."

Her expression changed. "Oh, I'm sorry, Wyatt. That accident was awful." She looked him up and down. "I hope you don't take this the wrong way, but you look really good."

Regan snorted. It was subtle, and he was pretty sure no one else caught it, but he did and frowned. He needed to get to the bottom of whatever the hell was up her butt, because the ice queen thing, though challenging, wasn't exactly the path he wanted to take.

"Regan, can I…"

"Can you what, Wyatt?" There it was. That whiskey-soaked voice he remembered.

"Well, we got off on the wrong foot in November, and it's kind of bugged me. I'd like to make it up to you."

"November?" Carly looked from Wyatt to Regan, one of her expertly shaped eyebrows arched imperiously high. "What the hell happened in November?"

"Nothing." Regan's tone was dismissive, but her eyes told an entirely different story. There was something there. And that intrigued him. "Wyatt came into the ER, and I discharged him. That's all."

Now, as a man who'd lived three decades, he'd had time to perfect his wit and charm. Born with an abundance of both, he'd honed these particular skills without much effort, and they were two weapons in his arsenal that he utilized when needed. Right now, the need was strong. He wasn't exactly sure of the why of it, but Regan Thorne had no use for him, and she sure as hell didn't like him. He got that their history wasn't exactly puppies and rainbows, but still, the fact he'd ditched her on prom night shouldn't account for her obvious dislike. There had to be another reason.

And dammit, he was going to find out what it was if it killed him.

"Why don't you ladies let me buy you another round?"

"And why would we do that?" Regan was pretty much shooting bullets at him. And maybe he should have ducked, but that wasn't exactly Wyatt's style.

"As a thank-you for taking care of me."

"I get paid to help people, Wyatt. I don't need your thanks. Anyway, I didn't lay a hand on you. Doctor McEachern did. All I did was send you on your way."

What was it about her voice? Shit. He could spend the entire night watching those pillow-soft lips wrap around whatever the hell she wanted to say.

A hand on his shoulder made him start, and he turned as Daisy Miller sidled up alongside him. "I'm going to pretend that you haven't been home for days and didn't at least send me a text message."

"Daisy." Hell. Thanksgiving. Accident. Hot tub. She'd taken him home from the ER and, well, things had gotten out of hand.

"You still have my number, right?" She slid her arm through his.

"If you're still in the mood to thank someone, buy Daisy a drink. She *is* the one who brought you in and, from the way I understand it, made sure you were good to go after your release."

Regan grabbed Carly's arm and pushed her friend past Wyatt without another word, leaving him staring at the back of her head, and yes (he was a man after all), at the soft curve of her butt.

"That was some arctic blast."

"Yes." His eyes followed Regan until she disappeared from view.

"She really doesn't like you."

"No shit."

Daisy was silent for a few moments and then extricated herself from his arm. "You know what they call her, right?"

He shook his head.

"Ice queen."

"Why?" He was curious. He didn't remember her that way.

Daisy shrugged. "She has a rep as cold as the north. Never lets anyone in. And as far as I know, she doesn't date."

"Huh."

"There's even a rumor that she's not into guys, if you know what I mean."

Somehow, that didn't jive for Wyatt, but he remained silent.

"So." Daisy smiled and then nodded toward the bar. "Drink?"

"Rain check? I'm kind of tired." His excuse was lame, and he knew it. One look at Daisy told him she did too.

Daisy took a step back and glanced in the direction Carly and Regan had gone. "You're wasting your time with Regan Thorne."

Wyatt didn't answer her, because he thought that she just might be right. And yet…

Daisy stared at him a few beats longer and then shrugged without elaborating. "Call me when it doesn't work out."

Wyatt watched Daisy melt into the crowd and felt like a shit for lying. But he wasn't into games, and leading a woman on wasn't his style. After the crash a few weeks earlier, he'd come back to Crystal Lake instead of staying in Daytona or Miami for a lot of reasons. The press alone would have driven him bat-shit crazy.

But this town wasn't exactly his favorite place either, though suddenly, things were looking up. Suddenly, he had a distraction, if you will. Something to keep his mind off the horrific images that haunted him at night and walked beside him every day.

Wyatt smiled to himself as he contemplated his next move,

because he needed to get this right.

Regan Thorne was five feet six inches of ice. He might be an arrogant son of a bitch to even think what he was thinking, but he was going to enjoy the hell out of melting it.

# CHAPTER FOUR

It had been snowing since the previous evening, and with clouds of the thick white stuff still falling outside her office window, Regan had a feeling it wasn't letting up anytime soon. She sat back and took a moment to enjoy the winter wonderland that stretched out before her. The parking lot had been plowed at least three times, but they couldn't keep up, and massive piles ringed the perimeter. The evergreens that surrounded the building were snow laden, branches heavy and hanging low, and the mountains that rose in the distance were no better. In fact, you couldn't see the top of the peak, so thick were the flakes.

A small smile touched her face as she thought back to her childhood. In many ways, small-town Michigan in the winter was straight out of a Rockwell painting. Snow forts, toboggans, and skates. Red cheeks, frozen toes, and hot chocolate by the fire. Snowball fights that lasted the afternoon and pond hockey until it was too dark to see.

Crystal Lake was an amazing place to grow up. She glanced out the window once more and giggled. If you liked snow, that was.

"Auntie Regan, when are we going to Nana's?"

She tossed her pen onto the desk and swivelled her chair around. Her brother's twins sat on the floor, Harriet with sheets of paper and crayons, Jordan with his dinosaurs. Her heart melted a little as she gazed at them, each so different from the other.

Harriet was the outgoing twin. Exuberant. Loud. Boisterous. Not to mention mischievous. She never stood still, was constantly in motion, and even now as she sat, her foot tapped impatiently on the carpeted floor. With delicate features and large expressive eyes, she was dark like her father, her long hair pulled back into a messy ponytail.

Jordan, on the other hand, was quiet. He was an observer. The kind of child who was hesitant at first, but once won over, gave his all. He wasn't into sports, instead preferred to spend his time with Lego or his beloved dinosaurs. There was something about him that tugged at Regan's heart. She had a soft spot for Jordan, most likely because she saw herself in him.

"Auntie Regan?" Jordan asked, pushing up his glasses and angling his chin to look at her. His copper hair couldn't be tamed, and he tugged on the cowlick near his forehead and tried to smooth his hair back.

"I'm not sure, pumpkin." Regan moved around her desk, a small frown darting across her face when she glanced back outside. Her brother had left Monday for business out of state, and Violet had decided to go with him. It had been last minute, so the kids had stayed with Regan, though they'd been due to go to her mother's tonight.

However, the weather wasn't cooperating. School had been canceled because of the snow. Regan wasn't so sure she'd make it out to her parents' place. They'd moved out of town the previous summer and had bought one of the new condos on the other side of the lake.

"You might have to stay with me one more night."

"Yay!" Harriet jumped up and began to dance around her brother. "And we can play with Bella and then have breakfast for supper and then we can have popcorn and maybe some sweet-and-sour candies, and watch a movie and…"

"Hold on there, Harriet-bean." Regan laughed and ruffled the top of the young girl's head. "Let's not get too far ahead of ourselves. I'll get hold of Nana and see if the roads have been plowed."

She grabbed the phone off her desk and tried her mother's number, but there was no answer. A glance at the clock told her it was nearly three in the afternoon. She hadn't seen a patient in the last hour. Most had canceled on account of the weather.

"I'll be right back."

Regan headed for the foyer and found her administrative secretary on her hands and knees behind her desk. The lounge was empty, and the doctor she shared the practice with had already called it a day.

"Everything okay, Lynn?"

The woman bumped her head and swore. "Sorry," she said with a half smile as she sank back onto her haunches and peeked over the desk at Regan. "I dropped my phone."

"Do I have any more appointments?"

"No. Everyone's rescheduled, and no one has called in over an hour."

"Okay. Let's close up. There's no point in staying, and the roads are only going to get worse." She frowned. "Are you okay to get home?"

"I'll be fine." Lynn got to her feet. A pleasant woman in her mid-fifties, she was an absolute darling who went above and beyond for Regan. "Teddy will come for me. He's only five minutes away."

"Good. I'll call you in the morning and let you know what's up. If this weather persists, we might have to remain closed until Friday."

Regan had the twins get dressed in their winter gear, and once Lynn was gone, she locked up and the three of them trudged through the snow. Her old Civic wasn't exactly ideal for this kind of weather, but the new winter tires would help.

The kids piled in while she cleaned several inches of snow from the car, and when she finally made it inside, the heat was on and Harriet was singing along to Taylor Swift. Jordan was oblivious, his nose still in his book. The kid had a thing for dinosaurs.

The roads were pretty bad, even the ones that had been plowed, and slowly she made her way across town. Crystal Lake was pretty much deserted save for the snow plow headed in the opposite direction and one truck. With dusk falling, an eerie mist hung over the small town. She shivered as she headed across the bridge and had just made it to the other side when her car hit a patch of ice. The Civic slid to the right, and when she overcorrected, the car went into a tailspin that saw them heading for a large snowbank. Hands tense, she yelled, "Hold on, twinners," and tried her best to soften the blow.

The car came to an abrupt stop, the front end half-submerged in snow, and Regan slowly exhaled. "You guys all good?"

"That was like riding a rocket ship!" Jordan peeked over his glasses, a huge grin on his face.

Heart thumping a mile a minute, she didn't exactly think it had been fun, but then again, she wasn't a five-year-old boy.

"Are we stuck?" Harriet poked her head over the seat.

"I hope not." Regan put the car in Reverse, and her heart sank as the tires did nothing but spin in the snow. She got out and had a look.

"Shit," she muttered, glancing around. She pushed her toque back and took a moment to calm her nerves. The car was sitting on sheer ice, and no way was she getting it out.

Just then, a truck pulled up behind her, and she turned with a smile, taking a few steps toward the black F-150.

Her smile slowly faded when she spied the man who stepped out of it. Seriously. She was stuck in the snow, and the only person in all of Crystal Lake to drive by was Wyatt-effing-Blackwell?

He took a few steps toward her, a lazy smile curling his bottom lip. Dressed in old, faded jeans, Kodiak boots, a blue turtleneck underneath a red-and-blue-plaid thermal button-up, the man looked sexy as hell. The black knit hat gave him a dangerous edge, and, coupled with a few days' growth of whiskers on his strong chin, she knew most women in her position would be ecstatic to have him come to the rescue.

But not Regan. No way in hell.

"You really got a thing for pink." His voice was deep and low, the words rolling off his tongue in a way that was intimate. Which was crazy. They were in the middle of a snow storm.

"Excuse me?"

He pointed to her head. "Your hat. It's pink."

"You got a thing against pink?" Okay. She sounded like a defensive bitch, but for the life of her, Regan couldn't seem to help herself where Wyatt was concerned.

"No." There was that smile again. She'd never noticed how straight his teeth were before. Like Hollywood-movie-star straight. And they were white. As white as the snow that blanketed the area for miles.

He walked toward her, slow and steady, like an animal on the prowl. Seriously? The man stood on sheer ice and by every right should be flat on his ass. What was he, part arctic cat?

She wrapped her arms around her midsection, suddenly hot and cold. Shivers rolled over her skin like waves butting the edge of the dock, and her teeth began to chatter. She was cold, yes. And kind of hot. And more than a little uncomfortable.

She could blame all that on the man in front of her.

He stopped a few inches away, and though she lowered her eyes, it didn't much matter. She'd already had a look at a mouth sculpted by the gods and bone structure fit for Hollywood. Even the scar that cut into his left eyebrow gave him an edge—made him more attractive than he already was.

Why did she feel the pull so badly? She didn't even like him.

"Regan?"

Slowly, she met his gaze. A snowflake clung to his lashes, and an unmistakable current of *something* jumped between them. His expression shifted—just for a moment—and she wondered if he felt it too.

He took another step, and she automatically stiffened. But he walked past her and hunkered down beside her car.

"You got any kitty litter in the trunk?"

"What?"

"Litter." He pointed to the tires. "Helps with traction."

She shook her head and grimaced. "No." That would have

been smart.

Wyatt straightened, that smile back on full display. "Huh." He rubbed his chin. "That's surprising."

She arched an eyebrow.

He grinned. "Well, I would have thought anyone who's such a big fan of Hello Kitty would, I don't know, maybe have a bag or two of litter in her car. Especially during a Michigan winter."

"How do you…" She fumbled over her words, confused and off-kilter. Hello Kitty was her thing. And yes, it was juvenile and her brother teased her about it, but hey, a girl had a right to cling to some eccentricities.

"I saw your shoes in the fall. The ones you wore at the hospital. It made me remember something. From senior year."

Cheeks suddenly hot, Regan cleared her throat and did what she always did when flummoxed. She changed the subject.

"I think we'll be fine, Wyatt. You can head home."

"We?" He bent to peer through the window.

"My niece and nephew."

Harriet's face was now pressed against the window, mouth open, nose flattened, her eyes huge as she stared up at Wyatt.

"These must be Adam's kids?"

"Yep." She nodded and moved closer to the car. "The twinners." She pointed to the squishy face. "That's Harriet, and her brother, Jordan, is in there somewhere."

Wyatt was silent for a few moments. "This thing isn't moving, and tow trucks are hours behind on calls. So how you getting home?"

"We can walk."

"No." He shook his head. "That's not going to happen."

Hackles up, she glared at Wyatt. "Excuse me?"

He pointed up the street. "None of the sidewalks are cleared, and it's too dangerous to walk in the road. Visibility is poor. I'll call Dominic at the garage and let him know your car is here and give you guys a lift to your place."

"I don't need you to bail me out of this situation. My house isn't far. We can walk."

His face darkened. "You'd rather walk through this crap than hitch a ride with me?"

"Yeah. I would."

"You dislike me that much." It wasn't so much a question as a statement.

"I don't think it's a secret." The retort fell from her lips before she could stop them.

They stared at each other for several more moments, Regan's heart nearly beating out of her chest. And just when she thought he might go away, Wyatt squared his shoulders and walked past her. He opened the rear door of the Civic and poked his head inside. "Hey guys, you want a ride home?"

"What are you doing?" Okay. Her voice was shrill, like, on-the-edge shrill, but he ignored her.

"We're going to Auntie Regan's," Jordan said quietly.

"Who are you?" Harriet asked, stepping outside.

"I'm Wyatt."

"That's a weird name," Harriet replied, face scrunched up as she studied the tall man in front of her.

Wyatt shrugged. "That's a first, but hey, I like your honesty."

"I have to go to the bathroom," Jordan said, inching forward on the seat.

Regan moved in front of Wyatt and fought the urge to elbow him as she did so. She peeked into the car. "Sweetie, you can go behind that snow pile. No one will see you."

Jordan's eyes got so big, she thought they'd pop. "Um, I can't. I have to go number two."

"Oh."

"Really bad."

Face tight, she was silent for a few moments.

"Regan." Did he have to say her name as if each syllable was soaked in sex? She tugged on her scarf, suddenly feeling more than a little constrained.

"I get that I'm not one of your favorite people, but maybe you can put that aside for the moment. We need to get these kids to your place before the storm gets worse. I'll call a tow truck and they'll come by when the can and return your car."

He was right. Of course, he was right. And now she felt like a complete tool. With no other choice, she nodded. "Okay. You win."

"I always do." A half smile clung to his mouth.

"Doesn't count when someone lets you."

"Does in my books."

Regan bit back a retort and chose to ignore him. "Come on, kids." She got her purse and laptop from the front seat and then ushered the twins over to Wyatt's truck. Once they were buckled in, she climbed into the passenger side. The truck was warm, but as she reached for her seat belt, she paused.

She gave him directions to her home and clasped her hands in her lap. She was tense and wired, and suddenly, another thought hit her.

"What were you doing driving around town in this weather anyway?" she asked.

"I was looking for you." He didn't miss a beat and kept his eyes on the road. Which was a good thing, because if he'd been looking in Regan's direction, he would have seen her tonsils on account of the fact her mouth hung wide open like a barn door.

"Looking for me." She was dumbfounded. "Why?"

"I want you to like me."

That was the last thing she'd expected to hear come out of his mouth. She licked her lips nervously. "Why does it matter so much to you what I think?"

He pulled into her driveway and put the truck into Park. For a few seconds, Wyatt sat with his hands on the steering wheel, and when he looked her way, his dark eyes were unreadable—gone was the lightness in his voice.

"I'm not exactly sure." His brutal honesty made her mouth go dry. He shrugged. "Could be my ego, but I think it's more than that. I want us to be friends."

"Friends." She was missing something. She could feel it.

"Yeah. Friends." He smiled then, a dazzling, curl-your-toes-and-punch-you-in-the-stomach kind of smile. "The kind of friends who invite each other inside on cold, blustery, winter days. You know, for a coffee."

Again with the smile, but she wasn't falling for it. "It's not that cold out."

"But it is blustery." He paused. "What are you afraid of?"

"Auntie Regan, I really have to go." Jordan was squirming in his seat.

Regan would have been an idiot not to acknowledge the fact that Wyatt Blackwell confused the hell out of her. On one hand, he seemed genuine. On the other? She didn't trust him. She still saw the arrogant, self-involved, man-boy who walked on clouds, while she trudged along in the trenches. And yet…

She was wavering.

*Don't do it.*

He winked. And smiled. And holy hell…she was wavering.

"I only have decaf," she said abruptly, getting out of the truck.

She didn't wait for Wyatt. She grabbed the twins and headed for the front door, totally aware of the man behind her. He hadn't lost one bit of his charisma. Not. One. Bit. In fact, his masculinity seemed more potent than ever, and his charm? He had it in spades.

She shoved her key into the door, muttering and calling herself every name she could think of. But she wasn't eighteen anymore. She was a grown-ass woman. She could do this. Coffee with Wyatt. It wasn't as if she'd invited him over for sex.

Shit. Sex? Where the hell had that thought come from?

*What am I doing?*

She was crazy. Had to be. She'd taken leave of her senses and crossed to the dark side. She would regret inviting Wyatt Blackwell into her home. She knew this. The man was a player and didn't commit to anything but racing. He scored just as many wins off the track as he did on it.

No way would her name end up on his scorecard.

She took a deep breath and opened the door, moving aside as Jordan rushed past her. She would give him a coffee and kick him out. They weren't friends. Hell, she didn't even like him.

She just had to make sure to remember that.

# CHAPTER FIVE

Not much surprised Wyatt Blackwell. The NASCAR scene alone was enough to open his eyes to a world not many of his friends knew. As one of its rising stars, he'd seen and done just about anything and everything. He'd learned early on to observe and to know each and every person's number that he crossed. Ninety percent of the folks he came into contact with wanted something from him. A win. An autograph. A night between the sheets, or a smile to sell their product.

His life was about being a winner and keeping his ass in the winner's circle. It was no secret that once you stopped crossing that finish line first, all the other stuff faded away. It was an illusion, really—none of it was real. None of it would last.

The world he lived in could destroy a weaker man. But Wyatt supposed his ability to disconnect helped his sanity. That, and the fact that up until a few weeks ago, his ass *had* been in the winner's circle.

Of course, there were those who would argue that point. Some would say he was an arrogant, narcissistic bastard who only cared about himself and winning. He didn't pay attention to any of that. He had his own reasons for doing what he did. His own demons to outrun. As far as Wyatt Blackwell was concerned, most people could think what they damn well wanted to. If someone didn't like him, so what.

Except…

Except for Regan Thorne. She was the kicker. The surprise in his otherwise orderly world.

For some reason, the fact that the woman didn't like him and made no effort to hide it, well, that got under his skin. Him. Wyatt Blackwell. The man some said had ice in his veins. The guy who had no problem taking a corner at one hundred and eighty miles an hour.

"Are you Auntie Regan's boyfriend?"

Wyatt had just doffed his boots and paused, midway between shrugging off his thermal button-up. The girl, Harriet, stared up at him with big eyes and an expectant look on her face.

"Oh my God, Harriet. No." Regan was already in the kitchen pulling out the coffee machine. Guess she was in a hurry to do the polite thing and send him on his way.

Wyatt winked at the little girl and grinned when she did a pirouette.

"Nice place," he said, walking toward the large granite island separating the kitchen from the rest of the living space. Her home was open, with high tray ceilings and lots of windows that overlooked a snow-filled yard. Tasteful décor and neutral colors, coupled with wide plank flooring, stainless steel appliances, and light gray tiles in the kitchen, gave the place an urban, modern feel. Yet as he sat his butt onto one of the chairs at the island, he saw a few things that were all Regan.

The Hello Kitty cozy over her kettle.

The Hello Kitty tea towels that hung from her sleek gas oven.

Oh, and the Hello Kitty artwork on the wall near her fireplace.

"Your house looks new."

"It is. I moved in a few months ago." Her voice was neutral. He supposed it was better than the biting tone she'd had earlier. "Jarret's family built it."

Regan grabbed two mugs from the cupboard, affording him a perfect view of her butt. She filled out a pair of jeans the way a woman was supposed to, and he took his time studying them, liking her curves and the way the small of her back dipped as she stretched to get the mugs.

Harriet pulled herself up onto the chair beside him and leaned on her elbows, looking up at him.

"You have pretty eyes."

The little girl had moxie, and Wyatt chuckled. "So do you."

"I know."

He liked this kid.

"My daddy tolded me I have the prettiest eyes ever." She giggled. "Even prettier than Mommy's."

"Your dad's a smart man."

Her lips pursed. "If you're not Auntie Regan's boyfriend, then why are you here?"

"Harriet Grace Thorne. Inappropriate." Regan frowned from across the kitchen.

"My mommy tells me that too," Harriet whispered, eyes on her aunt. "That I'm appropriate all the time."

"The word is inappropriate, Harriet. And your mother is right," Regan said dryly.

Wyatt hid a smile. "I believe it." He cleared his throat. "To answer your question, your aunt and I went to school together."

Regan placed a steaming mug in front of him, along with cream and a sugar bowl.

Jordan trotted into the kitchen with a bundle of fur on his heels. His cheeks were flushed and a lopsided smile curved his mouth. "That was a big one," he said, huffing for breath.

"Thanks for sharing." Regan rolled her eyes and shook her head, a small smile on her face. Wyatt liked it. The smiling. The way it softened her eyes. The way it drew his gaze to her mouth.

The kid climbed onto the only seat left, leaving Wyatt boxed in by the twins.

"You feeling better?" Wyatt asked, sipping his coffee.

"Oh yeah." Jordan grinned.

Regan pulled out a tray of muffins and poured each of the twins some milk. After a few protests, she managed to usher them over to the living room, and they settled in to watch a TV show.

"Your dog only has three legs." Wyatt leaned down to scratch the little dog behind her ears. "What happened?"

Regan leaned against the counter, cradling a hot mug in her hands. "No one knows for sure. Bella was found on the other side of the lake, and best we can guess, she was hit and lost her hind leg." At the sound of her name, the little dog wriggled away from him and ran to her owner. "No one wanted her." Regan scooped up the little dog and kissed the top of her head. "So I adopted her. No way could I let her be put down."

"Lucky dog. Not many folks would take on an animal with injuries."

"Honestly, I'm the lucky one. She's the sweetest little thing."

She glanced up then. Gone was the dislike. The dismissiveness. The cold arctic blast and the guarded look. Her eyes shone, their depths glimmering with a vulnerability that wasn't expected. It was gone just as quickly as it had come, but it made him wonder about all the other things she kept hidden.

As if realizing she might have revealed more than she wanted to, Regan cleared her throat and let Bella down. The little dog scampered toward the kids and settled between the two of them, angling for any crumb they let fall.

There was an awkward silence as the two adults watched the kids.

"So, how's your father doing?"

Wyatt swung his gaze back to Regan. "He's okay." With a shrug, he set his coffee down. "I guess."

"You guess?" She seemed surprised by his answer. "Haven't you talked to him?"

"We don't talk much."

"But aren't you staying with him?"

"Hell no." He shook his head. "We wouldn't last one night under the same roof. Last I heard, John and Darlene were thinking of heading to Florida for a few weeks."

She held her mug and looked at him. "They're not going."

That surprised Wyatt. "That's news to me."

"Well, your father…you know he's had health issues."

"I do, but Regan, I didn't come here to talk about John Blackwell."

She opened her mouth and then closed it. But he saw the wheels turning, and suddenly, he realized this whole thing—him coming here—was a mistake.

"Why do you call him John?"

"Why do you care?" he shot back.

"I don't. I was just trying to make conversation."

"Yeah, well, my dad is off-limits." The anger that burned just beneath the surface boiled over, and Wyatt glanced away. He had to take a few moments to get it under control. "I'm sorry. He and I…" Wyatt sighed and drained his mug. This wasn't turning out the way he thought it would. "I should go."

She didn't move to stop him, and that only added to his blackening mood. Wyatt headed for the door and shoved his feet into his boots. He grabbed up his plaid jacket, slipped it over his shoulders, and said good-bye to the twins. Both were engrossed in some show about dinosaurs, and he wasn't even sure they heard him.

"Thank you." Regan hung back a bit. "It was nice of you to give us a lift home." She shifted her feet. "I'm sorry if…" She sighed and shrugged. "I didn't know your father was a sore subject. I just assumed…"

That got his hackles up. "Assumed what?"

Her chin shot up, though she was silent for a few moments as if deciding what to say. Her wide, expressive eyes pierced him. Wyatt took a step back, uncomfortable with the notion that she could see right through him.

She tucked a dark strand of hair behind her ear—she had long, elegant fingers—and then she spoke. Her voice was soft, so damn soft…

"He talks about you boys."

"I'll bet he does." He couldn't help the sarcasm that laced his words.

"A lot."

Wyatt knew where this was headed because he knew his father's MO. "I'm sure he's told you a lot of stories. Hell, even I remember some good ones. But sometimes stories are just stories. They're vague reflections of moments in time that don't always add up. John Blackwell likes to present a certain image to the world. One of strength. Unity. Family." He shook his head. "But that wasn't our reality. In fact, it was far from it."

Regan cocked her head to the side, and he could tell she was struggling with something. He got it. His dad was a charmer. Always had been.

"A word of advice?" He didn't wait for an answer or an acknowledgment. "Don't fall for his bullshit. He's damn good at doling it out. Hell, he even got to Hudson. My brother might be willing to give him a second chance, but…"

His words trailed off as he backed up toward the door.

"But?"

Wyatt reached for the door and opened it. "I've no interest in taking up with him again."

"Then why are you back in Crystal Lake?" Regan's gaze never wavered.

Wyatt stared at Regan for so long that his shoulders tensed up, causing his collarbone to throb. It was enough time for the wind to whistle inside and bring with it a flurry of snow and ice. Pellets hit him on the cheek and galvanized him into action. He tipped his head, slid on his knit hat, and left without answering.

Dusk was settling early, brought on by the haze of snow and wind and ice. Driving conditions weren't ideal, but Wyatt never gave them a thought. He could handle the road. That was easy. It was the other stuff that was hard. The life stuff.

He couldn't relax, and his hands clenched the steering wheel as he headed out along Lakeshore Road. Regan's voice echoed in his head—her question haunting him with its simplicity. After the crash, he'd been told to take some time. Get his shit together. The driver who'd died hadn't just been a colleague, they'd been close friends.

Wyatt had never questioned his need to return home. He hadn't given it any consideration at all. Until now.

Exactly one week after graduation, he'd left Crystal Lake behind, not even bothering to glance in the rearview mirror as he did so. He hadn't been back until the previous Thanksgiving, and that had been a disaster. He couldn't be in the same room with John Blackwell without all the old hurt and resentment taking over.

As his truck headed up the mountain toward the cabin he'd claimed for the next few months, his mood was dark, his thoughts reflective. He had a place of his own in the sunshine that most folks would kill to have. Women by the boatload, if he so desired, and more than a fair share of vices to while the time away. For most men, staying in Florida would have been a no-brainer.

So why the hell *had* he decided to come to Crystal Lake?

# CHAPTER SIX

By the time Regan made it to the alumni dance on Saturday evening, it was close to eleven and she was bone tired and mentally exhausted. She'd planned on skipping the event entirely, but Carly and Violet had given her such a hard time, she decided it would be easier to show up for half an hour and leave than not to come at all.

Even so, as she gazed across crowded gym and listened to the band's epic performance of some classic Green Day song, she regretted her decision. She'd spent all afternoon with the Bergen family and their young son, Patrick. One of the first patients she'd ever cared for after taking over Doctor Hogan's practice, the eight-year-old had come to mean a lot to her. He'd been diagnosed with an aggressive form of brain cancer the previous summer and had been through surgeries, chemo, and radiation. They hadn't been able to get all of the tumor, but things had seemed hopeful.

After a routine trip to the Children's Hospital, an MRI, and several meetings with his treatment team, the Bergens had been told the tumor was growing. Patrick's road to recovery had been hijacked in the worst way possible.

And still he smiled through it all.

A knot formed in Regan's throat, and she swiped at the corner of her eye. "Let's get this over with," she muttered, standing on her toes, searching through the crowd for her sister-in-law and girlfriend.

She spotted the vibrant hue of Violet's hair across the room and slipped through the people on the dance floor, her intention to say hello to her friends, smile, and make nice for a few minutes and then leave. She was halfway there when someone grabbed her arm, and with a grimace, she turned. Sean McAdams.

He smelled like a brewery, and from the look of his dilated pupils, he'd indulged in more than just beer.

"How about a dance?" He attempted to pull her close, but she brought her hands up and thumped him in the chest, eliciting a wink and a smile for her effort. "I like a woman who plays tough to get."

"I'm not playing anything, Sean. Take your hands off me."

Realizing his strong-arm tactics were getting him nowhere, Sean let go but made no move to get out of her way. When she would have sidestepped him, he followed suit, effectively blocking her route.

"Jesus, Sean. I'm not in the mood for you tonight." The guy hit on her every chance he got. Normally, she could handle him, but tonight she didn't have the energy to pierce through his thick skull.

"Come on. Give me a chance. I know how to show a woman a good time." He slurred his words a bit, and disgust roiled in her stomach.

She glared at him and fought the urge to punch him in the throat. The guy was an idiot. He was the typical man who'd peaked in high school and never got the memo that real life required something other than cheesy lines and an attitude that would make a caveman look like Prince-freaking-Charming.

"Not happening, Sean."

"What the hell's your problem?" He took a step toward her, but Regan had nowhere to go. She was surrounded by her peers, and none of them paid the least attention to her. They were caught up in the music, the party, and good times. Seriously. It felt like she'd somehow managed to fall back in time and it was prom night all over again.

Chest tight, she gritted her teeth. Screw this yahoo. She *would* punch him in the throat and maybe kick him in the gonads if that was what it took. She actually brought up her hands and fisted them. And maybe she would have punched Sean McAdams in the throat, but Wyatt Blackwell stepped between them, and she froze.

His dark eyes looked at her in a way that made the hair stand up on her arms. And he studied her—holy hell, did he study her. The band slowed down, and an old Maroon 5 song spilled over the crowd. Its haunting melody reached out grabbed everyone, and bodies slowly melted together. Hands crept up to necks and shoulders. Sank into hair and slipped around waists.

She shouldn't have come.

She was angry. And sad. And confused. She was everything rolled up into something she couldn't name, and for a scary moment, she thought she was going to lose it. What the hell was wrong with her?

"Are you okay?" Wyatt's quiet voice managed to cut through the noise in her head, but she couldn't answer him. And dammit, those *were* tears welling up in her eyes. She shuddered and shook her head, trying like hell to dislodge the knot in her throat.

"You want to get out of here?" His question was soft, the words only for her. There wasn't anything remotely sexual in them. Nothing to beguile or persuade. There was only…concern.

A heartbeat passed. And then another.

He held out this hand, and with a small nod, she let Wyatt take hers. The two of them slipped through the crowd, and with his large, warm hand holding hers tightly, they didn't stop until they reached his truck. Once there, she climbed inside, teeth chattering, eyes closed, and she didn't say a word. Not when the truck roared to life. Or when he pulled out of the driveway. Or when they hit the open road.

She turned slightly, gaze on the full moon and the light it shed across the snow and frozen lake. Stars blanketed the night sky, a velvet canopy of diamonds, and they mesmerized her. So much so that she wasn't aware the truck had come to a stop until Wyatt cleared his voice and spoke.

"Maybe I should have said something before bringing you out here."

Blinking slowly, Regan turned and gazed out the windshield. Snow was piled up several feet on either side of the driveway, but the headlights showed it had been recently plowed, and a few feet away, a small cabin nestled against a stand of pine. In the distance, to the right, the lake spread out.

"Where are we?" she asked, sitting up straighter.

"The old Coleman resort. My brother Hudson bought it, and I'm staying in this cabin."

"Yes," she murmured. She'd heard that.

"I like it out here. It's quiet. There's nobody for miles." He fiddled with his keys, a small crease between his eyebrows. "I just thought of your dog. This is probably a bad idea."

"No." She shook her head. "No, Bella's with..." Her voice trailed off as she pictured Bella wrapped up in Patrick Bergen's arms. "She's with a friend." She was aware Wyatt watched her closely, and her heart sped up.

"I can take you home." He spoke quietly. "Just say the word."

If she was smart, she'd tell Wyatt Blackwell to take her home. But Regan wasn't feeling particularly smart tonight. In fact, she wasn't altogether sure what it was she was feeling. The tiredness in her bones—it ached. And yet there was a flair of something inside her. Some small little flame that smoldered.

"I don't want to be alone." She whispered the words, not realizing she'd spoken them aloud for several seconds. "If that's okay?" When she did, she tilted her head and met Wyatt's gaze. The moment their eyes connected was like a punch to the gut. Mouth dry, she couldn't look away.

"Totally okay." He turned off the engine, and she slid from the truck. Wyatt waited for her, and, with his hand at the small of her back, he guided her up the steps and into the cabin.

It was one large room with a stone fireplace on one end, a kitchen on the other, and a dining area in between. There were two doors at the back, one for a bathroom, the other most likely a bedroom. The furniture was worn and old, a large plaid sofa, a faux leather chair in the corner, two end tables that looked like they were on their last legs, and an area rug that looked suspiciously as if rodents had gnawed on the ends.

She turned as Wyatt headed to the kitchen area. The cupboards were chipped white with blue trim, the countertop was a rust color that was faded in several spots, and the table only had three chairs. It looked retro, from the fifties, and she wandered over, fingers trailing across the cracked laminate top.

She'd not bothered to take off her boots, but then neither had Wyatt.

"This place is cute."

He turned at her words and smiled. "It needs work. I told Hudson I'd tackle the other stuff as soon as I can, but I insisted he put in some decent appliances. They're not new, but they're twenty years younger than anything else in here." He winked. "And they work."

Wyatt opened a cupboard and reached inside. "You want some wine? I've got a stash of some good California red."

"Sure," she said slowly. "I didn't really picture you as a wine kind of guy."

"I'm full of surprises." Wyatt grabbed two glasses from the cupboard and opened a bottle of wine. He offered one of the glasses to Regan. "Here's to learning new things about each other." He took off his jacket. "You hungry?" he asked.

She began to shake her head, but then realized she was hungry. Taking a sip from the wine, she arched an eyebrow. "What do you have?"

"I made chili earlier. I'll heat it up."

Wyatt busied himself in the small kitchen, and once the chili was on the stove, he grabbed his wine and headed for the fireplace. Regan slid onto the sofa, which was decidedly comfortable, and watched as he loaded up the fireplace with kindling. It didn't take long for flames to lick over the logs. Once that was done, Wyatt headed back to the kitchen, where he promptly pulled together garlic bread with cheese and set the small table.

By the time the food was ready, Regan's stomach rumbled, embarrassingly loud.

"I don't think I've eaten since lunch," she murmured, her mouth watering as she sat at the table. Wyatt passed a bowl of grated cheese, and she topped her chili with it before reaching for a piece of bread. The food smelled amazing, and she took a spoonful.

It was a little slice of heaven in her mouth.

"This is delicious," she said. "Surprise number two. I never would have thought of you as a guy who spends a lot of time in the kitchen."

Wyatt reached for some bread. "And why's that?"

"I…" She was at a loss. "I don't know. Not many men I know cook." Heck, her brother could handle soup from the can and that was about it. As for her father? Well, the kitchen had always been her mother's domain.

"You're obviously not hanging out with the right men."

"I guess not." She laughed and finished her wine. "Who taught you to cook?"

Wyatt was silent for a few moments. "My mom loved to be in the kitchen. In that great big house, it was the one room she ruled. Dinnertime was family time, and no excuses allowed. We all had to be in our places, faces and hands clean, at five o'clock, or there would be hell to pay. At least, it was like that in the beginning."

He paused, a faraway look in his eyes. "After she died, I thought I could still feel her in that room. I mean, I knew she wasn't there, but all the things she loved were, so I hung out in the kitchen a lot." He shrugged. "Then Darlene came along, and she loved to cook as much as my mother. Maybe more." A soft smile tugged up his lips, and Regan's heart jerked.

"She put me to work, and I guess I had the knack for it."

"Well, you make a mean chili."

"This is nothing." Wyatt sat back in his chair. "Anyone can make chili."

Regan shook her head, accepting a second glass of wine. "Um, I wouldn't say that. I can handle pasta and sauce and that's about it.

Cooking is definitely not my forte."

"Maybe not, but you save lives."

Just like that, reality kicked in. *Not everyone.*

Shit. That knot was back in her throat, and the tears she thought she'd banished poked at the corners of her eyes. They were hot and sharp, and she blinked rapidly, turning her head slightly as she tried to get a hold on the rush of emotion that had come from nowhere.

"I try to," she managed to say. "It doesn't always work out that way."

Silence fell between them, and without a word, Wyatt got to his feet. He cleared the table. He put the food away and rinsed the dishes. He turned off the light and stood behind her, his heat radiating out and touching the back of her neck.

The fire was the only thing that threw light, and shadows danced along the wall, moving in rhythm to the crackling flames.

"You want to talk about it?" he asked. "Tonight? What made you sad?"

Slowly, she shook her head and whispered, "No."

"You want to sit in front of the fire?"

Again, she managed a whisper. "Yes."

She looked to the side, and his hand was there, open, palm up, waiting for her. Regan wasn't exactly sure what was happening or what she was doing, or if any of it mattered. She exhaled and slipped her hand into his.

Just like before, and yet…

Not.

They weren't at a dance surrounded by hundreds of people. They were here, in Wyatt Blackwell's cabin. Alone. With no one for miles.

She could tell herself that it didn't matter. That she didn't like Wyatt anyway, but she knew that was a lie. She didn't know what it was she felt for him, but the dislike and resentment were no longer at the top of the list.

He wasn't at all who or what she thought he'd be. And, weirdly enough, she kind of wanted to know more. But right now, in this moment, in this small dark room with the heat of the fireplace on her cheeks, all she really wanted was his arms around her.

They made their way over to the sofa, and as if reading her mind, Wyatt pulled Regan down and tucked her into his embrace. She settled back against him, aware of his body, of his strength and maleness. She felt warm and safe, and after a few seconds, she relaxed and closed her eyes. She emptied her mind and just enjoyed the feeling of being touched. Of being connected to something other than her dog or her job.

Regan didn't say a word and neither did Wyatt. By the time the fire burned itself out, they were both asleep.

# CHAPTER SEVEN

Wyatt woke with a start. The fire had long since died, and he could see his breath in the air. But he wasn't cold. In fact, with the soft warm body cuddled up against him, he was about as far from cold as he was from China.

He angled his neck and looked toward the kitchen. The glow from the clock over the stove told him it was just after three in the morning. The wind whistled, and the cabin shuddered against a ferocious push, as strong gusts rolled up from the lake. If he wasn't mistaken, the sound of ice pellets pinged against the windows.

Carefully, Wyatt slipped out from under Regan, and a quick look out the front window told him he was better off waiting until morning to take his guest home. There were definite signs of freezing rain. Until it stopped and the roads were sanded and salted, it wasn't a good idea for anyone to be out in that.

His gaze landed on Regan once more, and he crossed back to her side. She was curled into the corner of the sofa, her arms pillowing her head as she slept. Her long dark hair covered all her features except that delectable mouth, and it was open slightly as she exhaled. He was going to kiss that mouth if it was the last thing he did.

Mentally giving himself a shake, Wyatt considered his options.

He could leave her here with a blanket and pillow, but it would be freezing by morning, and that wouldn't do.

Before he could think better of it, Wyatt gently gathered her into his arms and headed to the bedroom. It was small—barely fit the queen bed and antique dresser—but he managed to get Regan into bed without waking her up. She immediately curled onto her side, and with deft fingers, he unlaced her boots and removed them. A smile touched his face, and his fingers lingered.

Pink Hello Kitty socks.

Slowly, his gaze traveled upward, and an unmistakable shot of desire rolled through him. Her hips were perfectly rounded, her ass begged for his touch, and that mouth….

"Jesus, get a grip," he muttered. He was acting like a damn fifteen-year-old kid, ogling the hot chick. He reached for the comforter and made sure she was tucked in. With one last look, Wyatt stepped out of the room and closed the door.

He wanted nothing more than to climb in beside her, but that would be more than a little presumptuous, and he sure as hell didn't want to scare her off, not when he'd made some headway into breaking through all that ice. He was pretty damn sure Regan Thorne wasn't the kind of woman who would take kindly to waking up in bed with him. He grinned.

At least, not yet.

Wyatt shed his boots and shirt and grabbed an extra quilt from the cupboard beside the bathroom. It wasn't nearly thick enough, and kind of itchy, for that matter, but it was all he had. He settled onto the sofa just as another gust of wind hit the window. He liked storms—always had—and he closed his eyes, listening to the wind and ice. A memory of his mom crawling into bed beside him as a wicked storm came up from the lake rolled through his mind.

It was bittersweet and, as always, accompanied by guilt and pain and a bunch of other shit he didn't want to deal with. With some effort, Wyatt pushed it all aside and eventually drifted off.

The next time he woke, the sun was shining, the wind had stopped howling, and a pair of soft green eyes looked down at him. Regan's hair was tousled with that just-rolled-out-of-bed look.

It was sexy as hell, and he wouldn't mind seeing more of it.

Maybe minus the clothes.

"Hey," he said sitting up, rubbing his hands across bleary eyes. He winced and swore under his breath. His neck was tight and sore, and the muscles in his back protested the lack of a mattress. His collarbone throbbed like a son of a bitch, and he had to wonder if he'd fractured the damn thing instead of bruising it.

"Good morning." Regan spoke hesitantly and shoved her hands in the back pockets of her jeans. Her pink socks stared up at him, and he couldn't help but smile.

"You really have a thing for Hello Kitty."

She followed his gaze and moved her toes. "Guilty."

He was silent for a few moments, that memory that had been digging around his brain since November now stirring.

"You have a tattoo. I remember."

"I..." Her head jerked in surprise, and she took a step back. "How do you know that?"

He slowly got to his feet, eyes not leaving hers. "It was prom, and we were dancing. A slow song..." He frowned, searching his mind.

"'Boulevard of Broken Dreams.'"

"Yes," he answered slowly, images turning in his mind. "How did you remember that?"

She gave a small shrug. "We only danced once that night."

Right. Because he'd been an asshole.

"How did you know about the tattoo?"

"Your hair was up, but long pieces hung down the side. I moved some of them aside, and I saw your tattoo behind your ear." He pointed to the right. "Your right one, if I've got things straight in my head."

Her hand rose, and she tucked a long strand of tangled hair behind that ear. "You'd be right again."

There was so much he wanted to say, and yet Wyatt knew he was on the verge of losing her. She was shutting down.

"Let me get this place heated. The bathroom is through there. I'll get some breakfast going, and if the roads are good, I can take you home after we eat."

He built the fire and then headed to the kitchen. Once the coffee was on, he grabbed eggs, cheese, green pepper, and onion from the fridge, before searching out a few potatoes from the bin. By the time Regan joined him, he had scrambled eggs on the grill, and was frying up potatoes and onion in the pan.

"Oh my gosh. Smells amazing." Regan wandered over. "Can I help?"

"Plates are to the right of the sink and mugs are beside them. Relax and get your caffeine fix. I've got this under control."

She made Wyatt a coffee and leaned against the counter, watching him as he added seasoning to the potatoes.

"You're not cold?" she asked.

"No. Why?" He glanced over and caught her checking him out. Which was when he realized he was still shirtless. "Never heard of the naked chef?" He grinned, flipping the potatoes over.

"No. Can't say that I have."

"Huh. Well, that takes cooking to an entirely different level. If you're comfortable with it, I'm more than happy to oblige."

She laughed. A straight-from-the-gut, no-holds-barred laugh. He kind of liked it.

"Oh my God, Wyatt. You haven't changed a bit. Always looking for an angle. Looking for that sure-fire way to win." She shook her head.

"When a guy wakes up with a beautiful woman in his bed, you can't blame him for trying, can you?"

Her laughter slowly died, and he glanced over to Regan. Her lips were parted, and he heard the breaths as they escaped. Each one of them caused her chest to rise and fall, and damned if he didn't sneak a peek. Those green eyes of hers darkened, and she licked her bottom lip, though she didn't take her gaze from his.

"About that," she said slowly. "I don't remember…"

Wyatt turned off the heat to both the grill and the frying pan. "I carried you."

"Oh." She pondered that for a moment. "But you slept on the sofa. Not many guys would have done that. Especially considering it's way too small for you."

"I'm not like most guys." Her focus had dropped to his chest again, and he fought the urge to pound it like an animal. "I'm taking this slow."

Her gaze jerked up to his. "This?"

Wyatt slowly nodded. "Yeah. This." He grabbed their plates from the table and began to fill them with food. "You and me."

"There isn't a you and me." Regan moved to the other side of the table and sat down.

Wyatt took his seat without a word. He'd let her have some room. Let her get used to the idea. And then he'd tell her how wrong she was.

"If you say so." He handed her a jug of OJ.

"I don't have to say so." She looked annoyed. "I know so."

"Okay." He couldn't help but smile.

She munched on her breakfast, eyes narrowed. "You're still arrogant as hell."

"Yep." He grinned and tucked in to his breakfast. "I am." He paused and arched an eyebrow. "You're still a bit of a snob. Definitely prickly and defensive."

Regan opened her mouth to reply but then shut it without a word. The two of them ate in silence for several moments, and after a time, she cleared her throat and sat back in her chair.

"I'm not prickly. Or defensive."

"Damn straight you are."

She tossed her napkin. "When have I... Give me an example."

Wyatt finished his potatoes and took his time drinking the last bit of orange juice. He was enjoying this...this back and forth. He wasn't used to women challenging every damn thing he said. The women in his life were pleasers, as in they lived to please him. They did what *he* wanted to do and agreed with whatever came out of his mouth. Hell, he was pretty sure if he told Miranda the sky was purple instead of blue, she'd agree with him if it meant him appearing with her at an event. There was no friction in his life.

Regan Thorne was friction. He was really digging the friction.

"Let's see." Wyatt watched her closely. He didn't have to think too hard. "In senior year when I signed up to volunteer for the food drive, you asked Mr. Tomlinson to disallow it."

"How did you…"

"He told me."

She pursed her lips but remained silent.

"You told him I was a meathead jock who had no business working on the food drive because my motives weren't…*pure*, I think is the term you used."

"They weren't." She was drumming her fingers along the top of the table.

"Says you."

"Says Lana Parson."

"There's a lot you don't know about me, Regan." He leaned forward. "She wasn't the only reason I volunteered for the food drive. When I came on board, you were so pissed, you treated me like trash and ordered me around like the help. Christ, you had me running in circles compared to everyone else. That last night, you had me stay and sort all the food. And there was a shit-ton of donations. No one else showed, and I found out later you'd told them all it was done. You wanted me to fail. I was there until two in the morning and had an exam the next day."

Regan grabbed her coffee mug. There wasn't anything in it, but he supposed she needed something to do with her hands. The woman didn't like losing, and he'd just called her out.

"What was your other reason?"

Wyatt pushed out his chair and got to his feet. "My mom started the food drive. It was one of her things, and each of us boys did our time." He placed his dishes in the sink. "She was my other reason. I did it for her."

"I didn't know." Her voice was small. Quiet.

"Like I said. You don't know everything about me. But don't worry about it. We were kids, right? We all did stupid stuff back then. It's part of growing up."

Regan got to her feet and joined him at the sink. He had hot soapy water ready and she dried as he washed. They worked in silence, and once the small kitchen was put back in order, he headed for his room.

"Give me five minutes, and I'll be ready to take you home."

Wyatt quickly brushed his teeth and changed his clothes. When he came back to the main room, Regan was dressed in her winter jacket and waiting quietly near the door. She followed him out into the bright sunshine. It took him a good twenty minutes to chip away at the ice on his windshield, and then they were on their way.

The roads had already been sanded and salted, so they were good to navigate, and he and Regan made small talk on the way into Crystal Lake. When they reached the community center where the alumni dance had been held the night before, her lone, ice-encrusted vehicle was at the far end. The sun was beginning to heat up a bit and melt some of the ice, but Wyatt pulled up alongside her car and overrode her protests. He got out and helped break up the ice.

When her windows were cleared and the car ready to go, she stood by the driver's side door and offered a small smile. "Thank you for…last night. I had a bad day, and it was good to get away from everything."

"No problem." He moved a little closer and shoved his hands into the front pockets of his jeans.

"Okay. Well…" Small puffs of air fell from between those lips of hers. Lips he wanted to taste. Lips he *would* taste if he was smart about things. If he was patient.

"So what time should I pick you up? And when is the best night?"

Those green eyes of hers opened wide, and he enjoyed the surprise that lit them up to a luminous shade of moss.

"Excuse me?"

He moved an inch closer, which left him with only another inch or so to go and he'd be all up in her business.

"The you-and-me thing. I want to continue that conversation." He bent forward—just a bit—and held his breath.

"Regan?" He waited for her to answer, inhaling that sweet scent that he'd noticed before. It had to be her hair. He was dying to get his hands into it.

"I don't know if that's a good idea." Her voice lowered, barely a whisper, and that sexy-as-hell rasp did all sorts of things to him. If she looked down, no way would she miss the erection he currently sported. It had been years since a woman could do this to him without even trying.

Wyatt leaned even closer, so that his mouth was nearly touching her right ear. "Why don't we try it and see? I'll pick you up Wednesday night."

"I'm at the hospital on Wednesdays."

"Okay." Wyatt took a step back. "What time Thursday?"

At first he thought she wasn't going to answer him. She reached for her car door and then paused. "*You* want to take *me* out on a date."

"Straight-up date."

"With me, the woman you think is snobby, prickly, and defensive."

"Yep. That's the one."

"Why would I do that?"

"Because I asked nicely?" He offered up the smile his mother had told him was dangerous. The smile that had seduced many a woman.

She slid inside her car and stared out the windshield for a few seconds. "I'll probably regret it."

"I'll do my best to make sure you don't."

She muttered something under her breath, but he didn't catch it. Regan started her car and, without looking at him, spoke. "I'll be ready at six."

"I'll be there." He closed her door and watched her drive away.

Wyatt whistled a tune as he headed back to his truck, a wicked grin touching his face as he headed for his brother's place.

Things were finally looking up. Date night with Regan Thorne. Hell had truly frozen over.

# CHAPTER EIGHT

"Sorry I'm late." Regan kissed her mother on the cheek and handed over a bottle of red wine.

"Carly and her parents are in the kitchen with your father." Katherine Thorne closed the door behind Regan, and Regan slipped out of her coat. It was Sunday evening, and her friend was leaving in the morning, headed back to California, so her mother had invited them for dinner.

Sunday night get-togethers were a tradition in the Thorne household, and the only excuse her mother would accept for missing it was one of the apocalyptic nature. Or, for Regan, if she was called in to the hospital.

In an era where most people led hectic lives, connected by mobile phones and other devices, it was something Regan looked forward to. Something that reminded her family was the most important thing and always should be.

"Are Violet and Adam here yet?"

Her mother nodded and led the way to the kitchen. "They're in the basement. Your father put together a new train for his track, and the kids couldn't wait to see it."

Regan's heart swelled when she spied her father. A hardworking man who'd spent his entire adult life in the lumber business, he was recently retired and spent most of his time listening to Johnny Cash and the like, and working on his model trains. In the summer, he made it out one night a week for nine holes of golf and dinner with his wife, but other than that, he was more than happy to stick close to home. He was a big man with a big heart and big hugs, and beside his love of family, God, and country, he had an obsession with plaid.

At the moment, he sported a pink-and-white plaid shirt and was deep in conversation with Carly's parents.

"Hey, you!" Carly enveloped her in a big hug and whispered, "We need to talk."

Great. The problem with small towns? Everybody's business pretty much belonged to everybody in town. Regan shouldn't be surprised that Carly already knew she'd spent the night at Wyatt's place. What she was surprised about was the fact her mother hadn't brought it up as soon as she walked in the door.

"Sure," Regan replied, pasting a bright smile on her face. "After dinner." She turned to her mother. "What do you need me to do?"

\*\*\*

By the time dinner was over and they'd cleaned up, it was nearly nine o'clock. Violet and Adam hadn't stayed for dessert—the twins were falling asleep—so once the coffee was made, the only ones digging into the strawberry shortcake were Regan and Carly. Their parents had retired to the family room, something about a show on the History Channel, and an easy silence settled between the two women.

Funny. She could go months and even years without seeing her best friend, and they could pick up as if they'd never been apart.

Carly licked her fork and set it down. "I slept with Jarret last night."

Regan froze, a hunk of shortcake perched precariously on the edge of her fork. That was not what she'd been expecting to hear.

"You what?"

Carly sighed. "I slept with him. Had sex. Did the funky monkey. The horizontal dance. The nasty—"

"Okay, I get it." Regan set down her fork. "I just… Wow. Jarret.

I didn't know you were interested in him. He's always had a thing for you—"

"He has?"

Regan looked at Carly. "Are you crazy? Of course he did. Everybody knew it."

"Well, I didn't." Carly studied her fork thoughtfully. "I thought he was a player like Wyatt."

The mention of Wyatt's name was a little too close for comfort, and Regan dove in, deciding to stick with Carly's bombshell before discussing her own. "How are you and Jarret going to work with you living in California and him living here?"

Carly snorted and shook her head. "Jesus. You've got us heading down the aisle and getting married. It was just sex."

Regan eyed her friend closely. "Was it, though?"

"Yes." Carly nodded. "Really good sex." She tossed her fork. "It was so good, I think I'm going to take him up on his offer of round two and go to his place after dinner." She frowned. "That's if you don't mind."

"No." Regan shook her head. "Why would I mind?"

Carly was watching her closely. "Because we were supposed to watch a movie or something? Hang out?"

"Don't worry about me. I'm not that girl, the one to stand in the way of her bestie practicing the horizontal dance."

Carly poked at her dessert. "It's just been so long since I've had an orgasm, you know? Like a real, hard, skin-on-skin orgasm. The blue-rabbit ones don't count."

Regan could only nod in agreement. "I can't even remember the last time I got naked with someone."

"What about that lawyer guy from the city? You dated him for a couple of months."

"Oh. Right. Colin." Regan shook her head. "That was nearly two years ago."

"Nooooo." Carly's eyes nearly popped out of her head. "Are you telling me that you haven't had sex in almost two years? Damn, girl. I thought my dry spell was bad. Four months is a walk in the park compared to you."

Her friend was right, and the thought was depressing.

"You know…" Carly carved off another hunk of cake. "You need to do something about that, or your hoo-haw just might seize up."

"My what?"

"Your hoo-haw."

Regan started to laugh. "Carly. Can we use big-girl words? It's called a vagi—"

"Nope. I like hoo-haw. Sounds cuter."

Regan made a face. "If you say so."

"Seriously, Regs. You need to do something about your situation because you're almost a virgin again."

"Yeah. I know."

"So what's the problem?"

Regan looked at Carly as if she'd lost her mind. "Problem? You *do* remember what it's like living here, right? There's no one to date."

"I call bullshit. I met a lot of new men last night. With all the folks moving to this area, the dating pool is one hundred percent better than when I lived here."

"Then why did you hook up with Jarret and not one of these new guys?"

Carly shook her head. "Um, we're not talking about me anymore. We're talking about you." Her eyes narrowed, and she pushed her plate of shortcake away. "And I'm still waiting to hear about your night. About why you left with Wyatt Blackwell."

Regan's mouth went dry, and her voice was small. "Oh. You saw that."

"Sure did."

"Who else noticed?"

"Pretty sure no one. You were there for like, five seconds." She paused. "So…Wyatt Blackwell."

Regan could only nod.

"I thought you hated him."

"I don't…exactly hate him."

Carly whistled and dropped her fork. It hit the table with a *clang* and bounced until it fell to the floor. "Are you telling me that Wyatt Blackwell has somehow managed to do the impossible and melt through all that ice that's encased your heart since, like, prom?"

"You're being dramatic."

"No." Carly shook her head. "I'm not. They don't call you the ice queen for nothing."

"The what? People actually call me that?"

"Sorry to say, but they do." Carly picked at a few crumbs on her plate. "I don't even live here anymore, and I know that. So? Are you going to spill or what?"

Annoyed, Regan grabbed their plates and tossed them into the dishwasher. "Nothing happened, if that's what you're asking."

"So he just gave you a lift home?"

"Not exactly."

"Well, what the hell does that mean?" Carly was on her feet and crossing the room until she stood beside Regan at the sink.

Regan dropped a tab into the dishwasher and turned on the machine. She knew Carly, and she knew she wouldn't be able to avoid the subject. Her best option was to just get on with it and spill. Besides, it wasn't as if she had anything to hide.

"I had a bad day at work and wasn't feeling the dance. I didn't want to be social and neither did Wyatt, so we left. We went back to the cabin he's living in for now, and had some food and then we fell asleep."

"You slept with him?" Carly squealed.

"No. God, no. It's all innocent. We fell asleep, and he made me breakfast in the morning. Brought me home, and that's all of it. There's nothing else."

Carly sighed, a dramatic sort of thing that brought a smile to Regan's face. "Well, that's too bad for your hoo-haw." She paused. "Seriously, though, I thought you hated Wyatt Blackwell. Like since fifth grade."

"Fifth grade?"

"Yes. When we were at Elise Martin's birthday party and you went into the closet with him and he told the entire class he touched your boob." Carly giggled. "I can still see how red your face was and how mad you were."

"God." Regan shuddered as the long-ago memory flashed before her. "I forgot about that."

"So did he?"

"Did he what?"

"Touch your boob?"

Regan's mouth dropped open, and then she laughed. "Of course he did, and I let him. I just didn't think he'd announce it as soon as the door opened."

"And then there was prom."

Regan met Carly's gaze. Carly was the only one who knew what had happened that night. Knew the extent of hurt and pain and humiliation Regan had suffered. Sometimes it seemed so long ago, and other times it felt as if the events of that night had only just happened.

She thought back to the night before and sighed. "I don't hate him exactly."

"So you don't have a box of voodoo dolls with Wyatt's name on it in your closet anymore?"

"Nope." Regan shook her head. "We're going on a date Thursday."

"Nooooo." Carly rolled her eyes.

"He's picking me up at six."

"So what made you change your mind about him?"

"I don't know. He asked, and I said yes." She sighed. "Maybe I'm tired of being alone. Tired of wine and Netflix. Tired of coming home from work night after night with only Bella for company." She shrugged. "Not that anything will come of this. I just…I feel something when he looks at me. At first, I thought it was dislike." She paused, a small frown on her forehead. "No it *was* dislike, but…there's something more and I…"

"Your hoo-haw is calling to him."

"My *vagina* doesn't know how to speak."

"Well, if it did, it would be telling you that you need to have sex with him." Carly grabbed Regan's hands. "You need to get down and dirty and get that hoo-haw of yours some action before it dries up and falls off."

Her girlfriend was too much, and Regan hid a smile. "My hoo-haw is just fine, thank you very much, but I was kinda sorta thinking the same thing. I don't really need to like the guy all that much to have sex with him."

"Okay." Carly nodded. "I like where you're going with this."

Emboldened at the thought, Regan plunged forward. "And he's not staying in Crystal Lake. He's only here for a little while until he heads back for NASCAR."

"Yep. You're a woman with needs. Go for it."

Regan bit her lower lip, strangely excited, mind racing at the possibilities she'd never allowed herself to think about until now.

"It would strictly be sex with no strings."

"Amen, sister." Carly raised her hands into the air. "*Hot sex* with no strings."

Carly grabbed Regan's hands and pulled her into a crushing hug. "Just promise me one thing. Be careful. Wyatt Blackwell is lethal. He's freaking sex on two legs. Got it?"

"Yes. I got it."

"The key to sex with no strings is that you have to make sure the damn strings stay unattached. The moment you get an inkling that feelings are involved, you bail. Promise me."

"You're being silly, Carly."

Her friend didn't look silly. She looked serious as hell. "Promise me."

"Carly. It's Wyatt Blackwell. There will be no strings."

Her friend arched a questioning eyebrow, which Regan ignored. Hell, at this point, she wasn't even sure if there would be sex. And if there was? Definitely no strings.

# CHAPTER NINE

A knock at the door caught Wyatt off guard. He checked his watch and frowned. It was nearly five thirty, and he had to get his ass in gear if he was to be in Crystal Lake by six. He grabbed his leather jacket from the chair where he'd tossed it days earlier, and strode from his room, making it to the front door in seconds. When he flung it open, he was surprised to find Darlene standing there.

A pretty woman, she wore a spring-green coat with a matching wool hat. Her simple boots were fur lined, and a soft smile graced her face. If not for the silver hair that hung around her shoulders in waves, she could easily get away shaving ten years off her age.

"Wyatt! I took a chance that you'd be here." Her gaze traveled the length of him, from the top of his head to the bottom of his black leather boots. "Are you going out?"

"I am, but I've got a few minutes to spare for one of my favorite ladies. Come inside." He enveloped Darlene in an affectionate hug. "Did you want something? Coffee or…"

She was shaking her head. And though she took off her hat, she didn't bother with her boots or coat. "I won't stay long."

"That sounds ominous." Wyatt kept his tone light, but inside, everything was tightening up. This had something to do with his father. It always had something to do with John.

"Well, I suppose I should get right to the point." Darlene gave him a look he was all too familiar with. She was a tiny thing—barely over five feet—and yet she managed to make Wyatt feel like he was ten again.

"You need to come home, Wyatt."

Shit. No holding back for this little lady. She was going for the jugular.

"Darlene—"

She put up her hand. "Sweetie, I don't mean to come and live with us. I know you're well beyond that scope. But you do need to see your father. You've been back in Crystal Lake for over two weeks and not once have you been by the house. Even Hudson is running out of excuses that John will listen to. Enough is enough, don't you think?"

Wyatt glanced away and took a moment. How in hell did he make Darlene understand the complicated relationship he had with John when he didn't even understand it fully? Sometimes there were no words.

"It's not that simple."

"Oh but it is." Darlene took a step closer. Her chin was lifted to that imperious angle she'd used many times when the boys were young. "It *is* that simple. He's your father, Wyatt. That has to count for something." She sighed, a painful sort of sound that tugged on his heartstrings. "I know things got…difficult for you boys after your mother passed. And I think, for you in particular, it was an especially hard road. But he's getting old, Wyatt. We almost lost him in the fall. You need to make peace with your father before something happens and you don't get the chance. Life is too short to carry around the kind of pain and anger that lives inside you. Let it go."

"Darlene." He tried to interject, but she wasn't having it. The woman was stubborn, always had been.

"No. Let me finish." She stepped toward him. "I see how you keep all your emotions bottled inside. It's not healthy. You keep everyone at arm's length. You take chances when you shouldn't and think you need to deal with life on your own. One day it's going to be too much for you to handle." She pressed her hands against his chest, and he wondered if she felt how fast his heart was beating. "All that stuff inside you, it *will* explode, and I'm so afraid for you."

"Darlene." His voice was thick, and he had to work to clear the knot in his throat. "I'm fine."

"Look, I didn't come here to start something. I don't want to upset you." Her voice was soft and cajoling. "But it's your father's birthday on Saturday. His seventieth. And we're having a get-together. Nothing big, just friends and family. It would mean the world to him if you could come."

Right. He'd forgotten about the birthday. "Darlene, I…"

"Please come."

She spoke quietly, and he knew he was done. How could he say no to her? The woman had come into his life when he'd needed someone the most. Within weeks of his mother's death, she was there, in the midst of the chaos that had been their home. In a storm that had become the norm for the Blackwell boys, she'd been the one to tame it.

She hadn't replaced their mother, but she had given them all something they needed. Unconditional love and a quiet sort of support that had sustained them when their father wasn't around.

"I'll be there. What time?"

She smiled at him and gave him a quick hug before tugging on her hat and slipping into her gloves. "Cocktails at four."

He followed her outside, inhaling a crisp shot of cold winter air. It was the kind of cold that made snow crunch beneath boots, and the crystals of ice hanging from the branches of the pine trees shimmered, illuminated by his headlights. Winter in Michigan wasn't exactly for everyone. It required a hardy soul with a love of the outdoors. A wave of nostalgia rolled over him as he climbed into his truck. He missed this place. A lot more than he thought.

By the time he reached Crystal Lake, evening had fallen and the night sky blanketed the town in a shower of stars. It was big and open and, on a night like this, pretty much perfect.

Bella greeted his knock, and he smiled to himself at the sound of her excited barks. He pressed his ear closer, opening the front door when he heard Regan shout at him to do so. The lighting was muted, and he bent down to scratch behind Bella's ears as the little dog danced around him. Considering she had only three legs, he was impressed with her agility, and laughed outright when she ran around the room and jumped at him.

"Sorry, Bella's full of beans tonight."

"It's okay." Wyatt straightened, and boom, everything inside him stopped and then sped up again. Regan stood a few feet away, her long hair in loose waves, those luminous eyes of hers sparkling in the low lights from the kitchen. She wore a silky black top, one that clung to her breasts and exposed creamy shoulders he would like nothing more to do than kiss. The top fit her like a glove and was tucked into a deep crimson skirt that, again, did nothing to hide the fact that the woman who stood in front of him was sexy as hell and sporting some serious curves.

"Regan." He had to take a moment, because the woman literally took his breath away.

"You look beautiful."

"Thank you." There it was, that soft husky voice meant for hot nights of sinning.

She smoothed the skirt, which of course brought his attention once more to perfectly rounded hips, and, as she turned to grab her coat, a mouthwatering butt. He really needed to focus.

"You might want to grab a pair of sneakers." She was wearing slim black boots that sported at least four-inch heels.

"Sneakers?" she asked, obviously surprised.

"Yeah." He nodded and smiled. "We should go, or we're going to be late."

Regan gave him a questioning look and then rummaged through her closet, grabbing—what else—a pair of black sneakers with Hello Kitty adorning the side. He took them while she pulled on a simple black wool coat. Less than five minutes later, he pulled onto the interstate.

"We're not staying in Crystal Lake?"

"Nope. I thought our first date deserved something more. Something special."

"First date. Huh. You're talking like there'll be a second."

Wyatt grinned. "And you don't think there will be?"

She shrugged, all nonchalant. "I don't know. Let's just get through tonight and see what happens. I can't promise anything until I know."

He shot her a look. "Until you know what?"

She looked straight ahead. "Until I know if you pass the test."

"What's the test exactly?"

Regan turned to him then and smiled. A full-on, no-holds-barred kind of smile that had all sorts of things popping inside him. "I'll let you know." She winked. "If you pass."

"You mean, *when* I pass."

"We'll see. The choice of footwear you requested I bring along has me a little concerned."

"Then we're golden. Because this is going to be the best date of your life."

"That's a pretty cocky prediction."

"I can be a cocky guy."

"That, Wyatt Blackwell, is an understatement."

Okay. This was flirting. This was a good thing. And maybe he should be wondering about it, considering the flirting was coming from Regan Thorne, who up until recently had been, well, thorny.

But it was the kind of flirting he hadn't enjoyed in a long time, and he liked it. Flirting was a lost art form in his world. Most of the women he met had an endgame in mind, and they bypassed flirting for straight-up sex talk. Being a red-blooded man, he'd enjoyed it at first—what guy wouldn't like to *not* have to do all that work just to get a woman into bed?

But lately he found it so damn mechanical and cold and premeditated. There was no challenge, and there was no fun in that. No getting to know someone before the sex part. But Regan? She wasn't so easy with her charms, and he was really digging that.

She fiddled with his radio until she found a station she liked—country was in her wheelhouse, it seemed—and they settled in for the ride, chatting about everything and nothing. By the time they got to the city, he'd learned a few things about Regan Thorne, and some of them surprised him.

She was allergic to dogs and took meds in order to keep Bella. She was also allergic to horses. And cats. And cows and pigs. Probably fish, if that were possible.

She'd wanted to be a veterinarian her entire life, but because of said allergies, thought it best she put her abilities to work saving humans. Which was the only reason she'd become a doctor.

She'd won the 100-meter race in fifth grade. A feat that surprised many, because Jessica Barnes could easily beat all the grade five girls—even if she started a few seconds later than the pack. Of course, it was easy to beat Jessica when she didn't show up for the race. However, the only reason she didn't show up for the race was because Regan had told her the final was scheduled for noon...an hour later than it ran.

"That's pretty damn devious and underhanded." Wyatt shook his head and navigated a turn.

"I know. I felt awful about it." She tried to hide her grin but was unsuccessful. "But I still have my red ribbon, and whenever I see it, it makes me feel good."

He liked this wicked side.

Regan volunteered at Children's Hospital in the city once a month. (Not a surprise.) She hated peas and carrots but loved brussels sprouts. (There was no accounting for taste.) She had a weakness for cheese fondue, dill-flavoured popcorn, *Seinfeld* and *The Office*. She thought Steve Carell was hot as hell, Christian Bale undoubtedly the best Batman, and that Wonder Woman could kick the whole of the Justice League's asses.

Wyatt could agree on the Wonder Woman thing. Most women he knew were fierce even if they didn't know it. He could even get behind the Batman thing. But Steve Carell? He shot her a look as they pulled into the parking lot and killed the engine. Now that, he couldn't figure out.

"What is this place?" Regan peered out at the large, cavernous building in front of them. The entire lot was empty, save for his truck and a bright red Volkswagen Beetle parked near the side entrance. Though recently plowed, the place looked abandoned.

"Jack's Place?" She turned to him, a slight frown on her face.

"It belongs to my buddy, Jack Turner. Grand opening is in a couple weeks."

"And we're here because…" Her voice trailed off, and that cute little frown was still very much in place.

Wyatt reached for the door handle. "Come with me and see."

He waited for Regan to exit his truck and, carrying her black-and-pink sneakers, followed her to the door. It was unlocked, and they let themselves in. The place was mostly in darkness, save for the neon signs that lit up a bar to their right and the pit area straight ahead. A mountain of a man appeared from nowhere, arms covered in tattoos, hair slicked back in a ponytail. He sported a full beard, a nose ring, and diamond studs in both ears. His smile was wide and inviting, and he eyed up Regan with an appreciative glance.

Jack Turner. The best damn mechanic in NASCAR. At least until his future wife made him choose life on the road or life with her. He'd chosen her and had ended up not far from Crystal Lake about a year ago.

Wyatt shook his hand and introduced him to Regan.

"Here's the keys. Lock up when you're done." Jack winked at Regan, grabbed a leather jacket from the bar, and headed for the door.

"He's leaving." Regan watched the big man go.

"He is."

"So, we're here alone."

"We are."

"With an open bar?"

Wyatt grinned. "Well, I'm driving, but help yourself."

"And is that…" She was looking toward the pit. "Bumper cars?"

"It's the only competitive vehicle I'm allowed to drive these days."

Regan turned in a full circle, a delightful, cute-as-hell grin on her face. She undid her wool coat and reached for her sneakers. "I should tell you that in my other life, I drive a go-cart like a boss."

Christ, he loved this side of her. "I believe it." Wyatt tossed his jacket and waited. She was bent over, tying up her sneakers, and, man, the view was heaven. Regan straightened slowly, as if knowing exactly where his eyes were.

"Okay, Blackwell. You've got one shot to impress the hell out of me. Grab me a drink, and let's do this."

She didn't wait for him but marched straight toward the bumper cars, leaving him standing like an idiot with his mouth hanging open, caveman knuckles pretty much dragging the floor, and a burgeoning hard-on that was going to be a son of a bitch to control.

Excitement thrummed through him, leaving him short of breath. But it was enough to get his ass moving, and just as the clock struck half-past six, Wyatt's date night with Regan kicked into high gear.

# CHAPTER TEN

Regan had shared a lot of things with Wyatt on the drive into the city, and that surprised her. The ease she felt in his company wasn't something she'd expected. Seriously. The guy must have some super-duper magic mojo hidden in his pocket or something, because she'd never told a soul about how she'd won first place in the 100-meter dash back in fifth grade. Not. A. Soul.

Not even Carly. And her best friend knew pretty much everything there was to know about her. All her deep dark secrets.

Like the fact she'd failed her driver's test *three* times. It still smarted to think about that particular humiliation. Because she *did* drive a go-cart like a boss.

She settled into her bright orange bumper car and placed her hands on the steering wheel. These were fancy machines, not like the ones she remembered from her childhood. They were plush, outfitted in leather, and turned on a dime. Rather, spun with the slightest bit of pressure.

Wyatt hopped into the only other one on the floor, a black-and-purple unit. "There's a cold beer on the table over there. You want to have a drink first?"

Regan's answer? She slammed her foot on the pedal and flew at him. He didn't have a chance to react, and she sent him spinning in the opposite direction, cursing all the way as he struggled to get control of his machine. Oh yeah. This was going to be one hell of an adventure.

\*\*\*

"Okay. That was the most fun I've had in…" Regan flopped back onto her seat, more relaxed than she'd been in ages. "In I don't know how long." She took a sip from her beer and glanced over the rim of her glass. "Years maybe."

They'd banged around in the bumper cars for well over an hour. It might have been two for all Regan knew. Not once had she glanced at her phone to check the time or messages—she'd been too busy ramming into Wyatt as often as she could. And she'd rammed him a lot, though she'd taken her fair share of hits in return.

She felt like a kid again. The kid she'd been before high school and peer pressure made her life crazy.

And now? A slow burn slithered along her skin as she pushed her plate away. Now she was ready for something else.

"My burger was amazing," she said softly. After their round of bumper cars, he'd led the way to the kitchen, where she sat and watched him prepare made-to-order burgers (she wanted peppers and guacamole, he preferred cheddar and tomato), onion rings, and homemade french fries. Not exactly the healthiest of meals, but hey, one was allowed to cheat every now and again.

"I don't want to sound arrogant or anything, but my culinary skills are legendary." Wyatt paused, his dark eyes causing all sorts of zigs and zags to explode inside her. "Among other things."

"Huh," she said. "I find it hard to believe there's more of you that can get to the kind of level your cooking does."

He smiled at that. A slow, sexy lift to a mouth that was, without a doubt, somewhere in the aforementioned legendary category.

"Do you want me to list them?" Wyatt asked.

"Do we have time?" she shot back, raising an eyebrow.

All serious like, Wyatt glanced at his watch and shook his head. "Probably not."

She laughed at that. "Oh, come on. Share a few."

"I'm not sure if you're ready for that kind of conversation." He was enjoying himself. She could see that. And holy hell, Wyatt Blackwell in this state was something to see. He'd worn a plain black button-down shirt, black jeans, and boots. His hair was longer than he normally wore it and had that messy just-got-out-of-bed look. His chin sported at least a days' worth of whiskers, and his dimples deepened as she gazed at him. For a few quiet moments, she drank him in, and that was enough.

"I promise you I am." Her words were husky, and she hoped like hell he hadn't heard the tremble she felt in her bones. She couldn't remember ever being this aware of a man.

And she didn't even like him.

Regan smiled at the thought. Sometimes she was an idiot.

"What?" he asked, leaning toward her.

"Nothing." She shook her head and shrugged. Should she be candid? Or coy. "Why did you ask me out?" Well hell, there you go. Candid it was.

"That's an easy question. There's something between us. I can feel it, and I'm pretty sure you can to. You're one hell of a woman, and I want to know you." Wyatt didn't hesitate. "Sometimes things can be that simple. Don't you think?"

Regan knew nothing was that simple where Wyatt Blackwell was concerned. At least not in her world. And yet she was willing to look past that because he'd surprised her. And that meant something. When was the last time someone had done that? Surprised her?

"Tell me something else you're good at." Regan decided coy would be easier than candid and changed the subject.

Wyatt gave her a look, and she knew he knew exactly what she'd just done. "Well, I can do one hell of a belly flop off the boathouse dock into the lake."

"That's impressive."

He nodded. "Right? I can also touch my nose with my tongue." He held his hand up. "I know what you're going to say, it's weird." He flashed a grin that kick-started those damn zigs and zags again. "But the girls always seemed to like it."

*I bet.*

Regan cleared her throat and tried to banish the images in her brain. Images of his tongue…his hands and mouth…and lots of naked flesh.

"Let me see." Wyatt sat back in the booth. "I'm pretty sure I hold the record for most time-outs in the focus chair."

Regan cracked up at that. "Oh my God. The focus chair. That was—"

"Mrs. Baird's kindergarten class. That woman must have sent me to the focus chair at least once a day. She even gave me a plaque when I"—Wyatt air quoted with his fingers—"'graduated to grade one' and wished me well. She told me I was the cutest kid she'd ever had the pleasure of teaching, but that I would have to learn charm doesn't always win the day. Hard work does."

Regan tried to keep a straight face but feared she was failing miserably. "She might have something there."

"She was wrong." Wyatt got to his feet and held out his hand.

"She was?" Regan slowly got to her feet and, after a moment's hesitation, put her hand in his. Her breaths were coming more quickly, and it would be a small miracle for Wyatt not to hear the fast-beating heart responsible for the state of her lungs.

"Totally wrong." Wyatt pulled her with him until the dim lighting over the booth they'd been sitting at faded, and they were alone in the dark. His warm breath ruffled the top of her head, and she shivered. Not because she was cold, but because she was hot as hell and suddenly throbbing in places that hadn't throbbed in ages.

*"Two years!"* Carly's voice shot through her head, and she shuddered.

"Hard work wins the day, that's true. But charm makes it a hell of a lot easier to get there." Wyatt's arms slipped around her, and he pulled her closer. Music erupted into the silence, a slow, sensual song of love and lust. She realized it came from his phone, left on the table of their booth, and when his hands settled at the small of her back, she closed her eyes and leaned into him.

"This is another thing I do real well."

"Dance?" she replied breathlessly. They'd gone this round once before, but prom night was nothing compared to the heat between them now.

His lips were by her ear, and her mouth went dry. "Among other things."

They began to move slowly, their bodies melted into each other. Her head fit just under his chin, and she rested her cheek against his shoulder, eyes squeezed shut, hyper aware that every inch of his hard body was pressed against every single part of hers.

They didn't speak, because they didn't have to. The music was haunting, a melody heavy on minor chords that brought a lump to her throat. Her chest was tight, and the want that bloomed there took her breath away. The want for human contact. The want for a connection. The want for *more*.

Wyatt's hand slid along her jaw and settled at the back of her head, his long fingers buried in her hair. Gently, he tugged until she was forced to look up at him. And it was then that all that want inside her tumbled over. It became something bigger and bolder. Something she couldn't deny. Something she didn't *want* to deny.

Regan lifted her face, and Wyatt met her halfway. He groaned—or maybe it was her—either way it didn't matter, because finally, she was getting some of what she'd been wanting for days now.

The kiss started out slow and sensual. A taste of a tongue. A nip of teeth. Hot lips searching and finding pleasure spots. Warm breath. Hard bodies. And hands that knew exactly where to caress.

It was one hell of a first kiss, and Wyatt didn't stop until her head spun. Until she was weak in the knees and her lady parts shouted for more. Until she gasped and tore her mouth from his, chest heaving, heart racing.

"What's wrong?" His voice was unsteady, and she knew he was as affected as she was.

"Nothing," she managed to say, inhaling deeply because she thought she just might faint. Imagine that. Fainting from the effects of a Wyatt Blackwell kiss.

"Good," Wyatt murmured, head dipping, mouth finding the racing pulse at the base of her neck. "Because I'm just getting started."

His tongue flicked out, and he licked her skin, a growl low in his throat that reminded her of an animal. But this thing between them had ramped up something fierce, and it felt animalistic. Primal. It was a reaction to touch and taste. To smell and, yes, sound. This attraction was stripped down to the basic need of a man and woman who desired each other. And everything about it made Regan feel wild and free.

She moved slightly, reaching for the buttons on his shirt. She was ready to throw away all her inhibitions. In this moment, she didn't give a crap about them. She'd worry about it in the morning.

Right now, she wanted Wyatt Blackwell so badly, her knees shook, and as she tore at his buttons, her fingers did as well. She had them almost all undone when his hand grasped hers and he held her still.

"Regan." She saw the desire in his face because he made no effort to hide it. He exhaled a shaky breath. "I'm not going to lie. I've been thinking about getting you naked for days now. But shit, I hadn't planned on doing it here. I just…" He ran a hand through the hair at his nape. "Are you sure about this?"

Regan held his gaze for several moments, reveling in the power that thrummed through her body. She'd brought him to the edge, and she licked her lips in anticipation. This was gonna be so damn good.

"I want you," she said slowly, the rasp in her voice much more pronounced. She splayed her hands against his naked chest and licked one of his nipples, smiling when she heard him gasp. "Right. Now."

That was all it took. One second he was staring down at her, a questioning look in his eyes. The next, his hands were all over her, followed by his mouth. He lips trailed fire down her throat and within seconds, her blouse hung open. He didn't stop and opened hotly over her breast, his mouth and tongue teasing until her nipple hardened painfully.

He made a noise—a primitive sort of thing that had her blood singing—and with one deft movement, he undid her bra, giving him access to her soft flesh.

"Christ, you're beautiful." Wyatt's breath was hot on her skin, and his wet mouth closed over her nipple, immediately setting off a firestorm of desire. She swelled beneath his tongue and offered herself to him with an abandon that maybe, under different circumstances, would have made her pause. Made her think that maybe she'd taken leave of her senses. But right now, with his hands and mouth wreaking havoc with her body, she didn't give it a second thought.

Regan's head dropped back, and she whimpered when he began to suckle. Each pull and thrust of his tongue against her flesh sent bolts of need straight through her body. It settled between her legs, and she gyrated against him, biting her tongue to stop the groan that sat in her throat, when his free hand reached back and cupped her butt, pulling her in even closer.

His erection was unmistakable, and as he nibbled along her jaw and teased the corners of her mouth, she pushed against him, her only thought to have him buried deep inside her.

His eyes darkened as he slowly looked her up and down, and never had Regan felt so powerful than she did in this moment.

"I gotta tell you, Regan. This right here is a picture I'm going to carry in my head until the day I die." His teeth flashed white in the gloom, a wicked curl to his mouth that pulled at her very core.

His hands found their way to her hips and slid down her thighs before curving around back, long fingers splayed possessively. He dipped his head once more and closed his mouth over her nipple, his fingers reaching for the edge of her skirt.

His tongue was relentless, his hands firm and sure, and Regan had no idea how long her cell phone rang until the Foo Fighters pierced the haze that clouded her head.

In an instant, desire turned to dread, and she pushed at Wyatt, chest heaving, mind whirling.

"Hey," he said roughly. "Am I going too fast?"

"No," she managed to say as she grabbed the edge of her blouse. "I just…" She glanced at the table. "I have to get that." Her voice trembled, and she exhaled raggedly.

Wyatt didn't say a word but nodded slowly as she straightened her clothes and jogged to the table. Her cell had stopped, but as she neared the booth, it started ringing again. Foo Fighters. The Bergens' ringtone.

"Yes." With shaking fingers, she did up her blouse, listening intently as Patrick's mother began talking in rapid-fire sentences.

Her heart sank. It sank all the way to her toes and left her feeling sad, frustrated, and so damn helpless.

"I'm coming. I'll be there as soon as I can." She glanced at Wyatt. "I'm in the city, actually. I won't be long."

Regan stared at her cell for a few seconds and then inhaled, trying to calm her nerves. She needed to get her shit together. Not just for herself, but for Patrick and his family.

"I need to go to the hospital."

Wyatt didn't hesitate. "Okay."

"Children's Hospital. It's on…dammit." She ran a hand over her temple. "I can't think. Can't remember the name of the street, but we can google the directions."

"I know where it is."

She gave him a questioning look.

"After the accident with my mother, I was laid up there for nearly two months."

"Oh, right," she whispered.

"They were great, and I try to get there at least once a year and drop in on the kids." He gave a half smile. "For some reason, some of them think race car drivers are cool."

She saw it in his eyes. He knew the drill. What the hospital represented for most of its patients. He knew the battle because he'd fought one of his own. These were the things he never talked about. The things she'd somehow forgotten.

Wyatt Blackwell continually surprised her.

# CHAPTER ELEVEN

The drive to Children's Hospital took about twenty minutes. Wyatt pulled up to the front doors and put his truck in Park. A light snow had begun to fall, but, driven by a strong wind that blew in from the north, it whirled and ripped past his windshield. He had the heat on but felt cold, and as he studied Regan's pale face, he grew concerned. She'd been worrying at her cell phone since they left his buddy's place.

"Are you— Do you need me—"

She reached for the door and cut him off. "I've got to get inside, Wyatt. Thank you so much for bringing me here. I'm sorry about…" She sighed and shrugged, those big eyes of hers beseeching. "Everything."

"I'll come in with you."

She shook her head and opened the door. "No. I have this patient and…" She tugged on her hood and offered a small smile. "I'll get a cab home later."

Like hell she would.

But before Wyatt could say another word, she slammed the door shut and hurried into the hospital. He spun the truck around and headed for the parking lot, and not more than five minutes passed before he found himself inside the hospital. He shook the snow from his boots and realized a few things.

    A.  He had no idea where Regan was and…

    B.  He had no idea what patient to inquire about.

He glanced around and shoved his gloves in the pocket of his jacket. The entrance was large, painted with soothing pastel colors and murals of animals that any child would love. At the moment, the place seemed deserted, so he headed for reception and smiled at the young woman behind the counter. Dressed in peach scrubs, she was a cute little thing, with a messy blond ponytail, large wire-framed glasses that magnified pretty blue eyes, and a welcoming smile that made him feel hopeful.

"Hey," he said, flashing a smile. She blushed, and that was a good sign. "I'm hoping you can give me some information."

She sat up a little straighter. "Sure. What do you need?"

"My friend, Regan Thorne, she's a doctor. Do you know her?"

"I'm sorry. Not personally, but I only started here a few months ago."

"Gotcha. Well, I just dropped her off. Did you see her come through?"

"Um, no one came to reception, so I'm not sure. There were a bunch of people in here a few minutes ago."

"Okay. Well, she's here to see a patient, and I just need to know where she is."

The girl hesitated for a second, and he flashed a smile that should make a nun's panty's melt. Her blush deepened, and she started typing on her keyboard, a small frown marring her forehead.

"Hmm. There's no Doctor Thorne listed in our system. Not even for privileges."

"Privileges?"

"Yes. Doctors who don't practice here, but they have permission to perform procedures, etc."

"I see." He leaned in a bit closer. "That kind of makes sense because her office is in Crystal Lake. But I think one of her patients from home has been admitted."

"That might be the case, but it would mean she's not here in a professional capacity."

He wasn't sure, but considering the whole privilege thing, he was going to go with no.

"Do you know the name of the patient?" she asked, watching him closely.

"No, but—"

"So, you're not a family member."

Shit. This was going sideways faster than the last bend he'd taken before his crash. "No. I just…" Wyatt stood back. "Look, Regan and I were on a date when she got called in here. I have no idea who she's seeing or why, but I can't leave her stranded."

"I understand that, but aside from the fact I don't have any information to give you, I wouldn't be able to if I did. You're not a family member. I'm sure you can appreciate my dilemma."

Wyatt wasn't the kind of guy to pull the celebrity card. And he wasn't even sure she would know who the hell he was. But he had a feeling in this instance it wouldn't do him any good and he'd only come off looking like an asshole.

He fingered his cell. He could call Regan, but there was a part of him that knew she'd ignore it. Not to mention it was in bad taste to disturb her when something obviously had gone so wrong.

"Okay, thanks." He turned and walked back to the main entranceway. He would sit his ass down in the lounge and wait. Not exactly an enticing prospect, but what choice did he have?

He dropped into a seat facing the elevators and was just about to get comfortable when he heard his name.

"Wyatt?"

He turned around and spied a man juggling coffees, a set of car keys, and an overnight bag. Tall. Dark curly hair with silver at the temples, and shoulders as wide as the Grand Canyon. Brad Bergen. The guy was a few years older than Wyatt and had been a mean son of a bitch on the football field. Along with Nash Booker and Wyatt's brother Hudson, he'd helped their hometown Cannons win State their senior year.

A good-looking guy, he'd always been up for a good time. He played hard and partied harder. And right now, Bergen looked like shit.

"Hey." Wyatt crossed the lobby, and suddenly things began to turn in his head. Brad's eyes were red rimmed, the lines on his face pronounced. He hadn't shaved in more than a few days, and his clothes looked as if they'd been slept in. He looked like a man who'd been put through the wringer, and since he was here, at a facility that dealt with sick children, things couldn't be good for someone close to him.

Regan had to be the connection.

Unease filled Wyatt, but he masked it, offering a simple smile and taking the bag from the other man so he could balance the three coffees without spilling anything.

"I heard you were home, Blackwell. Ran into Booker a few days ago." He frowned and looked around. "What are you…do you know someone in the hospital?" Brad sounded tired, and his shoulders slumped a bit. He looked like the weight he carried was about to do him in.

"No. I…was with Regan Thorne, and she got a phone call." Wyatt watched the man closely. "I dropped her off and went to park my truck, but I don't know where she is, and the cutie at the admission desk won't give me any information. Which I get. So, I'm just going to wait here for her."

A pained expression crossed Brad's face, and he sighed heavily, pointing to the elevators. "I'll take you to her. She's with my wife and son." His voice cracked. "Patrick is… He's not well."

Wyatt's heart sank, and he had no idea what the hell he was walking into. He thought that maybe this solemn, intimate family gathering wasn't exactly the place for him to be. "I don't want to intrude."

"Please, come up." Brad took a step forward. "Patrick's a huge fan. I think you could make this all a bit better. At least for my kid." He didn't wait for a response but headed for the elevators.

Wyatt followed him, and they made their way to the fifth floor. Once again the ward was painted with bright, cheerful colors that were meant to soothe. But there was a sadness hidden among the colors. It permeated the air, and he felt it in his bones. It was always the same. Every time he stepped foot in a hospital. And he didn't think there would ever come a time when it wouldn't.

They passed the nurses station, and by the time they reached the end of the hall, his steps were heavier, his chest tight. He glanced at Brad, but the man had put on his game face, and when they rounded the corner, Wyatt spied Regan with another woman. Tall and lanky, with straight red hair just touching the tops of her shoulders, she looked familiar. When she glanced up, Wyatt faltered.

Gwen Reynolds. *Right.* She'd married Brad Bergen.

She'd babysat him when Darlene or Hudson hadn't been around. She'd been his math and chemistry tutor. And he'd had a crush on her for years. Right up until she graduated and left Crystal Lake behind for college in the South.

"Wyatt?" Her pale lips barely moved when she spoke, and she took a step toward him, confusion warring with the welcome in her eyes. Tears sprang to her eyes, and she closed the space between them in seconds.

He enveloped her in a hug and felt how she trembled against him. "Been a long time, Red."

She squeezed his shoulders and stepped back. "It's been a long time since I've been called Red." She sniffled and blew out a long breath, glancing between him and Brad. "What are you doing here?"

"He's here with me." Regan's voice was low, subdued.

"Oh." Gwen's eyebrows furrowed. "*Oh.*" She shook her head. "I shouldn't have called you, Regan." She looked at her husband, voice trembling. "This could have waited. I just... This is a new doctor, and..."

"Don't be silly. As Patrick's family doctor, I'm happy to be here and help you through this process. I told you last week, you can call me anytime for anything."

A throat cleared behind them, and all four adults turned as an older gentleman with kind brown eyes came to a stop a few feet away. His silver-white hair was askew as if it hadn't seen a brush in a while, and his chin sported a full beard of white whiskers. A blue tie with purple polka dots peeked out from beneath his white lab coat, a direct contrast to the lemon-yellow pants he wore. Of medium build, the man looked like Santa Claus on Easter vacation, and he smiled as if he knew what they were all thinking.

"Doctor Hall." Regan stepped forward and offered her hand. "I'm Doctor Thorne, Patrick's family physician and a personal friend of the family. I hope you don't mind that I'm here."

"Not at." The older man smiled. "Shall we go somewhere to talk?"

"You guys go do your thing." Wyatt nodded to the room at the end of the hall. "Is that your son's room?"

Gwen nodded.

"Mind if I go in?"

"I think he would like that." Gwen gave him one last hug before disappearing down the corridor with the doctor, her husband, and Regan.

Wyatt poked his head in the room and spied a boy on the bed, reading a comic book. When he turned toward Wyatt, the face that greeted him was unmistakably all Gwen. It was big eyes, wide mouth, and freckles. He was pale, and there were circles under his eyes, but Wyatt saw the moment when recognition hit.

Wyatt edged inside the room as Patrick struggled to sit up. He looked about ten or eleven, the comic in his hand an old X-Men featuring Wolverine. He smiled at that. He was going to like this kid.

"Hey, Patrick," he said softly as he approached the bed. The boy was hooked up to an IV. "I'm an old friend of your mom's. Thought I'd pop in and say hello, maybe hang out for a little bit. That's if you don't mind?"

Patrick shook his head, a smile tugging one side of his face. His cheeks were puffy and swollen, and Wyatt's heart squeezed so hard, he had to take a moment to catch his breath. It was always like this—seeing a young kid so sick.

And yet, as the smile widened on Patrick's face, he couldn't help but return it and marvel at the ability for someone so young to cope with so much. He didn't know exactly what Patrick suffered from, but he was going to guess it wasn't anything good. And if he could somehow make the pain go away, even if only for a few moments, then he could leave here feeling he'd done something good. Something that mattered.

"You're Wyatt Blackwell."

"I am. Did you know your mom used to babysit me?"

Patrick nodded vigorously. "She showed me pictures of you when you were little. In your purple monster shirt."

He chuckled. "I forgot about that shirt." He pulled up a chair beside the bed. "You like cars?"

"Heck ya," Patrick replied. "NASCAR rocks. But…"

Wyatt cocked his head to the side and arched an eyebrow in question.

"Do you have any pictures to autograph? Like on you? Nathan and the guys will never believe this."

Wyatt grinned and reached for his phone. "I can do better than that, kiddo."

# CHAPTER TWELVE

Friday was pretty much a blur. Regan had a full day of patients to see, and after her office closed at four, she covered the remainder of Dr. McEachern's shift in the ER. His wife was not coping well, and with the new baby at home, she felt badly enough that she agreed. It was well past midnight when she pulled into her driveway, and the exhaustion she felt was bone deep. She grabbed a bottle of wine and, with Bella curled in her lap, barely made it through one glass before she fell asleep on the sofa.

When she woke, the sun filled her home with a brilliance that should have lifted her spirits. But it didn't. The weariness was still there along with a healthy dose of heartache. Her conversation with Patrick's doctor knocked around in her head, and she squeezed her eyes shut.

"Can't think about it right now," she muttered with a wince as she sat upright and rotated sore neck muscles. Bella barked, and she turned, groaning as she got to her feet.

The dog sat in front of the door, wagging her tail furiously, head cocked to the side and gazing upward. Regan realized Bella's barking had woken her. Regan followed the dog's line of vision and, through the frosted glass door, spied the outline of a tall, definitely male figure standing on the other side. Another soft knock sounded, setting Bella off once again.

"Come on, Bella. Enough," she said with a yawn. It was probably her brother. Walking out the kinks caused from sleeping on the sofa all night, Regan made her way over and opened the door.

Wyatt Blackwell stared down at her, arms laden with bags, and wearing a crooked smile that sent her stomach tumbling.

"Hey," she said, voice raspy from sleep. Surprised, she did nothing but stare up at him.

"Hey yourself." He took a step forward, and she was forced to back up and give him some room. The man could fill any space from the sheer force of his personality. Add to that the fact he was at least six foot four, and, well, she took another step back.

"You look like you slept in your work clothes."

She ran a hand through the tangled hair around her shoulders and glanced down at her wrinkled pants and blouse. Ugh. There were wine stains across her chest, and, shoot, was that ketchup on her lap? She was pretty sure every stitch of makeup she'd worn was rubbed off, and there was probably smudged eyeliner to boot. Her mouth was fuzzy, and she didn't have to do a sniff test to know she was wasn't exactly fresh.

"I…" She frowned. "What are you doing here?"

"I knew you pulled a major shift yesterday, and I figured you could do with a Blackwell special."

"A what?"

Wyatt stepped out of his boots and headed for the kitchen. "Breakfast."

"What's in all the bags?" She followed him to the kitchen.

Wyatt set them down and chuckled. "I had a look in your fridge the last time I was here, and, don't take this the wrong way, but you live like you're a starving college student. Go shower and let me get busy."

She stared at him, unsure and more than a little freaked out to have Wyatt here in her kitchen, acting like he *belonged here in her kitchen.*

"You feed Bella yet?" His dark eyes were on her, and that familiar shot of warmth flushed her cheeks. Regan shook her head, and he smiled. Damn if that didn't make things worse.

"Where's her food?"

She pointed to the cupboard beside the island.

"I've got her. Go." Wyatt grabbed a banana from one of his bags and pointed to the bedroom.

As she undressed, Regan was very much aware that a man was in her kitchen. Not just any man, but Wyatt Blackwell. That only a door separated them. And she was naked. In the shower. *Naked.*

Suddenly, she wasn't tired at all.

By the time she was done and grabbed a pair of sweats and a T-shirt, her heart was thumping against her chest, and it felt as if she'd just run a marathon. She was hot, flushed, and out of breath. All from the thought of the man in her kitchen.

And, well, her naked in the shower.

Not that it counted considering she'd been naked and alone. Still. She wondered if he was thinking about her being naked in the shower, and that got her all hot and bothered again. She exhaled, took a few more deep breaths, and then, after combing her hair back into a loose knot, headed back to the kitchen.

Not bothering with slippers, Regan padded barefoot, and Wyatt had no idea she'd joined him. He stood near the oven, tossing the odd piece of food to Bella—she was going to have to nip that in the bud—and whistling to himself. The place smelled heavenly, and her mouth watered just as her stomach rumbled.

But it was the sight of Wyatt that really got her worked up. Faded jeans that clung to an ass carved from stone. Seriously. She didn't care that his brother Travis was the hockey star. That right there was major hockey butt. Round. Firm. Delicious.

His faded navy T-shirt was so old and worn, it was threadbare. It clung to his shoulders and narrow waist. But there was something about a man in well-worn clothes—they made him look comfortable, as if he belonged right where he was. His side profile was as gorgeous as the rest of him, his long lashes sweeping downward as he laughed at Bella's antics. Hell, even her dog was enthralled.

"Smells good," Regan said softly as she slid onto one of the stools at the island. There were two bowls of fruit set there, salt and pepper, and fresh orange juice. "What's on the menu?"

He flashed her a smile and reached for a plate. "Mexican benedict."

"Yum." She stretched and tried to see over his shoulder. "Salsa?"

"Fresh."

"Really," she murmured when he set down her plate. "What exactly do you mean by fresh?"

Wyatt sat down beside her and passed a glass of orange juice her way. "I made it."

"You made the salsa." Was there anything he couldn't do?

"Yep."

"When did you do that?"

"In my spare time." He arched an eyebrow, a hint of a smile touching his mouth. "Dig in. I guarantee it's the best salsa you've ever had."

And it was.

They ate breakfast and chatted about pretty much anything that didn't matter. The weather. Restaurants. Favorite television shows. Regan? *Game of Thrones.* Wyatt? *The Voice.* That one surprised Regan, but then she couldn't help but think he'd been constantly surprising her since coming back to Crystal Lake.

Wyatt Blackwell was funny, charming as hell, had a great sense of humor, and with that sexy-ass grin, he could melt any woman's heart without even trying.

*I want him.*

Her mouth went dry at the thought, and she pushed away her juice, jumping to her feet and heading for the coffee machine. Once she had the brew going, she leaned against the counter, unnerved to find his dark gaze on her. The air was thick between them. Thick and heavy with things they'd been skirting for the last week or so.

She wasn't so sure that a casual hookup with Wyatt Blackwell was a smart move. The sex would be good. How could it not? But was good sex worth the fallout? Because there would be fallout. She stifled a groan and crossed her legs, suddenly aware of the heaviness between them. The friction and the ache.

In that moment, Regan did what she always did when she was confused and feeling up against the wall. She changed course and opted for new subject matter. One that would deflect.

"So, how come you're not racing?"

Wyatt froze, fork halfway to his mouth. He took a moment and then casually chewed the last of his breakfast before putting down his fork and settling back in his chair.

"I'm sure you know about the crash."

His tone was off, and that told Regan her instincts were correct. Something was up. Was she really going to open this can of worms with him? Get inside his head and deep into his personal shit?

She cleared her throat.

Guess so.

She picked at the edge of her T-shirt and watched him carefully. "The press is saying you have a concussion, or at least that's what they're guessing is the reason you're not driving. No one is really saying anything."

His mouth tightened, and gone was the lightness they'd shared moments earlier.

"I didn't know you were so interested in NASCAR," he replied.

"I'm not. I'm just saying you're not concussed."

"Really." He got to his feet and shoved his hands into the front pockets of his jeans. "You an expert on racing related injuries?"

"I'm just saying you're not concussed, and if you had the type of concussion that's been reported in the media, for one thing, you wouldn't be driving at all. You'd have double vision and a bunch of other things that would make it dangerous to be on the road, and they would have taken your license." She shrugged. "From what I can see, you're not presenting with any symptoms of the like."

"That's your expert opinion?" His voice was like silk, and it slid over her, soft and dangerous like.

"I already told you," she replied, watching him warily as he made his way toward her. "I'm not your doctor. I'm just observing."

He stopped a few inches from her, and she held her breath. "Do you know what I think?"

Regan barely mouthed a reply before his lips were near hers, his warm breath sending shivers dancing along her skin.

"I think that right now, talking about my racing career is the last thing we want to be doing." His tongue snaked out and left a line of fire along her collarbone.

"You're trying to change the subject," she managed on a gasp.

"Caught me." Again with the tongue, and just like that, she was on fire. "Is it working?"

Working? Understatement. Of the year. Regan's hands crept up to his shoulders. "Totally."

"Good," he murmured against her mouth before claiming it in an exquisite kiss that left her body limp like a noodle. Wyatt Blackwell kissed her until her head spun. Until all her brain emptied and her body took over. This was primal. Hot. Sexual.

His hands were under her shirt, fingers caressing, palms applying pressure. But, dammit, he wasn't going fast enough. Impatient, she knocked them away, ripped at the edge of her T-shirt, and tossed the damn thing on the floor.

He made a noise, a deep, male, possessive sound that had her blood singing. "Jesus, Regan." He lifted her up, and her legs curled around his midsection, her mouth seeking his because she was starving.

For him.

He set her on the island, and that allowed easier access.

Tongues danced. Fingers explored. Her bra ended up on the floor a few feet from her top, and when his hot mouth closed over her nipple, she sank her hands into his hair, holding him in place. Her head thrown back, body arched in pleasure, she began to grind against him, whimpering with need.

"Wyatt," she breathed, hands reaching for his jeans.

He pulled back abruptly, chest heaving, face flushed dark with desire, and ran a shaky hand through his hair. He stood back, as far as he could go with her legs still wrapped around him, and the look in his eyes was enough to set the entire place on fire.

She smiled wickedly and reached for him, loving the feel of his hardness through his jeans.

"Hey." He shook his head and tried to extricate himself from her grip. "I can't…" Unmistakable regret clouded his words and took a step back. He wanted her. She saw that.

"I don't understand." She barely got the words out. Her body was ripe. It was hot and aching, and she was so damn wet for him.

Wyatt shuddered and cupped her cheek. He reached for her, his lips grazing hers in the softest of kisses. "I really did only come to make you breakfast. Trust me, if I could stay and spend the entire fucking day in bed with you, I would."

He tugged on her until she was forced to look up at him. "And we will. This is so gonna happen. Just not right now."

"Okay," she whispered, more confused than ever.

"I have to be somewhere in an hour, and I don't want to rush this. No way in hell am I gonna do that. I want to take my time and worship every single inch of your body." He paused. "Rain check?"

"Yes."

Wyatt dropped a kiss to her swollen lips and rested his forehead against hers. "I promised Patrick an advanced copy of the new NASCAR game, and he's expecting me."

Her heart swelled so big and full that she nearly choked on the emotions that ran through her.

"He would love that," she said softly, angling her head back so she could see Wyatt.

He was quiet for a few moments and when he spoke, she heard the concern and worry in his voice. "He's a great kid who's been dealt a real shitty hand. Anything I can do to make him feel better, I will. Brad told me about the tumor and how the chemo and radiation haven't really done the job. He told me about this new infection and…" Wyatt took a step back and exhaled. "I just want the kid to smile."

"You're so not what I thought you were."

Wyatt held her gaze as he reached for his jacket, which was slung across one of the chairs at the island. "That's probably a good thing." He slipped into it and turned toward the door. He opened it and paused, tossing her a wicked grin over his shoulder.

"Nice tattoo."

And then he was gone.

Regan wrapped her arms around her chest and stared at the door for so long, she began to shiver. Only then realizing she was still half-naked. She glanced down, noticing her track pants had ridden low on her hips. And there on the right side, just below her bikini line, was a small pink Hello Kitty.

She slipped off the counter and pulled her cell phone from her purse. Quickly, she scrolled through her contacts until she found the one she wanted. A soft smile played around her lips as she began to type a message.

*The code to the front door is Bella.*

She paused, fingers tracing letters on the keyboard and then typed one more sentence before hitting Send.

*Use it.*

# CHAPTER THIRTEEN

Wyatt was late for his dad's birthday dinner. By the time he rolled up to the house on the lake, only a few cars remained in the driveway, and one of them was his brother Hudson's. He put his truck in Park, wondering why he'd come at all, and sat there for a good five minutes.

Light shone invitingly from inside, yet he felt nothing but cold and an overwhelming sense of sadness that left him weary. Why had he come? He glanced down at the seat beside him as his cell lit up for the tenth time in the last hour.

Right. Because he had no choice. Not only had Darlene given him the gears the other day, but his brother was hounding him. There was no sense in putting this off any longer. He slid from the truck and headed inside.

He hung up his coat and followed the low hum of voices to the great room off the kitchen. The space was huge and airy and wide open, giving him an unfettered view of the few guests left. Their neighbours the Edwards were chatting with Darlene, while John sat in a leather chair beside them. Hudson was near the fireplace, head bent, listening to Rebecca. The soft swell of her belly showed a burgeoning growth, and Hudson's hand rested there, protectively, possessively. It was a good look for his brother, and Wyatt was happy he'd finally figured out Rebecca Draper was the only woman he was ever going to be happy with. It had taken ten years, but then no one had ever claimed the Blackwell men were smart when it came to their personal lives.

He glanced around. There was no one else. Guess that was what happened when you were several hours late for a party.

The remains of the meal were tidied up in the kitchen, and soft music played in the background. Darlene glanced up just then, and he saw the disappointment in her eyes. She was gracious and quickly hid it, and it made him feel like shit.

"Nice of you to join us." Hudson straightened and walked over, followed by Rebecca. He offered his hand, which Wyatt shook. "Beer?" his brother asked.

"I know where they are." Wyatt kept his tone light and flashed a smile at Rebecca. "You look amazing."

"I feel amazing," she murmured, linking her arm through Hudson's. "A little nauseous in the mornings, but nothing I can't handle."

"Where's Liam?"

"He played shinny at the arena and then a sleepover at his buddy's."

"That's good," Wyatt replied with a wink and a hug. "This would have been boring as hell for the kid."

He made his way over to Darlene and his father, passing a long table filled with balloons, cards, and presents. Crap. He hadn't even bothered to pick up a card. Another fail to add to the long list of them when it came to his father.

He greeted the Edwards warmly. Like his own family, they were about as close to Crystal Lake royalty as you could get, and he'd known them his whole life. Marnie and Steven looked happy, healthy, and robust.

The contrast to his father was striking, and it was then he noticed the pallor in John's cheeks, the sickly tint beneath his flesh. It caught him unaware, and he found himself staring.

"We were just leaving," Steven said, slapping Wyatt's shoulder in the way that men did. "But I'm glad we were able to see you, Wyatt. Everyone's talking about our very own NASCAR champion and looking forward to your return to the track." He paused. "Any idea when that's gonna happen? My son Jake and I thought we'd do a weekend trip when you start back up."

"Not at the moment." He took his eyes off his father and attempted a smile.

"Of course," Steven replied. "That was some bad business, that accident."

"Yeah," Wyatt murmured. He said his good-byes and headed for the kitchen, rooting around in the fridge for a beer that wasn't imported. Jesus. Since when had his father decided that good old American brew wasn't up to snuff? He finally found a Bud and popped the can open before returning to the family room.

Darlene had walked the Edwards back to foyer, along with Hudson and Rebecca, leaving him alone with his father. Silence fell between them, awkward and big and uncomfortable as hell. Wyatt glanced back, hoping to see his brother or Rebecca…or someone, but they were all still gathered in the foyer.

"Sorry I missed dinner," he said, turning back to his father. "I got held up."

John shrugged. "You know how Darlene is about these things. Birthdays and such. They're important to her. She's the one you need to apologize to, not me." The subtle reprimand hit home. Probably because his father was right, mostly because it came from John.

Wyatt took another pull from his beer. This was gonna be a fun one.

"A lot of people come?"

John nodded. "A fair amount. Apparently it's a big deal to hit seventy when most folks had you dead and buried months earlier."

That was a joke, and Wyatt almost said as much. John Blackwell would outlive them all. People that stubborn usually did. And yet, there was something about the pinched look in his eyes, the way his thin fingers clung to the edge of the chair. Wyatt thought back to something Regan had told him days ago.

"You guys aren't going to Florida."

"Nope." John glanced up at him. "We thought we'd sit it out this year."

"Any particular reason why?"

His father didn't look away. In fact, he leaned forward. "I prefer to die at home. No way will I go in Florida. Too hot."

"I don't think that really matters when you're dead. The heat and all."

"Well, I plan on going in my own bed. And damned if I let Regan get me back in that hospital."

Right. Regan was his family doctor.

Regan. Doctors. Hospital. All three of those things made his gut tighten. He took another swig and sighed, glancing at his watch and wondering...

"You don't have to stay."

He raised an eyebrow at his father. "Darlene would have my ass if I left right now, so no thanks."

John Blackwell chuckled at that. The sound was like a returning memory, and Wyatt had to shake his head a bit in order to clear it. No sense in dwelling in the past. Even the good shit led to pain.

The two men fell silent. It was always like this between them. Sparse. Cold. Complicated. He doubted it would ever change. Wyatt wandered over to the large floor-to-ceiling windows. They gave an uncluttered view of the lake, and the winter beauty of it was breathtaking. The moon shone from above, creating shadow and light depending upon where it hit, making small snow drifts look impossibly huge. Making the lake look mysterious, dangerous, and inviting. It was a contrast he loved and one he missed a hell of a lot.

He wasn't sure how long he stood there, staring out at the lake, but it was long enough for him to finish his beer. He turned around just as Darlene, Hudson, and Rebecca returned to the great room.

"Can I get you anything to eat, Wyatt?" Darlene seemed overly bright, her voice a tad high.

"I'm good, thanks."

She grabbed a silver-gray afghan and placed it across John's legs. "Well, I'm glad you were able to come and see your father. It's lovely, isn't it, John?"

"It's unexpected is what it is." John didn't bother to look his way. "I'm tired, Dar. I'd like to go to bed." He gave a small wave to them all and slowly got to his feet, holding tight to Darlene as she led him toward their bedroom.

"I'll just... I'm going to call Liam and see if he needs anything before we head home." Rebecca gave a small smile and disappeared.

Huh. Nothing like a Blackwell family reunion to get everyone's spirits up. Wyatt crunched the empty can in his hand and sighed heavily.

"He doesn't mean to be an asshole." Hudson stood beside him, hands in his pockets. "He just can't help it sometimes."

Wyatt wanted to punch a wall. "Since when do you make excuses for him? He wrote the book on being an asshole."

"Wyatt—"

"Hudson, I don't want to dissect our family bullshit. I don't want to talk about John or Darlene or any of that stuff right now. I know you've found some sort of peace with him, but you need to hear me when I say it's not gonna happen between him and me. That right there is an old horse you need to stop beating. Because if you don't, she's gonna kick back, and things are going to get messy."

"Okay. Let's forget about Dad. Let's talk about you."

"There's nothing to talk about."

Hudson was silent for a few seconds, his gaze on the lake. "We haven't talked about the crash."

A muscle worked in Wyatt's jaw, and his teeth clamped down so tight that it ached. "There's not much to add to what everyone already knows. Diego Sanchez died. He hit the turn too fast and took me out. I walked away. He didn't." He paused, thinking of his mother. "It's something I'm getting used to."

"Wyatt, it was a shit deal, that's for sure. I just..."

"What?" He turned to his brother and scowled fiercely.

"I just want to make sure you're okay. That couldn't have been easy. Not after Mom."

Wyatt pivoted abruptly and headed for the kitchen. He tossed the can into the recyclable bin. "I told you I'm not doing this right now. I shouldn't have come."

"Flash. Come on. Listen to me."

He stopped dead in his tracks. Hudson hadn't called Flash that since they were kids. He'd been the one with no off switch. The to do everything full tilt and fast as hell. When had things gone so wrong?

Hudson followed him into the kitchen, and they stood staring at each other for so long, Wyatt's eyes began to burn.

"If you need to talk. I'm there for you. I hope you know that." Hudson cleared his throat, and Wyatt could see he was struggling. It was hard for them. Hard to be here. Hard to be open. Hard to be honest.

"Don't worry about me, Huds. I'll be fine. I always am."

"That's the thing, Wyatt. I don't think you are." His eyes narrowed. "Did the nightmares ever go away?"

Jesus. Fucking. Christ. Did Hudson always have to bring that shit up? Why couldn't he just let things be? The anger that rolled through him was hot and furious and absolute. It took his breath away, and he had to take a moment to calm himself.

It was the kind of anger that could be a game changer. The kind that stayed with him.

Wyatt needed to shut this shit down. He backed away and attempted a smile. "Give my best to Darlene and Rebecca. I'll see you around." With that, Wyatt headed for the door and grabbed his coat along the way. He didn't bother putting it on; in fact, he got out of the house so fast, he was surprised the door didn't slam shut and hit his ass on the way out. He drove away, not caring that his tires squealed. He headed not toward the mountain and the cabin he'd claimed as his, but to town.

Ten minutes later, he was parked in Regan's driveway. Her car was there, but her place was in darkness. Even though it was barely ten, he couldn't be sure if she'd already gone to bed. Her work hours made his head spin.

He thought of her text message. Of her urging him to come by.

But was it fair to her? To come to her home when his head and his emotions were all over the place? Shit. What to do.

Screw it, he thought.

Quietly, he let himself into the house, shedding his boots and coat at the door. A lamp was on in the family room, its muted glow casting barely a shadow. With stealth, he made his way to the back, to where her bedroom was.

Bella hopped from the bed, her odd gait bringing a smile to his face as she came for some loving. He gave her a scratch and then leaned against the doorjamb, drinking in the sight of the woman fast asleep. She was on her back, her hair spilled across most of her face. Her chest rose and fell evenly, and bare legs peeked from underneath the covers. She looked so damn relaxed and warm... so damn right. In this moment, she was everything he needed.

Quickly, he tossed his shirt and jeans and socks onto the floor beside the bed. He eyed his boxers, but, with a wicked grin, decided getting naked right off the bat wasn't exactly fair. He slipped into bed and under the covers, gathering her close to his body.

Wyatt wasn't sure how long he lay in the dark, listening to her breathe, watching her lips move as she had some imaginary conversation with herself. But it was a long time. Long enough for him to get lazy. Long enough for the demons in his head to fade away and for him to fall asleep.

More importantly, long enough for him to finally find some sort of his own peace.

# CHAPTER FOURTEEN

Warm. So incredibly warm.

Slowly, Regan came awake with a smile on her face and a feeling inside that made her feel strange. It was unfamiliar, and at first, she wasn't exactly sure what it was.

The only thing she did know was that she didn't want it to end. Didn't want to open her eyes. Didn't want to do anything to stop this feeling. She sighed and stretched—or at least tried to—and it was then that her eyes flew open and she found herself staring into the face that had haunted her dreams.

Her sweet, hot, erotic dreams.

Wyatt was on his side, facing her, one of his arms tucked around her midsection, the other flung above his head. Her legs were caught between his (hence the not being able to move bit) but she didn't mind. At all.

She relaxed against her pillow, enjoying the sensation of another human being in her bed and the warmth that came with it. This was nice. So nice.

He looked much younger asleep, more like the boy she remembered from high school. But the body, well, that didn't go with a teen boy. *Hell no.*

She bit her tongue and lifted the blankets for a peek.

He was naked, save for a pair of plain black boxers, and her eyes traveled the length of him. *My God, he's beautiful.* She watched him closely, her tongue caught between her teeth as she leaned back a bit in order to see better. The thin line of hair below his belly button disappeared under his boxers. And those boxers did nothing to hide a bulge that made her hot.

And bothered.

And horny as hell.

Already she throbbed between her legs, and gently, she traced his pectorals, down his chest and lower, until she hovered over that delicious bulge. A quick glance up told her Wyatt was still asleep, but she hesitated. It wasn't her nature to be bold, to throw caution to the wind and just do what it was she wanted to do.

Normally, her brain didn't work that way. But right now? In this moment? A new kind of Regan took over. She threw back the covers all the way.

His eyes were still closed, and that was probably a good thing, because if they were open, he would have seen the uninhibited glee on her face as she eased her hand inside his boxers.

He was semi-hard, and as her fingers closed around him, he swelled beneath her touch. It was amazing, really, how men were so hard, and yet, as her fingers rolled over the top of his penis, so silky soft.

She caressed him, slowly, methodically, until he was fully erect, and because she couldn't help herself, Regan gently wriggled her legs free from his. Wyatt made it easy; with a groan he flopped onto his back, murmuring something she couldn't understand. But he didn't wake up.

She licked her lips, got to her knees, and stared at the most beautiful man she'd ever seen. His boxers strained against his erection—the sight hypnotized her. Her breaths came hard and fast, and the friction between her legs was getting harder to ignore. She whimpered, gyrating her hips slightly in an effort to alleviate the pressure as a wicked thought struck. A wicked, naughty, very un-Regan-like thought.

She glanced over her shoulder—which was ridiculous; there was no one here except Wyatt. Then, with slow, precise movements, she gently tugged down his boxers, and his cock sprang free.

Holy. Hell.

She could now confirm, unequivocally, that every single inch of him was beautiful. Like Michelangelo's David kind of beautiful. She giggled. But bigger. Much, much bigger.

Regan rested her butt on her heels and spread her legs slightly. She fingered the waistband of her pajama bottoms as another wave of heat hit her core. Those un-Regan-like thoughts circled hard, and she bit her lip.

He was still asleep. He wouldn't know.

She eased back, using her left hand to help lever her body, and her right inched downward, deep between her legs and straight to the swollen flesh between them. Slowly she exhaled, her deft fingers sliding across slick skin. Slowly she massaged her clitoris, eyes on the man in front of her. She imagined it was his hands on her. His fingers inside her. His body pressed into hers.

The thought emboldened her. Heat suffused her skin in another wave that took her breath.

*I can't believe I'm doing this.* She squeezed her eyes shut, ignored the voice in her head, and found a rhythm that worked. Her fingers coaxed and massaged, while her hips slowly gyrated, adding to the friction between her legs.

Long ragged breaths escaped from between her lips, and she bit down hard when she would have groaned out loud. Deep inside, that familiar pull began in earnest, and her fingers pressed into her flesh, rubbing, massaging feverishly as it continued to build.

Her head rocked forward, her eyes flew open and…shit…

Dark eyes stared down at her.

"Don't fucking stop." His voice was low and hoarse. He made no effort to hide his desire or the pleasure he took in what she was doing. "This is the hottest thing I've ever seen and one hell of a wake-up."

Regan was breathing heavily, and slowly withdrew her hand from between her legs.

"Babe, I told you not to stop." His expression was fierce.

She tilted her hips, acting totally on instinct, and pulled her pajama bottoms all the way down. She tossed them to the floor and sat back on her butt so that she was facing Wyatt. He physically jerked when she spread her legs, leaving her fully exposed to him.

"Shit," he muttered, sitting up higher so that he could see better.

Never had Regan felt such power. Felt so full of her feminine self. She reached down once more, her clitoris full and aching, her body in need of release. She was wicked. Wanton. She smiled and spread her lips, taking pleasure in the sound he made as she did so.

It didn't take long. Not with Wyatt watching her like he was starving. The muscles in his neck stood out, attesting to how close he was to losing control. When she began to whimper, when her orgasm bloomed hard and heavy, he inched forward, like a predator after prey. Never taking his eyes from her.

His hand joined hers, big, hard, and warm, and he held her as she came. He cradled her against his chest, as her body shuddered with aftershocks. And kissed the top of her head when it was over.

For the longest time, the only thing Regan heard was her frantic breathing and the beat of her heart echoing inside her head. Slowly, two hands crept up along her cheeks, and she could do nothing but look up.

A slow, wicked grin spread across Wyatt's face. "Good morning."

She tried to look away, but he wouldn't let her. She cleared her throat. "Good morning. When did you…"

He was shaking his head. "No. That conversation is for later. Right now, we need to take care of business. Because as much as this has been a good morning so far, I'm thinking we can do better." He dropped his head and nuzzled just below her ear, and delicious shivers raced across her skin. "I know I can." He tugged on her earlobe. "I'm betting you can too."

Wyatt tucked a long strand of hair behind that ear and nibbled his way back to her mouth, taking her in a hot, hard kiss that made her head spin. When he broke it off, all that heat was back, faster, hotter, and more urgent.

"What say we get rid of this top," he said, that wicked grin still in place. "I think they're missing the bottoms." His large hands slid down her shoulders and caressed her breasts through the thin cotton before reaching for the edge and pulling it over her head.

This was it. They were both naked. In her bed. About to make love.

God, she'd touched herself in front of him. Suddenly, a host of overwhelming thoughts crowded her head, and she blinked rapidly, unsure, confused, and so turned on, it was killing her. Was she doing the right thing? Would sex make things complicated?

*Of course, you idiot.*

"Hey." He gripped her chin once more. "We can take this slow. We don't have—"

She didn't give him the chance to finish his sentence. Regan reached for Wyatt. She put her hands on him, pulled him close, and kissed him with all the passion, with all the want and need that was in her. Tongues tangled. Hands roamed. Bodies melted together.

It was hot. It was real. It was skin on skin.

And she was doing this.

The part of her that had been asleep for years, or maybe forever, that un-Regan-like part, it roared to life. With a soft growl, she pushed at him until he was flat on his back.

"So this is how you want to play it," he said, a half grin on his face. His cock stood up, big and strong and ready for her. His chest rose and fell rapidly, and the fever that lit his eyes struck an answering chord in her.

She couldn't wait for the intimacy. That could come later. Right now, the need in her clawed at her insides. It messed with her brain until all she knew, all she wanted was Wyatt at the most primitive level.

"This is how it's going to be." She didn't hesitate. Regan straddled him, welcoming the hands that clutched at her breasts. His fingers sought out pebbled nipples and tweaked them—none too gently, but she was okay with that.

She was so wet and ready, and she sank down on Wyatt, taking all of him deep inside. She immediately began to ride him, up and down, thrusting forward, giving her clitoris that friction she needed.

"Dammit, Regan. Let's go slower." His hands were on her hips, and he tried to do just that. But Regan was having none of it. It had been too long since she'd been with a man. And she'd never had this kind of connection before. She wanted all of him, and she wanted him now.

"No." Through half-lidded eyes, she gazed down at him. "Touch me, Wyatt."

She leaned back on her hands, thrusting her breasts upward, once more giving him access to the part of her that needed him most. His greedy fingers found her right away, and as she increased the tempo, his fingers slid across her slick center, tugging, rubbing, and driving her to the edge.

It was too much. He filled her completely—stretched in such a way that shards of pleasure spiked out with each thrust. They pulled at her, begging for release, and she knew she couldn't hold on much longer.

"I'm so ready," she said hoarsely, her voice breaking. "Wyatt."

With one hand on her hip, the other where they were joined, he kept pace. "I'm right there with you, babe."

Regan's body buckled forward, her control so thin that for a second, she saw nothing but haze. Her vision cleared just as that delicious pressure bloomed and spread like wildfire. Wyatt's eyes were closed, his gorgeous lips pulled back, ferocious and so damn primal. His muscles bulged, his pulse raced at his neck.

She did this to him. Her.

Regan came so hard that the aftershocks trickled through her body in pulses that kick-started another orgasm. One after the other. She collapsed on top of Wyatt, and the two of them stayed like that until she slid from him, limp and sated and all used up.

"That was..." She couldn't articulate the thoughts in her head.

"I know." Wyatt pulled her close. He slid his arms around her and pulled the covers up until they were warm and comfortable.

Bella barked, and they both looked over the side of the bed, where they spied the small dog watching them, tail wagging, tongue lolling to one side.

"Your dog is a pervert." Wyatt pressed a kiss to her forehead.

"Apparently," she managed. God, she was out of breath.

"She's going to have to wait a bit for round two. I need to recharge the batteries."

"It's Sunday, right?"

He nodded.

"No problem. We have all day."

# CHAPTER FIFTEEN

Monday night rolled around much too quickly. Wyatt spent the day hanging new cupboards in the kitchen. The job was labor intensive, but he enjoyed the hell out of it. He'd forgotten how much he liked to work with his hands. Some would be surprised to know that before racing had taken over his life, carpentry had been an interest he'd seriously considered.

He stood back, a critical eye on the cupboards. If he remembered correctly, it was the only thing he and Mrs. Lee had agreed on. The crusty old guidance counselor had tried everything in her power to get him to enroll in a local community college, but Wyatt had resisted. At that point in his life, all he thought about was leaving Crystal Lake. Coupled with the fact fast cars and racing took up most of his time, it was an easy decision.

Thinking back made him wonder, though. Where would he be if Mrs. Lee had won?

He glanced at the clock and shook the memories away. If he didn't get his butt in gear, he'd be late, and hell if he'd give Jarret a reason to ride his ass. Plus, he'd worked up an appetite and was hungry as hell. Chicken and beer were on the menu, and it had been way too long since he'd chowed down on greasy wings.

His cell pinged just as he got out of the shower, and, with

a smile, he grabbed it off the table beside his bed. It wasn't the green-eyed brunette he'd been hoping for, and his smile slowly faded.

He stared at the name. Rob Tracy. The team manager and boss. He'd been calling steadily for the last few days now. And though Wyatt knew he needed to deal with him, he decided to do it later. All it took was that number to light up and deflate the good mood he'd been enjoying since he'd crawled into bed with Regan. With a scowl, he tossed the phone.

At exactly seven o'clock, Wyatt strode into the Coach House, automatically glancing to his left. But Sal wasn't there. Instead, a mountain of a man with a full-on Grizzly Adams beard kept the customers happy. Ironically, he was known as Tiny. He was a good guy, but there wasn't a regular who didn't miss Salvatore. The old man used to dish out advice as quickly as he'd pour a draft. Most of the time, you didn't want to hear his opinion, on account of most of the time he was right. Most guys didn't like having that particular fact pointed out.

It was sad he was gone, but Nash Booker was doing a fine job keeping things up to Sal's standards.

The Coach House was full, largely due to the half-price wings and the fact that there wasn't anywhere else in town that catered to pretty much everyone. Townies. Seasonals. New bloods. Moneyed folk and not. It was the kind of place that smelled of stale beer and grease. The kind of place that had dark corners and bathrooms that hadn't been updated since the early seventies. It was the kind of place Wyatt could walk into and no one gave him a second glance. They didn't care that he was NASCAR or that he owned a fancy house in Florida. No one could give a goddamn that he had more money from racing and endorsements than he needed or knew what to do with.

It didn't matter because he was born and bred in Crystal Lake, and on any given day of the week, he could walk into this place and run into an old friend.

None of the new establishments that had sprung up downtown or across the lake came close. Coming here felt like coming home.

And it was that ease that Wyatt enjoyed.

He spied Booker behind the bar, four bottles of whiskey in his hands and a large bag of peanuts clenched between his teeth. He nodded at Wyatt and made a gesture with his head that had Wyatt moving to one of the tall tables near the stage. Jarret and Sean were there, a jug of beer in the middle of the table, along with three large baskets of wings. The boys were tucked in but good and barely grunted as Wyatt slid onto a stool and poured himself a beer.

"You guys look like a couple of meatheads," he said with a chuckle, reaching for a plate.

"You're late," Sean mumbled, swiping at the sauce on the corner of his mouth. He missed but didn't seem to care. Instead, he grabbed another wing.

"I was busy."

"Doing what?" Sean asked with a crooked grin before tearing into his wing. "Seriously, Blackwell. What the hell do you do, holed up in that cabin? Why the hell are you here anyway? Christ, if I were you, I'd be living it up somewhere warm, knee-deep in pussy and booze."

Wyatt reached for a wing. "That I don't doubt."

"Lots of pussy." Sean grinned.

Jarret reached for a napkin and made a face. "And that's why you're still single, McAdams. You're a pig."

"Yeah?" Sean chewed on a bone before pointing it at Jarret. "What's your excuse?"

Jarret topped up his draft and filled a mug for Wyatt. "My excuse lives on the West Coast."

That got Wyatt's attention. "Carly?"

Jarret shrugged, but the lopsided grin on his face told a story Wyatt wanted to hear. "You guys get together when she was here?" Wyatt asked.

"We might have hung out."

"Hung out?" Sean sat back in his chair. "Who gives a shit if you hung out. Did you bang her? That's the question my friend."

Jarret turned to his pal. "Again. The pig thing. You need to grow up."

Sean didn't get the sarcasm. "So, you banged her but you don't want to talk about it." He looked at Wyatt, eyebrows raised comically. "I'd say that means something."

"Yeah," Jarret mumbled. "It means I'm not a dumbass twenty-year-old eager to share every detail about the girl I'm with. You might get there one day."

Wyatt chuckled. "If he's lucky."

Sean shook his head and carried on with his wings. But Wyatt sat back and sipped his beer thoughtfully. "So, this thing with Carly is more than just a random hookup."

"We'll see," Jarret said slowly.

"So, you did bang her." Sean barely got the words out before Jarret punched him in the shoulder.

"Hey. What the fu—"

"Grow up, McAdams," Jarret growled.

"Fuck you." Sean made a face.

"And that is the reason you still live with your parents," Wyatt said with a grin.

Sean stopped chewing and eyed up the both of them, and was silent for the next little while. The boys made small talk, and eventually the conversation centered on the new sports complex being built across the lake. Jarret's family had won the contract three years prior, and the plans he outlined were impressive. The complex would feature both indoor and outdoor activities, as well as use of the water.

The arena had already been finished and would have an adjacent indoor pool as well as a new community center.

"You should invest," Jarret said, looking to Wyatt. "Jump in while you still can."

"Invest? In what?" Over the course of his career, he'd been asked to invest in numerous ventures—restaurants, health clubs, night clubs—but Wyatt always deferred and kept his money in stocks. He owned a few homes, two of which were rentals, but other than that, he didn't really pay much attention to that sort of thing. Maybe it was short-sighted, but he'd always been of the mind that he had time for that stuff.

"There's lots of options. Restaurants."

"Nash would love that," he replied dryly.

"Competition is healthy for everyone, Blackwell." Jarret sat back and looked serious.

He supposed that was as good a comeback as any, and there was probably more than a little bit of truth in there. Wyatt shrugged. "You want my honest opinion?"

Jarret looked at him as if he had four eyes. "Well, I don't want your dishonest one."

"I like Crystal Lake the way it is. Or rather, the way it was. I'm not sure all these imports coming into our town is a good thing."

Jarret's mouth tightened. "Well, that's pretty ballsy considering you haven't actually lived here in years. Fact is, the tax dollars rolling in are good for the town coffers, and more people living here means more people spending money, which is good for business. Tourism is up, which your brother Hudson is happy about. It's a win for everyone."

He had a point, but Wyatt wasn't giving in just yet. "Don't you think building a huge sports complex is going to take away from the town? What the hell is going to happen to the old arena?" He looked at Sean. "The ballpark we played in when we were kids? The football field?"

"Hey, don't look at me." Sean shrugged.

Okay. McAdams was an idiot.

"The town won't suffer. There are limitations in place. The council is committed to making sure Crystal Lake retains the spirit that attracted folks here in the first place. Hell, your brother is on the council, and he approved the plans." Jarret frowned. "I'm surprised you care is all."

If Wyatt was honest with himself, he would have to agree with his friend. As it was, he didn't get a chance to elaborate or reply because Daisy Miller appeared out of nowhere. She pulled up a seat alongside Wyatt and was joined by a girlfriend she introduced as Trish. Trish, Wyatt didn't know, but Sean McAdams did, and the two of them cozied up together sharing laughs, beer, and wings.

Daisy sat a little too close to him, but she made no overt moves, and the five of them chatted about nothing in particular.

The band started up just then, a local country act that covered everything from Johnny Cash and Hank Williams to Zac Brown and Florida Georgia Line. Wyatt was thankful for the distraction because it took Daisy's focus from him. They ordered another round, more wings, and sat back to enjoy the show.

Near the end of the set, the band slowed it down with a haunting, romantic sad sap of a song that had Sean and Trish up and moving toward the dance floor. Jarret had already flown the coop. He'd gotten a call and left twenty minutes earlier.

"So," Daisy said, eyeing him over the rim of her glass. "I think we should dance."

He hesitated, and she smiled.

"Hey. It's just a dance, nothing more. And I really like this song." She paused. "Please?"

Okay. It was just a dance, and he was being silly as hell. They headed out to the dance floor.

"So, you're still in town."

"I am."

"You forget my number?" She offered up a slow, sexy smile. But Wyatt saw the hopeful look in her eyes and glanced away, feeling more than a little guilty.

"I've been busy."

"With anyone I know?"

Daisy wasn't giving up, and Wyatt needed to nip this in the bud. The thing was, he didn't know where he and Regan stood. Was Sunday just a one-off? They'd agreed that maybe dinner on Thursday would be good. Regan had a busy week, so they'd left things causal. But hell, nothing about what had happened between them was casual.

He scowled. At least not for Wyatt.

The song ended, and he took a step back. It wasn't late—barely eleven—but he faked a yawn and stretched out his neck, rolling it from one side to the other.

"It's been nice catching up, Daisy. But I should go."

Daisy smiled and looked up at him. The move was coy, playful, and he knew where it was headed before she opened her mouth. "You want some company?"

There was a time when Wyatt would have been all over this. Hell, up until a few weeks ago, he wouldn't have thought twice. He would have said, *Hell ya*, grabbed Daisy, and taken her back to his place for a hot night of sex and no regrets.

But a lot can change in a few weeks, and even though she was sweet and nice and a good time, Wyatt wasn't into it.

"I don't think that would be a good idea."

She watched him closely, that small smile slowly fading. "Okay," she whispered, a thoughtful look on her face. "Can I ask you a question?"

"Sure."

"Did you manage to melt the ice queen?"

The thought of Regan did all sorts of things to him. Things he didn't want to think about too closely. He shrugged.

"I'm trying."

"And how's that working out for you?"

"Honestly, I have no idea."

"Well." Daisy stood on her tiptoes and pressed a kiss to his cheek. "Let me know if you crash and burn."

Wyatt watched her walk away. He pulled out his wallet and tossed cash onto the table. Sean was tonsil-deep in Trish's mouth—some things never changed. He checked his phone, but there was nothing from Regan.

He thought about calling her, but she was most likely in bed. And he didn't want to come across as a needy son of a bitch. Wyatt decided it was better to let her come to him. She was a strong woman, and if this—whatever this was—was going to work, she'd be the one driving the car so to speak. Not him.

Wyatt smiled at the thought as he headed out into the Michigan cold.

# CHAPTER SIXTEEN

Regan was irritated.

Hell, she was beyond irritated, and the fact that she'd jumped over that particular line made her more irritated than whatever the heck described how she felt. What that word was exactly, she didn't know. All she did know was that irritated didn't quite cover it. She thumped her fingers along the edge of her desk and decided not to think about it anymore.

Damn Violet and her thirst for gossip.

Regan jumped out of her chair. She had one last patient to see and then a visit with her favorite youngster. The infection surrounding Patrick's brain had responded to his new meds, and he'd been released the day before. She passed Lynn in the hallway and, after a quick conversation, headed to exam room two. She knocked once and entered, smiling when she spied one of her favorite people ever.

Mr. George Darville.

He was a small man of French descent, who was approaching ninety with the same ferocious attitude he did every new decade. He was a no-holds-barred kind of man. He loved life, made no promises, and gave no excuses. He smoked a cigar every night on his porch while enjoying a nice bourbon, and he ate food rich in taste and calories.

He'd been married five times—happily, he claimed. He'd divorced three and outlived the other two, including his first wife, who was the love of his life. He had a pack of kids, many grandchildren, including Margot, a friend of Regan's, and all of them loved him with a fierceness that brought a lump to Regan's throat.

He was a character, and it was always a pleasure to see him. He, and folks like him, were the reason she opted to go into general practice. It wasn't as glamorous as specializing in something like neurosurgery, which she'd considered, but she loved where she was.

"Good afternoon, Mr. Darville." Regan sat in her seat and had a look at the computer screen.

"George to you, girlie." He winked.

"Okay, George." Regan clicked a few times. "I see your blood pressure is good."

"I could have saved your nurse the time, but she insisted." He winked again. "I think she likes me."

"Everybody likes you, George." Regan studied the notes and frowned. "You're complaining of pain? In your abdomen?"

"Bah." He shook his head. "It's nothing, but Margot insisted I come see you."

"Okay." Regan got up. "Let's have a look."

It took Regan about twenty minutes to finish her examination. George's abdomen was slightly distended and definitely tender. She sent him to the hospital for further tests—with someone his age, she didn't want him to wait—and called Margot to fetch her grandfather. After conferring with her for a few moments, they were on their way, and Regan could do nothing more until the results were in.

She made a few notes and shut down her computer before gathering her purse and jacket. Bella was asleep on her bed, tucked away in the corner of her office, but one whistle and her little three-legged bundle of fur jumped up and happily followed her from the office. They climbed into her car just as her phone pinged.

She glanced at her cell. Crap. Her mother.

She sighed and sank back into her seat, waiting for the vehicle to warm up. "Shit," she muttered, reaching for her cell. There was no sense in putting this off. Her mother was stubborn as hell and had been calling since Sunday evening. The evening she'd spent doing all sorts of things with Wyatt Blackwell that, apparently, she shouldn't have been doing. She should have had her ass parked at her mother's, enjoying a nice roast beef. If she'd done that, she wouldn't still be searching for that word that kicked "irritated" out of the ball park.

She sighed and answered her phone.

"Regan?"

"Wrong number? Were you looking for Adam?" A girl could be hopeful.

"I'm not in the mood."

"No. I can hear that." And, boy, could she ever. Her mother's tone was full of attitude, and Regan gazed out the windshield, wishing she hadn't bothered to answer. She loved her mother. So much. But Jesus, the woman was relentless.

"You missed dinner Sunday night."

"I did."

There was a pause. "You didn't call to tell me you wouldn't be coming for dinner. I set out the good china. The rosewood pattern that will one day be yours. I even made Yorkshire pudding because it's your favorite."

"Sorry. I was busy."

"So I hear."

Regan perked up at that comment. "What do you mean by that?"

"Regan Ophelia Thorne." Okay. The middle name had been thrown down, and that was never a good sign. How in hell did her mother manage to get under her skin like this at the ripe old age of twenty-nine? Heck, her birthday was coming up. She would be thirty in a month. It was ridiculous.

"Mom." She went for a soothing tone. The kind she used with little kids when they came in for a needle.

"Don't you *Mom* me. I'm hurt, Regan."

*Unbelievable.* "Hurt? Mom, I missed regular Sunday night dinner. It's not like it was Thanksgiving, or Christmas or Easter or freaking Lent, when we don't get to eat anything good anyway."

"Regan."

"Also? I'm an adult and—"

"We always have something good to eat whether it's Lent or not."

She gripped the steering wheel and took a moment. "That's not even the point."

"Then what exactly is?"

Regan exploded. "How the hell should I know? You're the one who called, pissed off because I missed Sunday dinner."

"That's not why I called." Her mother sounded as cool as a cucumber, and that just about sent Regan over the edge. She banged the steering wheel—several times—and the horn sounded each and every time.

"Shit." She glanced outside and spied Lynn by her car. The look on her nurse's face was comical, and Regan was going to guess she'd witnessed her mini meltdown. She gave a quick wave and watched her drive away.

"Language, darling."

Oh. Now it was darling. That was somehow worse than the use of her middle name.

"Mother." She counted to three. "Why *did* you call?"

"Well, let me see." She paused dramatically, and Regan could picture her mother with a smug look on her face, perched on the edge of her off-white sofa. The one in the front room that no one was ever allowed to sit on.

"Aside from the fact that you did miss Sunday dinner, something that is not only a tradition in our house, but something that's important to your father and me…" Again. Another dramatic pause. "I found out something that hurt, and I'm not happy about it."

Seriously. Katherine Thorne could have been a politician. She talked in circles, and it took her forever to get her point across.

"Honestly, Mom. I need to be somewhere in ten minutes."

"I bet you do."

"Just tell me whatever it is you called for, and I'll say I'm sorry, and we can move on." Regan pointed her index finger to her temple and looked down at Bella. The dog cocked her head to the side, ears perked up.

"Okay. I'll be frank."

Hallelujah.

"I ran into Joanne Wheeler at the grocery store."

This was not being frank, but Regan wasn't about to point that out. It was all she could do not to hang up on her mother. She'd done that before—it only made things worse.

"Joanne proceeded to tell me that Susan Avery told *her* a black truck was in your driveway all Saturday night until well into Sunday evening."

Busted. Her eyes slammed shut. Great.

"Mom."

"Now, Regan, you know I've been after you to be more social. To put yourself out there and have some fun. There are a lot of eligible men in this town, but Wyatt Blackwell? I know he's a handsome young devil, but he's a race car driver, for God's sake. *NASCAR*. He's never going to stay here for you. Don't you remember how he crushed you prom night?"

Wow. "Mom. Prom was over ten years ago. Can we not bring that up?"

But her mother went on, as she was prone to do. "Because I remember. I remember you coming home, crying and upset. And that pretty dress of yours ruined."

Irritated was no longer even in the universe of words to describe the feelings that coursed through Regan.

"I'm not discussing this with you."

"Regan."

"No. My privacy is just that, private. I appreciate you're looking out for me in your own special way, but my sex life is none of your concern."

"Oh God. You've already had sex with him."

Regan's eyes nearly popped out of her head. "What the hell did you think we were doing for twenty-four hours?"

Silence greeted her outburst. "I'm not a prude, Regan. I hope you were smart about things and used protection."

Regan's cheeks burned. They had used protection, but not the first time. Or the second. It wasn't until they'd come out of the incredible sex haze that had settled over them that she'd realized her mistake.

Sure, she was on the pill. Sure, he claimed he wasn't hiding any nefarious STDs. But still. She was a doctor, for God's sake. She counseled teenagers on being responsible, yet one touch from Wyatt Blackwell and all her good sense had gone out the window.

And then to hear that he'd been at the Coach House, slow dancing with Daisy Miller…

Her mother was right. She was an idiot. Tears sprang to the corners of her eyes and she swiped at them angrily.

"Regan?"

"I have to go, Mom." She put the car in Drive.

Her mother sighed, and that made Regan feel worse. "I just worry about you, and I want you to be happy."

"I know." And she did. She and her mother had a history of butting heads, but they always had good intentions.

"Are you okay?"

"Never better," she quipped.

"This wasn't about dinner. Although I would appreciate a heads-up if you're not coming. We might have ordered in Chinese takeout."

"Noted."

"I love you, sweetheart. Just be careful. Your heart is worth more than you know. Don't give it away to someone who doesn't deserve it."

"It was just sex."

Her mother's voice lowered. "It's never just sex with someone like Wyatt Blackwell. Be careful."

Again, the tears stung her eyes. What the hell was wrong with her? "I really do have to be somewhere."

"I love you, Regan."

She cleared the lump from her throat. "I know, Mom. See you on Sunday."

She tossed her cellphone onto the seat and headed out of town. The Bergens lived in one of the new subdivisions that had sprung up around the golf course on the other side of the lake. She'd been so pleased to learn Patrick had been released, and when Brad called to let her know, she'd accepted his offer of dinner. She couldn't wait to see the little guy.

By the time she crossed the bridge and headed for Crystal Lake Road, darkness had fallen and her mood had improved substantially. That was the effect one darling little, Patrick Bergen had on her. If she could do anything to make him smile, or ease his mind, she would. She turned to Bella.

"Ready?"

She'd put a Redwings sweater on the dog because the Detroit team was Patrick's favorite. Bella jumped into her arms, and she headed for the house. There were two trucks in the driveway and a sinking sensation hit her stomach as she stood on the porch and rang the doorbell. She glanced back at the black truck. She knew the red one was Brad's.

It couldn't be… Could it?

The door opened, and Brad greeted her in a Budweiser apron and a spatula. He had on a cowboy hat, and an unlit cigar was clamped between his teeth. "Right on time." He stood back, and she walked inside. Their home was big, open, and spacious. Decorated in light creams and grays, it was soothing and contemporary.

"Gwen's in the kitchen, and I need to grab the stuff off the barbecue off back. Western night, if you couldn't guess. Patrick likes it when we have theme nights, so who am I to say no to my son?"

Her heart melted. A lot. For such a big guy, he was all mush when it came to his son.

"You and Bella want to get Patrick? He's in his bedroom with Wyatt."

She slipped out of her coat. "Blackwell?"

"Is there any other?" He flashed a smile. "He's been real good to Patrick."

She waited until Brad disappeared down the hall and then headed upstairs. The landing was large, and she knew Patrick's room was the last one on the right. Bella ran ahead of her, and she pasted a smile to her face as she followed the dog inside.

Her smile faltered and fell away at about the same time her heart lurched and broke open. Wyatt's large body took up nearly all of Patrick's bed. He was asleep—they both were—his arms around the slight boy, whose head lay on his chest.

Bella barked, and Regan jumped, skin going hot and cold as Wyatt's eyes slowly opened.

"Hey," he said, carefully sitting up. He smiled at her then. The crooked, sexy-as-hell half smile that was enough to make any woman lose her mind.

It made her feel things, and that wasn't a good thing. Her mother was right. Wyatt Blackwell wasn't the kind of man she should be tangling with.

Patrick woke up, and Bella did her best to scramble onto the bed, but with her limited skills, it wasn't easy.

"How ya feeling, bud?"

"I feel good," Patrick replied with a yawn. "Wyatt came to play NASCAR with me. He's on the cover of the new game." The boy's voice was weak and a bit raspy, most likely because he'd been intubated a few days earlier for surgery. But his eyes were bright, and the look he gave Wyatt was filled with a healthy dose of hero worship.

She felt Wyatt's dark eyes on her. "Dinner's ready. Can you..."

"I got him." Wyatt swung off the bed and scooped the youngster into his arms.

Regan turned back toward the stairs, heart thudding painfully in her chest. For the third time in less than an hour, she felt as if she were on the verge of tears. What the hell was wrong with her?

But then she knew...didn't she?

Of course she did. The answer was six foot four inches of male perfection that would cause a lot of trouble for her if she wasn't careful. It was excitement and temptation and trepidation rolled into one. It was two words.

Wyatt. Effing. Blackwell.

Okay. Three words.

# CHAPTER SEVENTEEN

S omething was off. It didn't take a rocket scientist to figure
that out. Wyatt watched Regan as she chatted with Gwen. The
women were in the family room, cuddled up on the sofa with Bella
and Patrick. She was warm and open with them. All of them. But
every time she'd been forced to interact with Wyatt, she'd been
polite. Too polite. Plastic.

He didn't like it.

Something had happened between Sunday and now. He just
had no idea what the hell it was. And until he got Regan alone,
there was no way for him to find out.

"I'll take this out." Wyatt grabbed two garbage bags from the
kitchen and headed to the garage. He tossed them into the large
can and nearly tripped over Patrick when he turned back.

The kid's big eyes were wide and shiny, and there was color in
his pale cheeks, which was nice to see. But there was also fatigue.
Wyatt saw it just under the skin, paper-thin bruises beneath his
eyes.

"Hey," he said, tousling the kid's hair. "It's cold out here." He
was dressed in flannel pajamas and socks, but still...

"I'm not cold." But Patrick's teeth were starting to chatter. "I
wanted to ask you something."

"Sounds serious." Wyatt pointed to the door. "Why don't we talk inside?"

Patrick was visibly shaking now. But he shook his head and looked around, whispering, "I don't want anyone to hear."

"Huh." Wyatt scratched his chin. "This sounds like a man-to-man talk."

Patrick nodded. "It is."

"What say we head inside? Your parents and Regan are in the family room. We can have our man-to-man in the laundry room, like all real men do."

Patrick made a face. "My dad never hangs out in the laundry room."

Wyatt grinned. "Neither do I, but that doesn't mean we can't."

He guided the kid back inside, and the two of them kept on down the hall until they reached the laundry room.

"So what's this all about?"

Patrick was still shivering, and Wyatt pulled off his thermal Henley, placing it over the boy's head and tugging on it until it was down past his knees.

"Looks like my nana's muumuu," Patrick said, holding his arms wide with a grin.

"Yeah, but it will keep you warm." Wyatt picked him up and set him down on the dryer.

"Whoa. Cool tattoo. What is that?"

Wyatt glanced down at his right arm. Wrapped around his bicep was the only ink he had. It had been there since the day he turned eighteen and had caused one hell of a fight between him and his father. John Blackwell had been of the opinion that tattoos were only for certain types of folks, and the Blackwells weren't in that particular group.

Wyatt wondered what John thought of Hudson's tats. Hell, the man's entire right arm was filled with ink. He trailed his fingers over his own, suddenly somber.

"I got it for my mom. See here?" He pointed. "If you look real close, you can see a lion." Wyatt moved a bit so the kid could have a better look. "And here? That's the word Leo. It was my mother's astrological sign."

"I see it," Patrick breathed, reaching for the artwork. Wyatt moved a bit more so Patrick could touch it. "It so cool." He grinned, those big eyes of his flashing. "Does your mom like it?"

Wyatt couldn't take his eyes from the tattoo. Weird. It had been there for years, but he hadn't actually paid attention to it in ages. Looking at it now through the eyes of a young boy made him feel a lot of things. Most of which he didn't want to deal with. Things he wanted to forget.

At least, right now.

"I ah... My mom never saw it." He cleared his throat and glanced up, more than a little unnerved by the look in Patrick's eyes. There was knowledge there. A maturity that a kid his age shouldn't have. Patrick held his gaze for a couple of heartbeats.

"Did your mom get sick?"

Wyatt shook his head. "No."

"But she's in heaven?" Those little hands were on him now, and, dammit, Wyatt had to clear his throat again before he could answer.

"Yeah, Bud. She's in heaven."

Patrick traced the outline of the lion, and when he spoke, his voice was barely above a whisper. "I'm going to heaven too."

"Hey." Wyatt frowned, not liking the turn the conversation had taken. "Let's not talk silly."

Patrick nailed him with a look that said *cut the bull.* "I am." He shrugged. "It's okay. Father O'Reilly says heaven is really cool and I won't be sick up there. And our dog Molly went to heaven last year, so..."

Choked up, Wyatt had a hard time replying to that, so he did what most men would do in that situation. He waited a few moments for the emotion to clear and tried to change the subject.

"Patrick, what did you want to talk about?"

That little hand fell away from his tattoo, and a shiver rolled through Wyatt. He'd known this boy for barely a week, and in that short span of time, Patrick had managed to worm his way into the one place Wyatt kept guard over. The one place he allowed no one to enter.

His heart.

"Well…" Patrick ran his hands through his unruly hair. Wyatt heard the strain in his voice and knew the kid's strength was waning. He needed to get him back inside the family room, bundled up and warm with his parents.

"My mom and Dad are sad a lot." He looked up at Wyatt, and there went his heart again, tumbling through his body and hitting the floor with a *thud*. "Because of me. They're sad because I'm going to heaven and they don't want me to."

Wyatt could do one of two things right now. He could dismiss everything this kid was saying. Gloss over it as if it didn't matter and try to make Patrick forget the shit deal he'd been dealt. Or he could let Patrick say what it was he needed to say, because obviously, something was on his mind. And if Wyatt could help ease his burden, he'd damn well try.

Throat tight. He took a shot.

"First off, Patrick, I don't think you're going to heaven for a long, long time. Just my opinion, of course, but that's something I want to put out there, okay? And yes, your mom and dad get sad. They get sad because you're sick. They're sad that you have to go the hospital and that you missed hockey this season. They know sometimes you feel like crap, and that makes them feel helpless. It makes them sad because they love you."

"I know." Patrick picked at the edge of Wyatt's Henley. "I hate that stuff."

Wyatt leaned against the dryer and shoved his hands in the pockets of his jeans as a sudden thought struck him. "So what are we going to do about it?"

"Well." Patrick looked serious as all get-out. "I was thinking that because you're famous…"

Okay. This was good. He could do something to make Patrick feel better about things. Maybe take him to the next NASCAR race if he was up to traveling. Even if it meant meeting with Rob Tracy. Agreeing to see the damn shrink. He would do that for his kid.

"I was thinking you could get tickets to one of your brother's hockey games. Like, maybe my mom and dad could go?"

"My brother. This is about Travis."

Patrick flashed a half grin. "He's like the best goalie in the league and plays on my dad's favorite team. It could make them happy again. I just don't know how to get tickets. I don't have one of those cards."

Wyatt nudged him. "And you don't like hockey?"

"Yeah, I do. But my mom says it's not a good thing to be greedy. She says that greedy monsters have sticky fingers and that bad things stick to sticky fingers."

Wyatt laughed. He remembered something similar coming out of her mouth when she babysat him. "I think your mom might have been talking about sweet and sours. I used to eat them by the bag full and always had a sore stomach."

Patrick shrugged as if he had no clue what the heck Wyatt was talking about. "Can you ask your brother?"

"I think I can help you out."

Patrick smiled, obviously relieved. "Could you do it before I go to heaven? Just so that I know they went and had fun and weren't sad?"

In one moment, all that emotion was back, and Wyatt could do nothing but nod. "Sure. We'll get it done as soon as we can. I'll call Travis tonight. Right after his game."

Patrick seemed to consider his words, but when he spoke, his mind had obviously gone in a different direction.

"How old were you when your mom went to heaven?"

Shit. They were back to this.

"About your age."

Patrick's eyes widened, and he was silent for a bit. "You must have been really sad."

Wyatt nodded. "Yeah. I still am."

"I bet she was pretty."

His eyes smarted, and he swiped at the corners. "She was. Just like your mom."

"Did she smell like vanilla beans? My mom does."

"No." Wyatt slowly straightened as a memory washed over

him. "She smelled like green grass when it's just been cut and warm summer breezes off the lake. Sometimes she smelled like honeysuckle. It grew in the garden out back. I remember it crawled along the trellis."

"I like vanilla beans." Patrick shuddered and yawned.

"Hey, we should get you to bed." Wyatt scooped the little guy up and turned to leave the laundry room, only to come face-to-face with Regan. Her eyes shimmered with unshed tears, and her bottom lip trembled.

"I…" That husky tone he liked more than most things was there, and she took a step toward them, pressing a kiss to Patrick's cheek. "Your mom was looking for you. Time for your medication and bed." She paused, a soft smile playing around her mouth. "Do you want Bella to spend the night?"

Patrick nodded but didn't bother to answer. It was as if all his energy had been used up and he had no gas left in the tank.

"I'll take him up."

Wyatt slipped past Regan and carried the boy upstairs, Bella on his heels. Gwen was up there—she'd just put clean sheets on his bed—and she raised an eyebrow when she spied his naked chest.

"You like to show off your muscles or what?" she asked lightly.

"Your kid's wearing my clothes." He placed Patrick on his bed, and Bella immediately jumped up beside him. "He was cold."

Gwen tugged off Wyatt's shirt and handed it back, holding his gaze a heartbeat longer. "Thank you. I'm going to stay with him for a bit, so I'll say good-bye now."

He hugged her close. "He's one hell of a kid, Gwen."

She nodded. "I know."

"I'll talk to you tomorrow."

Wyatt headed downstairs, pulling on his shirt so that he was decent by the time he reached the foyer. Brad was chatting with Regan, their voices low and subdued. The man looked tired, worn out, and sad as hell.

Wyatt thanked him for a great evening and slipped into his boots and jacket, watching Regan as she followed suit. They said their good-byes and headed into the dark, Wyatt unsure how to proceed and one hundred percent off his game.

He paused by his truck, and just as he was about to say good-bye, Regan spoke. "Are you headed back to the cabin?" Small pockets of mist fell from her lips, her warm breath coming alive in the cold.

"That depends," he replied.

"On what?"

"On you."

A heartbeat passed. And then another.

She opened her car door, slipped inside, and waited a few moments before closing it. It was quiet out. The kind of quiet that hides in the snow. But then she spoke, and her words were crystal clear.

"I think you should stay in town."

Wyatt watched her taillights disappear down the road as he climbed into his truck. He backed out of the Bergens' driveway and hesitated for all of two seconds. He could have turned left and headed back to the cabin. Could have called it a night, taken the sleeping pills he'd been avoiding, and drifted off to a place where nothing existed.

Instead, he wheeled his truck right and headed back to town.

# CHAPTER EIGHTEEN

Regan was up early, which was saying something after the night she'd had.

It was early enough that she had time to lie in bed and enjoy the feel of Wyatt beside her. She turned onto her side and watched him sleep. It was a simple pleasure, really, and she indulged herself because she wanted to. Because she had no idea what it was they were doing, which meant she had no idea how long it would last.

*It won't last.*

The thought rifled through her head, and with a sigh, she slipped from bed and headed to the shower. It was still dark out, and the windows rattled from the force of the wind. Slivers of ice wound their way up the panes, and she knew it was going to be a cold one. Regan would have loved nothing more than to cuddle back up with Wyatt and fall asleep, but that wasn't a good idea.

Something was going on with him. He'd kept her up with his tossing and turning. And the man talked in his sleep. Nothing she understood, but still, he was troubled. Another reason why all this—whatever this was—wasn't a good idea.

With one last look at the sleeping man in her bed, she closed the door and turned on the hot water. Exactly thirty minutes later, she was showered, hair dried, and body lotion applied everywhere.

She ached in a few spots, but that was okay. She smiled. It was a good ache.

When Regan walked back into her bedroom, the bed was empty, the rumpled sheets and indentation on the pillow beside hers the only indication she hadn't been alone. She glanced around the room. Wyatt's clothes were gone.

Lovely. He'd up and left as soon as he could, and maybe that was a good thing. Last night had been...well, different.

They'd made love in silence. With furious ardor. It was as if they each needed something only the other could give, a connection that didn't need words. A touch that made things right in a world so unfair, a young boy would most likely not see another year.

And now in the harsh light of day, all the things left unsaid—her doubts, whatever it was he was hiding—well, they were there front and center.

It was enough for Wyatt to bolt. She shouldn't be surprised.

She quickly got dressed, pulling on dark gray slacks and a soft green sweater. She wrapped a scarf around her neck, grabbed her wool coat, and headed for her car. She'd be early for work, but the quiet and alone time would give her the opportunity to get her shit together.

The sun was coming up when she pulled into the parking lot of her office. Mr. Parker the cleaner was just leaving and let her in with a smile.

"You're early. I don't usually see your pretty face, so this is nice."

He was a sweetheart. "I've got some work to catch on, so I thought I'd get a head start."

"Well, you have a good day. I hear it's going to be another cold one."

"I know. It is only the beginning of February." She winked.

"It is," he said with a grin. "Florida is looking mighty fine right about now."

She flipped on the lights and headed to the back of the building, unloading her winter gear and pulling out her work shoes. Regan waited for her computer to boot up and was just thinking she should make a pot of coffee, when a loud rapping on the front door had her heading from the kitchen area to reception. She checked her watch, but it was at least an hour before Lynn or anyone else was due in. Maybe Mr. Parker forgot something?

She took exactly three steps before coming to a full-on stop.

Wyatt was on the other side of the glass door, a brown paper bag in one hand, a tray of coffee in the other. He'd pulled on a black knit hat, which only emphasized the cut of his jaw, the dark hair that shadowed it, and that mouth that had brought her so much pleasure the night before.

Regan's heart did a weird little flip, and she did her best to push that aside as she crossed reception and unlocked the door.

"I was going to make breakfast while you were in the shower, but your fridge made that kind of impossible."

"Sorry."

"No worries." He walked past and headed to the back, leaving her to lock the door behind him and follow. She found him in her office, and he handed her a coffee when she walked in.

"Black, just the way you like it."

"Thank you," she murmured, moving to her desk. Things were easier with a barrier between them. She felt safe—which was silly—but there you have it.

He took the seat across from her and set down his coffee so that he could empty out the bags. Her stomach rumbled as she accepted a bagel with egg, cheese, and bacon.

"This smells amazing."

"I swung by Coffee Corner. That place hasn't changed at all. I know the Nelsons don't own it anymore, but the new people seem real nice."

"They are. Milo and Angie are very sweet."

"From LA, she said." Wyatt hadn't touched his bagel. Instead, he stared at her from over the top of his coffee cup.

"Yes. They moved here a few years ago. Right around the time I came back and took over this practice."

"Harry Anderson was in there. Motorcycle accident, wasn't it?"

Again, Regan smiled politely and nodded. "He likes to help out. I think keeping busy calms his mind."

"I know Hudson's helping him out with some work."

"Your brother is a good guy."

"Yep. He is."

Abruptly, Wyatt sat forward and placed his coffee on her desk. The air suddenly changed. It became heated, charged with something she couldn't quite place. It wasn't anger, really, but it wasn't exactly rainbows and unicorns either.

"What's going on?" Gone was any pretense of niceties. Wyatt's eyes were hard and his mouth tight.

"I don't…" Shit. How was she going to handle this when she didn't exactly know how to articulate what it was she was feeling? "What do you mean? You want to talk about last night?"

He stared at her for a good five seconds and then sat back in his chair, nodding. "I sure as hell want to talk about last night."

Deflect. Deflect. Deflect.

"Okay." The word rolled around her head, and she put down her bagel. "You talk in your sleep."

She could tell that surprised him, and his face darkened with a scowl.

"That's not what I want to talk about." He practically growled the sentence.

"Right now, it's all I've got."

"Okay. If that's how you want to play." He studied her for a few moments and then shrugged. "Well, darlin', I hate to tell you this, but you snore."

"I do not." She sat up, her back ramrod straight, and glared at him.

"Yep." He was grinning now. "You do. Really loud, by the way."

"No one has ever told me that."

"So I'm lying?" His smile was wider, and that made her more irritated.

"I'm just saying no one has ever said that to me before."

"First off, no guy is going to block his own cock by telling a woman she snores. A guy will ignore that stuff to get what he wants. And secondly, when is the last time you slept with someone other than me?"

"I…" She stumbled over her words. How in hell had he managed to turn this around in the space of a minute? "That has nothing to do with it."

"No. You're right about that. It doesn't. So why don't you say whatever the hell it is you wanted to say to me last night. At Brad and Gwen's. You know, before the night of sex and more sex and the no-talking thing. Because, hey, most guys like the no-talking thing. Most guys would be all over that. But I gotta tell you, for me, it made things seem a little cold."

"Really?" Her back was up. "You didn't seem cold last night."

"I probably didn't because even when you're cold, you're still hot as hell. Even when you're cold, I still want you." He held her gaze for a heartbeat or longer. "But the thing is, Regan? I like talking with you. I like it. All of it. Even when you're driving me crazy. So, tell me what the hell changed between Sunday and last night?"

She didn't hesitate and leaned forward. "Violet told me you were at the Coach House Monday night with Daisy Miller." Her heart was beating nearly out of her chest, but she gripped the edge of her desk, watching him closely.

He didn't give anything away. And he sure as hell didn't look surprised at her comments. In fact, a slow smile crept over his face, and she envisioned her fist hitting his throat. That should knock that smug look off his face.

"You're jealous of Daisy Miller?"

"I'm not jealous of Daisy Miller." Holy hell was she jealous of Daisy Miller.

"Good, because there's no need for you to be. I was at the Coach House. I met up with Jarret and Sean for beer and wings. Daisy and her friend Trish—'"

"Trish McMaster?" She rolled her eyes. "Wow. Great company you're keeping these days."

That damn smile tugged at his mouth again, infuriating her even more.

"I wouldn't know," Wyatt said slowly. "She was playing tongue tag with Sean. And as for Daisy, we danced to some sappy song she liked and that was it."

"That was it." She so didn't believe it. She knew Daisy. And she knew the two of them had gotten together when he'd been home for Thanksgiving. It was a small town. Folks talked.

"She wanted to come back to my place, but I said no."

Regan said nothing to that because she couldn't. And Regan didn't have to look into a mirror to know her cheeks were scarlet. Why the hell hadn't she just zipped her mouth and shut the hell up?

"Do you know why I said no?" His voice was low. Dangerously low. It hit at all sorts of things inside her, and Regan swallowed hard, glad there was a piece of furniture between them.

Slowly, she shook her head, unable to answer.

Wyatt got up and walked around her desk and—boom—there went the barrier between them. He turned her chair and placed both of his hands on either side of her cheeks. She couldn't look away if she wanted to. Which she didn't.

And that was crazy.

"I said no to Daisy Miller because she's not you. It wasn't hard to do, and it *was* that simple." He leaned closer, his breath warm on her face. "Are you reading me here?"

She leaned into his palm and closed her eyes. "But what are we doing?" She thought about what her mother said. About how she'd placed Wyatt into a narrow category that suddenly didn't seem to fit. "What's the point if…"

"If what?"

So here she was. About to lay it on the line. About to let Wyatt Blackwell know that this thing between them wasn't casual for her. It just wasn't.

"Whenever you deal with whatever it is you're dealing with…" She slowly opened her eyes. "You'll leave and go back to your life. We don't fit, Wyatt. We never did."

"I think you're wrong." He sighed and stood, running a hand across his chin. "I know you're wrong."

"What if I'm not?"

Just then, the door opened, and Lynn walked in, rambling off a list of patients coming in before noon. She stopped when she spied Wyatt.

"Oh. My. I didn't see you there."

He grinned and winked. "Hey, Lynn."

"Good morning, Wyatt Blackwell." She set down a folder on Regan's desk, mindful of the food and coffee. "Nice to see you. I heard you were back in town." She glanced at Regan, a knowing twinkle in her eye. "I guess you don't need a coffee."

"No…I…we're good."

"Okay, then. I'll leave you guys to it." She winked once more and reached for the door. "Although you only have ten minutes, because your first patient will be here soon. Mrs. Waters is always twenty minutes early."

The door clicked behind her, and Regan got to her feet. "I should…" She pointed to the folder.

Wyatt didn't budge. "Are we good?"

Before she could answer, he leaned forward and swept his mouth over hers in a scorching kiss. It was a slow sort of assault that had her head spinning and her knees shaking. And when he gently let her go, Regan nodded.

"Yes. We're good."

He dropped one last kiss on her nose before grabbing his coffee. "Good. I'll see you tonight."

There was no question in his tone. The man wasn't playing games. She nodded and watched him leave. She wasn't playing games either, but unlike Wyatt, she wasn't so sure.

Unlike Wyatt, Regan was a little bit afraid.

# CHAPTER NINETEEN

Wyatt spent the morning buying food for Regan's home. The girl had no idea how to feed herself, and he was more than happy to stock up. After that, he tracked down his brother Hudson and drove out to the lake and the family home for a meet-up. Darlene was out of town for some woman's retreat at a spa, and Hudson had spent the night.

"You don't answer your damn phone," Wyatt said, stomping the snow from his feet and undoing his jacket.

Hudson was in the kitchen and shrugged. "It's nice to unplug sometimes. As long as Becca knows where I am, I'm good."

"I get that."

Wyatt hung up his coat. "Another cold one out there."

"Yep. Weather's not supposed to break until next week." Hudson offered him a coffee, but he was pretty much done with caffeine for the day. "Nothing us Michigan boys can't handle."

Wyatt took a seat at the island and watched his brother. "The domestic thing. How's that working out for you?"

Hudson sat across from him. "I'm guessing you didn't come here to discuss the ins and outs of my day-to-day living. What's up?"

Just like Hudson to cut to the chase.

"I did some digging and was surprised to find out Blackwell Holdings bought the old arena from the town."

"Yes." Hudson sat back and crossed his arms. "With the new one already up and running, the old place wasn't being used. Some money from out of state came sniffing around, and I didn't want just anyone getting their hands on the property. The town didn't have the funds to maintain it, so we bought it."

Wyatt let that settle a bit. "You got any plans for it?"

Hudson shrugged. "We've rented it out for a few functions, but I haven't really had time to take a good hard look. Why?"

"I'm guessing there's no ice right now?"

"No. All town sports were moved to the new arena. It's a quad rink, so we were able to accommodate a larger pool of teams and leagues."

"Is the equipment still there? For the ice?"

Hudson frowned. "What are you getting at, Wyatt?"

"I've got an idea. Something I'd like to do for someone, and I was hoping to use the facility."

"I don't see that being a problem. You'd have to look at insurance and liability and such, but the place is sitting there empty at the moment. I'd rather it be put to use, even if only for an evening. How soon you looking at?"

"As soon as possible. Within two weeks. I just have to line up a few things and talk to some people."

"Okay. Run with it. If you need anything, just let me know."

"I appreciate it." Wyatt looked over his brother's shoulder. "What're you cooking up there, anyway?"

"I didn't cook anything. You were the one who wore the chef's hat in this house." Hudson grinned. "Darlene left Hungarian chicken stew. Want some?"

"Hell yeah."

The two men got serious about eating, and an hour later, they'd put a good dent in the stew and had eaten half a loaf of homemade bread.

"I remember Darlene would make this every Saturday night." Wyatt grinned.

"With dumplings."

"God damn, her dumplings were good."

Hudson grabbed Wyatt's empty plate and carried it to the dishwasher, while Wyatt scooped up a rag and wiped down the island. When he was done, he rinsed it out and hung it in the sink. The hook was still there, and he stared at it for a few seconds, thinking how some things never change.

"Are we going to talk about the crash?" Hudson leaned against the counter, a no-bullshit look in his eyes.

Wyatt swore under his breath. No. Hell no. "Hudson. I appreciate you looking out for me, but I don't need you too. We're not kids anymore, and I'm good."

His brother was silent for a few moments. "It looked bad, Wyatt. I can't imagine how it was for you to be involved in that. To see that."

*Again.*

His brother didn't have to say the word. It echoed in Wyatt's head, so loud he wanted to scream. Ever since Diego's crash, he'd been thinking of nothing but that. The day his mother died.

"Rob Tracy called me," Hudson said.

Wyatt's head shot up at that. "What the hell did he want?"

"He's concerned. Said it was mandatory that you see a sports psychologist after Diego died. He said you left halfway through your session. Rob told me that's why he hasn't cleared you to race."

"Rob Tracy should keep his mouth shut. My personal situation isn't any of your concern."

"You're wrong about that." Hudson looked angry. "I don't care if you're ten, twenty, thirty, or one hundred years old. You'll always be my little brother. And I'll always look out for you."

Wyatt made a sound of frustration. "Hudson, just leave this alone. I'll be back to racing before you know it."

"Not according to Rob."

"Sorry to point this out, brother, but when it comes to the world of racing, you don't know shit."

"Then fill me in."

"If Tracy doesn't clear me to drive soon, Stu Randall, the owner and the guy who signs my paychecks, will. Denver Gilroy hasn't placed in the top five since I've been gone. Rob Tracy has a hornet up his butt because I didn't do things his way. Because I won't listen to his bullshit. I don't need to talk to some stranger about my feelings. Diego died. It was tragic and sad as hell, but it's part of the job. Every time we get on that track, there's the possibility of getting hit with bad mojo. It's the nature of the beast. Stu will get sick of losing, and I'll get the call."

Wyatt had to take a moment, because there was a fire in his gut and it was spreading. He hadn't come here to fight. Hell, he'd come here to do something good. Something that had nothing to do with racing.

"Hudson, let's drop it."

His brother must have known he was waging a losing battle, because he gave up on the racing thing and dug in on something else entirely.

"What's this I hear about you and Regan Thorne?"

Christ. He should have skipped out as soon as he was done eating. He sighed and shook his head. "You say it like it's a bad thing."

Hudson frowned. "I'm just a little surprised is all. She's not exactly the type you've been known to hook up with."

Annoyed with his brother's attitude, Wyatt shoved his hands into the pockets of his jeans. It was either that or hit something. And the problem with hitting Hudson? He would hit back.

"Didn't know I had a type."

"Oh yeah." Hudson nodded. "You do. Tall. Blonde. Big tits and no brains."

"That's pretty generic."

"Up until recently, you were pretty generic about the women you dated."

"A guy can change."

"True." Hudson followed him back to the foyer. "But usually there's a reason. And while Regan Thorne is one hell of a reason to change, I don't get you and her. I thought she hated your guts."

Wyatt reached for his coat. "Hate is a pretty strong word." He zipped up and shoved his feet into his boots, not liking the way Hudson was looking at him. His gaze was piercing and thoughtful, and just like that damn eye in *The Two Towers*, it was all-seeing.

"What?" he asked casually, slipping on his thermal gloves.

"She's the real deal, Wyatt."

"Jesus, Hudsy. You sound like a wuss."

"I'm not joking."

"I can tell."

Hudson opened the door for him. "Look. All I'm saying is that a girl like Regan Thorne doesn't give her time easily. Hell, I've been home for months now, and I don't know one guy that's managed to snag her interest. So for her to be spending time with you says something. I like her, and I'd hate to see her get hurt."

Was he ever going to be forgiven for prom night?

Wyatt stepped onto the porch. "She's a big girl, Hudson. I don't think you need to worry about her. She can look after herself."

"She might be a big girl, but trust me, brother. All big girls carry around the shit they dealt with when they were little. I should know. I screwed up huge with Rebecca, and I have no idea how I managed to win her back."

The warning was subtle. And it was noted.

"Must be the Blackwell charm."

"Maybe."

Wyatt started toward his truck. "I'll let you know when I figure out my plans for the old arena."

"Good. I look forward to it."

He waved good-bye and got into his truck.

He was halfway to town when he realized he hadn't asked about his father. In fact, he hadn't thought about it at all. On a gray day with snow-heavy clouds dotting the horizon, it was a thought that left him feeling bleak and tired.

Hudson was worried about Regan's baggage, but the thing was, they all had baggage. Stuff from their past that definitely impacted the present. Regan had dealt with hers. At least it seemed to be the case. How long was Wyatt going to hold on to his?

# CHAPTER TWENTY

The week sped by. Flu season was well under way, and in addition to a full slate at Regan's practice, she'd taken two extra shifts at the hospital because several of the doctors were sick, and they were understaffed. She barely had time to think, let alone dwell on the fact that Wyatt Blackwell had become a habit.

No. Scratch that. Wrong phrase to use. A habit was something you could break. Something that happened *just because,* over and over and over again. With Wyatt, that wasn't the case. He'd become a fixture in her home. In her life. In her bed. And if she wasn't careful, he'd infiltrate her heart.

Case in point.

It was Saturday evening, and she'd spent her entire day off at the hospital. In addition to the cold and flu cases she'd seen, there'd been an accident on the bypass just outside of town, and several patients had come through the ER.

Most of them were okay. A broken arm. Cuts and bruises. But Dale Hubber hadn't been so lucky. He'd sustained a collapsed lung, a broken pelvis, and an internal bleed that had required surgery. The man was on the wrong end of eighty and had barely made it through.

Blair Hubber, Dale's son and current mayor of Crystal Lake,

was in a state. Regan had known the family her whole life, and though she'd seen her fair share of emotion and tragedy, it was still hard to deal with when a friend was involved. She'd stayed late, well after her shift was over, to make sure Dale was okay and to comfort Blair in any way she could. The old man was doing as well as could be expected, and sure, it was still touch and go, but Regan was hopeful.

She'd been exhausted by the time she'd pulled into her driveway—it was nearly ten o'clock—and all she wanted was a hot bath and her bed.

Wyatt and Bella greeted her at the door. Wyatt with a gentle kiss that brought tears to her eyes and a glass of red wine in hand. Bella with her three-legged happy dance and a wet nose pushed repeatedly into her hand.

Wyatt had called the hospital and had known she was on her way home, so he'd filled the whirlpool tub in her bathroom with hot water and gently nudged her in that direction.

Now, it was half past ten, she was still enjoying the hot bath as well as her second glass of wine, and Bella was asleep beside the tub. She sank lower into the tub, her big toe moving the lever, allowing more hot water to flow in, and closed her eyes as she rested her head on the bath pillow.

She wasn't sure how much time had gone by, but Regan's eyes flew open with a start. She shivered and glanced up, her heart lurching when she spied Wyatt leaning against the door frame, a big fluffy towel in his hand.

"I think it's time for you to get out." There was a teasing note to his voice. She liked that. Probably more than she should.

"You do?"

"Yes." He moved closer. "I do. Because if you don't, one of two things will happen." He sat on the edge of the tub. "One. You just might turn into a prune. And two, I might have to join you, and if I did that, you wouldn't have the energy to try my homemade chicken soup."

Her eyes widened at about the same time her stomach rumbled—loudly. It brought a smile to his face, and he held up the towel. Five minutes later, she was bundled up in her fluffy pink bathrobe, hair secured in a loose knot and a bowl of to-die-for chicken soup in front of her with…

"Did you make these biscuits?"

Wyatt grinned and sat down across from her. "Just one of the many things I can do."

They melted on her tongue. Like literally. And the taste… "From scratch?"

He shrugged. "Is there any other way?"

Seriously. The man could write the book on how to be the best boyfriend. Ever. *Boyfriend.* Was that what he was? She glanced away, stirring her soup. She was getting way ahead of herself. Sure, they'd fallen into a routine of sorts, but they'd both been so busy, the only time she saw him was at night, and they spent most of that making love.

"Why did you start racing?" The question just sort of fell out her mouth, and, surprised, Regan glanced up, watching him closely. He took a bite from his biscuit as if considering his answer and then spoke.

"John took me to the dirt track, next county over when I was about thirteen."

"John?" Now that was surprising.

Wyatt nodded and played with the edge of his napkin. "He thought it would be good for me. I was having a hard time with some stuff, and he…" He shrugged, his face shuttered, his jaw tight.

"We don't have to talk about this, Wyatt. I was just curious is all."

But he kept on as if he hadn't heard her.

"I was in the car when Mom died. We'd been to the grocery store. I remember she bought me a huge bag of sours and then told me not to open them until I got home." He smiled then, a sad, wistful sort of thing that tugged at her. It took hold and held Regan tight.

He looked up suddenly. "They were my favorite thing in the world. Mom used to tell me that it was a miracle my teeth weren't rotted out of my damn head, but…she still bought them."

He paused and cleared his throat. "I saw the whole thing. I was in the back, keeping an eye on my mom so she wouldn't see that I'd opened the bag of sours. I was stuffing them in my mouth, two at a time, trying to eat as many as I could before we got home." He frowned. "No. She said she had to meet someone. Someone Dad worked with. So, we're cruising down the road, and I see this car coming at us. Like a straight line. A shot of big, black American metal. I wasn't scared or anything. I mean, the car would pull back to his side. He had to, right?"

There was a long pause, and Wyatt's eyes dropped once more. He grabbed the napkin back and shredded the edges. "But he didn't. And my mother did nothing to avoid it. It was like she was driving the car but not really seeing anything. In that last moment, I tried to scream. I tried to warn her. I tried to get to her, to make her turn the wheel, but my seat belt… I couldn't get it undone."

Regan's heart broke for the little boy who still lived in this man. She was silent because she didn't know what to say. What words of comfort could she offer him now?

"After it happened, I guess I blacked out. Found out later I had a lot of internal injuries, and I'd lost so much blood that for a few weeks after, they called me the miracle kid. But the only thing I remember from that day, other than that big, black car headed toward us, was opening my eyes and seeing all those sour candies on the seat and the floor."

Regan sat back in her chair, suddenly cold.

"But that doesn't really answer your question about the dirt track. See, John was a hard-ass. After the accident, I had a difficult time being in a car. Being in any kind vehicle, really. If it had a motor in it, I was freaked out. Once, in the middle of the lake, I jumped out of the boat because the Sea-Doos buzzing around made me anxious. John yelled at me to get back in, but I refused, so he left."

"What?" Regan's mouth fell open in shock.

"I swam halfway across the lake to get back to shore. He didn't get it. The fear… It was a fear that would leave me sick to my stomach. Paralyze me. It made me weak, and he hated that. He thought that forcing me to drive would help."

"Wyatt," she breathed, getting to her feet. Her heart ached, and she needed to do something. She walked around the table and stood beside him, feeling unsure and inadequate.

"Thing is? The bastard was right. I was shaking so bad the first time I got into one of those cars, I could barely get the key in the ignition. But all it took was one spin around that track, and suddenly I was free. Free of the fear. Free of the memories. The images from that day." His voice lowered. "I was free of him, and I never looked back."

Regan's hands crept around his shoulders, and when he turned to her and placed his head against her chest, she damn near cried. They stood like that for a long time. So long she was pretty sure her delicious soup was cold and those biscuits were probably hard. Not that it mattered. She wasn't hungry for food. She was hungry for that connection only she and Wyatt shared. She couldn't explain it. And truth be told, she didn't give a crap.

Gently, she pulled away, loving the way his eyes darkened as she reached for the tie around her waist. One deft movement and the robe slid from her body to pool at her feet. His sharp intake made her feel powerful. Alive.

Wanted.

She reached for him and pushed him back in his chair. She positioned it the way she wanted and undid his jeans, her body already hot and wet and ready. He was just as ready, and she bent down, taking all of him into her mouth. Enjoying the feel of him, the hardness wrapped in velvet. The way he let go.

She wanted him to forget about the blackness. If only for a little while.

Regan licked and suckled. She took him deep and teased him until she knew his control was weak. She massaged his balls and moved her hands deftly up and down his shaft, then tore her mouth away and kissed him with a fervour she hadn't felt before. Something was different. This was somehow more real.

His hands were on her breasts, and his mouth trailed a line

of fire to join them. With breaths falling rapidly, Regan straddled Wyatt and sank down on him fully, taking every inch of his cock deep into her warmth.

"God, Regan. You feel like fucking heaven."

She gripped his shoulders and started to move as he looked up at her. Regan couldn't speak. Hell, she could barely keep the tears that threatened to fall from doing so.

"Hey," he said, hoarsely as he found her rhythm. "You okay?"

She nodded, her chest tight with emotion, her body on fire with need. She pressed her breasts against him and threw her head back when he closed his mouth over her nipple. Regan rode Wyatt for as long and as hard as she could. She tried to communicate all the feelings and thoughts she had with her body. With her hands and her mouth and her sex.

Their passion filled the room, and they came together in a shattering climax. Taking. Receiving. Holding on.

Regan pulled Wyatt close and kissed the top of his head, holding him, needing him as much as he needed her.

She didn't want to let him go, and that was a *hello* moment. It was a sobering thought, because she knew she would have to…

Eventually.

# CHAPTER TWENTY-ONE

Wyatt drove through a grand stone entrance and followed a gray-tinted, stamped concrete drive until he found the building he was looking for. He parked his truck in a spot reserved for visitors, eyes taking in a condominium complex that was quite impressive. Crystal Lake View was only a few years old, and Regan's parents had moved in not long after it had been completed. Built with a vision of stone, glass, and nature coexisting in a serene setting on the lake, he understood its appeal.

He didn't see Regan's car, but after checking his watch, he headed inside. They'd spent all morning in bed, and then he'd had to keep an appointment in the city. She was running errands and had asked him if he wanted to go to her parents for dinner.

Wyatt hadn't thought twice about it and answered yes. He thought that maybe she was a little surprised, but the cute smile she'd given him told him she was pleased. They'd agreed to meet at four, but with no car in sight, he was thinking he'd be on his own for a bit.

That was fine. Wyatt remembered Katherine and Frank Thorne as pleasant folks, though he was thinking he hadn't seen them since...

He rang the doorbell and frowned. Hmm. Not since prom

night.

He heard precocious giggling at about the same time the door opened. Regan's niece, Harriet, hung on the door and started to swing back with it, her eyes full of mischief.

"Nana," she yelled over her shoulder. "It's Auntie Regan's boyfriend." A pause. "The man with the funny name!"

"It's not funny, silly." She was joined by Jordan, who pushed up his glasses and gave a wave.

"Hey, Wyatt."

"Hey, Jordan."

Harriet was still hanging off the door, and it was slowly swinging back and forth. "Aren't you coming in?" Her voice was singsong, and something about the way she held her head or tilted her chin reminded him of Regan.

"I would." Wyatt winked. "But you have to move."

Jordan grabbed Harriet's sweater, which started a bit of a tug-of-war between the two of them. Wyatt took a couple of steps inside and scooped up both twins, one in each arm, enjoying the giggles and shouts. He pretended to drop them, and just as Harriet squealed loud enough for the entire complex to hear—hell, he was pretty sure it carried across the lake and into town—Katherine Thorne appeared.

A smart-looking woman, she had classic features and wide-set gray-green eyes. Her hair was still worn long, although instead of the brunette shade he remembered, she'd let it go silver gray. She'd always been a pretty lady. One of the moms who used to fuel a lot teenage fantasies, from what he remembered, and he noted she could still turn heads.

Her eyes narrowed a bit when she spied him, and he didn't exactly sense a warm welcome, even though she held out her hand and said hello. It was polite. But too polite. He got that. She was taking measure. Looking out for her daughter.

"I see you've met my grandchildren."

Wyatt nodded and set the children down. "I have. A few weeks back. There must be something in the water. A hell of a lot of twins in Crystal Lake."

Harriet made a loud, dramatic noise. She poked her brother and whispered, loud enough for Wyatt, Katherine, and probably anyone else in the house to hear, "He said a bad word. The H one."

"Shit."

Harriet squealed again.

"Sorry." Wyatt chuckled. "I guess I'm not used to being around kids."

Katherine took a step back. "No. I guess you're not." She turned to her grandchildren. "You guys go down and fetch your papa away from his trains. Tell him that..." She glanced back at Wyatt. "Tell him Regan's friend is here."

Harriet began to giggle and grabbed her brother's hand. Again, she whispered behind her hand into his ear. Again, it was so loud everyone could hear. "Auntie's boyfriend."

The kids ran down the hall and disappeared, leaving Wyatt with Katherine. She indicated he should follow her, so he doffed his boots and hung up his coat before following her to the family room at the back of the house.

The décor was tasteful, understated, and classy.

"This is real nice," he said, walking up to the windows that overlooked the lake. In the distance, he saw Pottahawk Island, and beyond that, the shores that touched his family's home base.

"It's certainly different from living in town, but I do love it out here. And the view is one of the reasons we bought." She paused. "Can I get you anything?"

"No. I'm good." Wyatt turned around. "Are Adam and Violet here?"

"Adam is out of town on business, and Violet is with Regan. You didn't know that?"

"No. I wasn't sure what Regan was up to. She just said she had errands and asked that I meet her here."

"Hmm."

Wyatt generally had a good read on people, and he got the feeling Katherine Thorne wasn't a fan. It annoyed him a bit—he wasn't used to people not liking him. Never mind that most people he met went out of their way to meet him, A) because of his celebrity status or B) because they wanted something from him. Thing was? Not too many folks that crossed his path didn't like him.

The front door flew open just then, and Violet and Regan stomped in like a herd of buffalo. They carried bags and boxes and a heck of a lot of snow on their feet. Their laughter was contagious, and he smiled as he watched them navigate the boots already at the door, the things in their arms, and each other.

Violet Thorne was a blast from the past, and he smiled when she caught sight of him. Her vibrant red hair was more colorful than he remembered, helped in part by streaks of black and blue, and her smile was as open and warm as he remembered.

He helped the girls bring in their bags. They'd obviously been to the grocery store, and just as they gathered in the large, bright kitchen, Frank and the twins joined them.

Regan's father had aged well. He looked like he was in shape, had a full head of hair, and a hearty laugh that put everyone at ease. He used to help coach football, and Wyatt had vivid memories of the loud, exuberant man yelling at the defense from the sidelines.

"Sir," Wyatt said, offering his hand. The man slapped him on the shoulder and shook his hand vigorously.

"It's Frank. Sir makes me feel ancient." He stood back, a wide grin on his face. "Nice to see you, son. It's been a lot of years." He winked. "Can I get you a beer?"

Wyatt smiled. Okay. This might be a win after all.

Turned out some of the bags contained Chinese takeout from a new place, Yin's, and they sat down right away, not wanting the food to get cold. The kids ate their way through an impressive amount of rice and chicken balls before repeatedly attempting to steal everyone's fortune cookies.

"No," Violet said for the fourth time. "We each get our own fortune." She gathered them in her hand, and everyone took a turn retrieving their own. The twins tore into theirs right away. They wolfed down the sugary cookies and didn't seem interested in their fortunes.

After all that.

"What does yours say?" Regan poked him as she broke open her cookie. "Oh. Mine's good." She leaned against him, and he peered into her hands. "A fortune for the lucky means a big win in your future." She made a face. Guess I should buy a lottery ticket."

"That would be a first," Violet said. She looked at Hudson. "She's cheap as hell, you know."

"Really?" He chuckled.

"You see the car she drives?" Violet made a face. "I rest my case."

Regan reached for his and snagged it before he had a chance to see what it said.

"Regan," Katherine said. "That was rude."

She shrugged and obviously didn't care. Neither did Wyatt. Watching her smile and be relaxed and happy, well, he would have given up a hundred million fortunes.

Her laughter slowly faded, and she crumpled up the paper before he could grab it back. "What does it say?"

"Just a bunch of numbers," she said. "You got a bum fortune."

"Are there any more cookies?" Harriet searched through the mess of wrappers and containers on the table.

"Okay." Katherine got to her feet and began to gather up the mess. "Is everybody done?" Frank insisted on helping his wife clean up, and while Regan and Violet stayed to help, Wyatt had no choice but to let the twins lead him downstairs. Apparently, their grandfather was quite the train aficionado, and there was an impressive display that Harriet and Jordan were dying to show him.

At least thirty minutes passed in which Wyatt learned a hell of a lot about trains. The kids had stories to tell—most they'd obviously heard from their grandfather, and their imaginations knew no boundaries. There was even a pink-and-purple caboose that was not only magical, sometimes (according to Harriet) it disappeared and went to the magical place full of cotton candy and root beer.

"I'd say I hope they're not talking your ears off, but I know better than that." Violet joined him and shook her head. "Don't worry. It gets easier. After a while, it all blends together and you learn to say yes and no, and..." She giggled. "Really?"

"They're great kids."

"Yeah. They are. I mean, they're a handful and drive me crazy sometimes, but I wouldn't trade them for anything."

She clapped her hands together. "Okay, guys. You need to put away the toys, and we have to go soon. School tomorrow."

They groaned and complained and made faces. But they listened to their mother and began to organize their mess and put the toys away.

"So...you and Regan." It wasn't a question.

Wyatt turned to find Violet's attention on him. Her gaze was a little unnerving—not unlike her daughter's—and he shrugged.

"Me and Regan."

Her eyes lingered a little too long, as if she were trying to figure something out. She rocked back onto her heels and shoved her hands into her pockets.

"I'm just surprised."

"Yeah?" He should have known he couldn't leave the Thorne house without a grilling. Hell, he should be thankful Adam wasn't here. The guy had always been a bit of a hothead where his sister was concerned.

"Why's that?" he asked, genuinely curious.

"Because of prom." She gave him a look like he was an idiot, and then her mouth dropped open. Slowly, she shook her head and took a step back. "You don't know what happened prom night, do you?"

The kids had stopped tossing their toys into the bin, but all it took was one look from Violet and they dug back into the job. Wyatt took those few moments to gather his thoughts.

He would have liked to have asked Violet more questions, but Regan appeared at the top of the stairs, and it was time for him to go. He said good-bye to the twins, promised Harriet he'd let her read to him the next time he saw her, and then headed up to join Regan.

She was in the foyer chatting with her mother when Frank joined them. The look of pride and joy and love on the man's face when looked at his daughter was something to behold.

If Wyatt were a pussy, he might wonder what that felt like to be on the receiving end of such unconditional love. But he wasn't a pussy, and he didn't much care to think of those things. What was the point? He'd only disappoint himself.

"Hope to see you again, Wyatt." Frank shook his hand and stood back, slipping his arm around his wife's shoulders. "Hey, sorry, I meant to ask earlier, but how's the old man doing?"

"He's…" Wyatt glanced at Regan as if she could help him out. The sad fact was, Wyatt Blackwell had no idea whatsoever. "I think he's doing all right. Hanging in there."

"That's good to hear. We've missed him down at the shelter."

"Shelter?"

"The animal shelter. Your dad likes to come and help out when he's feeling up to it. Problem is, the old ticker doesn't always cooperate."

Well, that was a new one. Hell, when he was a kid, he and his brothers had begged John for a dog, and the man always answered no.

"You tell him I said hello, and I'll try and stop in and see him real soon."

Wyatt didn't bother to tell Frank it might be days before he saw his father. He nodded and said he'd pass along the message, and then he and Regan left. They'd arrived separately, so he waited for her to pull out ahead of him, and he followed her back to Crystal Lake.

He had a lot on his mind, and he meant to have a conversation with Regan about prom night as soon as they got to her place. But that plan went south as soon as he walked into her house. She was there, in his face. All that hair and soft, warm skin. That mouth and that voice that drove him crazy with the sexy things she whispered in the dark.

They ended up on the floor in front of the fireplace, and as she stripped off all her clothes and pushed him back onto the soft fur rug, prom night and all that other crap faded from his mind.

There was only Regan, and in that moment, she was all Wyatt needed.

# CHAPTER TWENTY-TWO

Regan hadn't been to A Cut Above for a manicure since before Christmas. Even then she'd been dragged in by her mother because Katherine insisted her hands should look presentable for the holidays. As for a pedicure? She couldn't remember the last time. As she soaked her feet and gazed over her magazine at the girl sitting in front of her, she was pretty sure Dana was thinking the same thing.

"What color did you pick for your toes?"

Carly was back in town. Apparently, she'd flown back to Michigan the night before, and she'd shown up at Regan's place an hour earlier, coffee in hand, plans for the spa and a look that said she wasn't taking no for an answer. Luckily, it wasn't Regan's Saturday to cover the ER, so she could indulge her friend and spend the morning with her.

"I picked blue."

Carly made a face. "Boring."

"Jet Set Blue." Dana looked up with a smile. "I'll be right back. I just need to grab some tools."

"Gosh, your feet are rough." Carly shook her head. "But at least you shaved your legs." She licked her lips and made an exaggerated smacking sound. "Though from what I hear, you've got plenty of reason to make sure every inch of you is well groomed these days."

"Yeah?"

"Yep."

Regan closed her magazine and set it aside. "I could say the same about you."

Carly grinned. "The rumor mill must be working overtime."

"Not hard to do when you and Jarret were spotted making out in the drive-through of the Dairy Queen. Jesus, Carly. You're acting like a teenager."

"Right?" She giggled and wriggled her toes. "I don't know how it happened. I mean, I came home for the reunion and we just hit it off. He makes me feel like the sun is always shining, you know? I can be down and he'll call, and suddenly, the world is spinning the way it should be. Not too slow. Not too fast. Just perfect."

"Keep spouting stuff like that, and I'm going to think you've fallen in love with him."

Carly splashed the water a bit and lowered her voice when Dana sat back down. "I kinda think I have."

Regan opened her mouth to respond, but she didn't know what to say, so she shut it again. Carly and Jarret? In love?

"He's been into you since high school." Dana looked at both of them and shrugged. "Everybody knows it."

"Everybody but Carly." Regan finished her coffee and tossed it into the trash can. "Weird, don't you think? How something unexpected can happen, and suddenly your axis is off-kilter. Everything you thought you knew is wrong. And everything you need to know is out of reach. Like you're fumbling in the dark."

"That sounds deep," Carly said. "Too deep for a Saturday morning. Give me a couple of hours, and I'll come up with an appropriate answer."

Dana began to scrub Regan's heels. Her fingers were firm, and the sensation was lovely. So lovely, Regan closed her eyes and sank back into her chair.

"You talking about Wyatt Blackwell?"

She yanked her head up and was greeted by Dana's wide smile as she added more sea scrub to her heel.

"Excuse me?"

"Your axis killer. Must be Wyatt."

Dana Margolla was the younger sister of a girl she went to high school with. She was maybe twenty-four, small, cute and apparently quite nosy.

"Everybody's talking about you guys." Dana gave her a knowing look.

Carly snorted. "Sheesh. Guess we're the talk of the town, Thorne."

"Guess so." She watched Dana as she worked. "What are they saying? Like what have you heard?"

Dana paused, blowing up as a stray piece of hair swept across her face. "About you and Wyatt, or Carly and Jarret?"

"Oh no." Carly shook her head and laughed. "This is so not about me. Let's hear the juicy gossip concerning our very own Doctor Thorne."

Dana shrugged. "It's no secret you guys are together. Heck, his truck is like a permanent fixture in your driveway."

"Huh." Regan glanced at Carly and raised her eyebrows. "I didn't know folks kept such a close eye on my place."

"Not folks in general." Dana giggled. "Just Mr. Abercrombie. He's the biggest gossip in town, and in case you've forgotten, he lives right across the street from you."

Right. She'd been busted right from the beginning.

Dana shrugged. "He goes to Coffee Corner every morning and has a standing Friday appointment at Don's Barbershop. Ever since his wife passed, his greatest pleasure is keeping up with his neighbors and letting everyone in town know exactly what they're doing."

"Guess you've been keeping him busy," Carly teased.

"Only because you're still living on the West Coast."

"Not for long."

Wait. What? Regan turned in her seat. "You're moving back here? To Crystal Lake?"

"I'm thinking about it. I got a job offer a few months ago from a company in the city, but I turned it down. Moving back this way wasn't on my radar, and I was happy where I am. They contacted me again last week and made it really hard to say no. I'm meeting with them on Monday."

Regan squealed. "You're just telling me this now?"

"I wasn't going to tell you at all until I knew for sure, but yes, it's a definite possibility."

"Jarret will be happy to hear that."

Carly made a face. "I'm not moving across the country for Jarret Cavendish. I'm moving across the country because an opportunity has presented itself."

Regan leaned toward her. "So you have decided." If she could have added, *Ha!* and not sounded like one of the twins, she would have.

"Let me rephrase. I may be moving across the country because of an interesting job opportunity."

"And the fact that you've started up with Jarret has no bearing."

"No. It's just a perk."

Regan chuckled. "A bonus."

"Yes."

"Okay then."

"Enough about Jarret. What's going on with you and NASCAR?" Carly wasn't letting go. She asked the girl working on her toes for a few more options (couldn't decide between Fire Engine Red or Glitzy Ginger) and looked at Regan pointedly.

"Don't worry about me." Dana dried her hands and inserted a pair of bright pink earbuds before putting Regan's foot back in the hot soapy water and reaching for the other. She grabbed a generous scoop of sea scrub and got to work.

"Well?" Carly prompted.

Regan shrugged. "I don't know. We just sort of fell into this... this *thing*. I don't even know what to call it."

"So the big R isn't the word you're looking for?"

Regan looked at her friend questioningly.

"Really, Regan?" Carly looked at her as if she had two heads. "Relationship." Her friend strung out the word into at least ten syllables.

*Relationship.* It was a loaded word, ripe with so many meanings.

"I'm not sure I'd call whatever it is we're doing a relationship."

"Let's figure this shit out." Carly sat back and was silent for a few moments before she launched her assault.

"Are you guys exclusive?"

Regan nodded. "Yes."

"When was the last night you slept alone?"

"Weeks ago."

"Does he make you laugh?"

She nodded.

"Is the sex good?"

"Definitely."

"He treats you well?"

"Yes."

"Has he met the family?"

"Yes."

"Is he your king?"

Regan whipped her head up, eyebrows raised.

Carly giggled. "Let me rephrase. Is he your king of orgasms?"

"Yes."

"Does he make you laugh."

She nodded, a small smile touching her mouth. "Yes."

"And you know his family."

"I do."

"And the sex is good."

"Jesus, Carly. The sex is the most amazing sex I've ever had."

"Record number of orgasms?"

Okay, her friend was crazy. "In one night?"

Carly nodded.

"I don't know. Like seven? Eight?" Dana stopped what she was doing, just for a second, and Regan had the sneaking suspicion the funky pink buds she'd stuck in her ears did nothing to muffle their conversation.

"That question was just out of curiosity, by the way." Carly giggled. "But go, NASCAR." She settled back in her chair and sighed dramatically. "All kidding aside, sounds like a relationship to me."

Regan sipped her now-cold coffee, because she needed to do something with her hands. Her morning pedicure was giving her a lot to think about.

"What's up with tomorrow, by the way? Jarret said we were heading to the old arena for noon."

"I'm not sure. Wyatt asked me to meet him there."

"You're not going with him?"

"No. He's in Detroit and not back until late morning." She frowned. "He's been busy all week doing God knows what. Being real evasive about it all too."

"Guess we'll find out what all the fuss is about tomorrow." Carly winked. "What in the world are you going to do with yourself without the king of orgasms around?"

Regan made a face. "I did have a life before he came back to town, you know. I'm sure I'll come up with something."

"Netflix and wine?" Carly chuckled.

"Is there anything else?"

"Anyway, whatever this is he's got planned tomorrow sounds mysterious."

"Agreed."

For the next hour, Regan listened to Carly chat about Jarret, the new job offer, and the mysterious gathering at the old arena. Only with half an ear, because the other half of her brain was focused on something else entirely. She couldn't shake that one word from her head.

Relationship.

It carried a lot of weight and meant a lot of different things to many people. She just had to figure out what it meant to her. And hope that Wyatt was on the same page.

# CHAPTER TWENTY-THREE

There had been a general consensus among the folks in Crystal Lake that in spite of the tragedy suffered when they were young, the Blackwell children had managed to carve out a charmed life. To an outsider, they had money, prestige, a home on the lake that had been featured in several architectural magazines, and the toys that went along with such an estate. They had a father who provided for them, and a caregiver, Darlene, who was as sweet as could be. They were charismatic, well-liked among their peers (especially the girls), and each of the boys had that certain *something* that set them apart from the crowd.

Hudson, the oldest, was a born leader. Wyatt, the middle child, had a devil-may-care attitude and a recklessness some couldn't help but admire. And Travis, the youngest, was the most diligent, focused, and gifted athlete the town had ever seen. They were the kind of boys anyone would be proud to call their own. And they certainly did right by their mother, who'd been killed so tragically.

But life isn't a fairy tale, and in most cases, things aren't always what they seem.

Hudson was a leader because he had to be. As the oldest, his brothers looked to him for guidance, and he answered the call when he could.

Wyatt, on the other hand, took chances when others didn't. He lived life on the edge, and it was a good thing that his brother was there to pull him back. At least most of the time.

And then there was Travis. As the youngest, the effects of that terrible day weren't apparent until later. He turned to sports, a love he'd shared with his mother, and the ice rink became his second home. In some ways, it fulfilled a need in him he didn't quite understand. The need to be needed. The need to be important and part of something.

The Blackwell boys proved that it wasn't only parents and teachers who shaped a child. It wasn't just community. It was life. It was love and laughter, anguish, and tears. It was pain and heartache and failure.

John Blackwell felt the sting of failure every day of his life. It hung on him like a shroud. Sucked at his soul. And now that he was in the twilight of his life, he found it hard to breathe on account of the regret that choked him. It made him more determined than ever to right the many wrongs he'd committed. Because he was running out of time.

The only problem? You can't force forgiveness.

But John Blackwell could hope. He could hope that somewhere, buried deep inside each of his boys, a shred of compassion still lived—a piece of their mother, his darling Angel—and it would bring them back to him.

It was *that* hope that brought him home from the hospital all those months back. *That* hope that railed at him when he couldn't find the right words—when he stared into the eyes of his son and said the wrong things.

And it was *that* hope that kept him alive. Sometimes, in the quiet of early dawn, when he looked out his window at a world he no longer recognized, he felt as if it were the only thing he had.

The funny thing about hope was that one could carry it inside without knowing. Without realizing it had been there all along. And when a person least expected it, that hope would bloom. It would expand and get so big, you couldn't ignore it. It would fill your heart and your head until there was nothing left to do but act on it.

\*\*\*

Wyatt made it back to Crystal Lake in record time. He'd spent the previous afternoon and evening in Detroit, attending several charities his brother Travis and some of the other Detroit Red Wings supported. That had been the deal to get them to come to Crystal Lake on a rare day off, and he'd been happy to do his part. They'd visited a homeless shelter, a greyhound rescue center (man, the dogs were big but sweet as hell), and an inner-city sports complex.

He'd done his duty and had been happy to do so, but now it was time to get things started in Crystal Lake.

Wyatt checked his phone as he pulled in behind the two chartered buses he'd arranged for the Red Wings and their families. The old arena was a buzz of activity with the players arriving, their wives, girlfriends, and kids running around, and Hudson there to make sure things went smoothly. Aside from Jarret and a few others, he was the only person who'd known about Wyatt's plans, and they'd been sworn to secrecy.

There was a message from Regan. It was short. To the point. And so Regan.

*Bella misses you.*

He cracked a smile and slipped out of his truck, typing back a rapid-fire message before joining his brothers near the entrance.

*Ditto. See you soon*

"That is one hell of a goofy look on your face."

Wyatt glanced up at Travis. "Huh?"

Hudson elbowed the youngest Blackwell in the ribs. "It's a new thing. We call it the Regan Thorne look."

"Regan Thorne." Travis's eyebrows rose comically, as if Regan Thorne and Wyatt Blackwell being together was out of the realm of possibility.

Wyatt scowled at Hudson. "Will you shut up?"

But Travis wasn't letting it go. "Regan Thorne. Like, Doctor Regan Thorne."

"That would be the one," Hudson replied.

"Like hot Doctor Thorne. I ran into her at Thanksgiving and

seriously considered asking her out, but..." Travis looked at Wyatt, a frown on his face. "I thought she hated your guts?"

"Don't you have to go stretch or something?" Irritated, Wyatt shoved his cell phone back in his pocket.

Travis chuckled. "Yeah. I guess I'll get on that. See you boys in a bit."

He wasn't having this conversation. Not with Travis or Hudson, or anyone, for that matter. What he and Regan had wasn't for public consumption. It was private. It was...

His scowl deepened. Hell, he didn't exactly know what it was, and maybe it was time he did something about it.

Wyatt watched Travis walk away, not taking his eyes off his brother until he joined his teammates.

"Jarret got the last modifications done?" he asked, turning back to Hudson.

"All done."

"Transportation?"

"Pickups scheduled. Dixon Grady down at the taxi service was over the moon to get the business. He broke out the old Cadillac and hired his grandson to help out."

"Catering?"

"Yep. Put in a call to Angie at Coffee Corner, and she's got it covered. Sandwiches, sweets, coffee, and tea. Just liked you asked for. She's setting up inside as we speak. Nash is helping out with burgers and dogs, and I borrowed two deep fryers from the community center for fries and onion rings."

"Good." Wyatt was pleased.

"All the food, by the way, was donated."

"Yeah?" That surprised Wyatt. He'd planned on covering the costs himself. "By who?"

Hudson shrugged and shook his head. "Hell if I know. I mentioned invoicing to both Angie and Nash, and they said everything was covered. When I pushed for a name, both of them clammed up."

Wyatt didn't have time to dwell on it, but he made a mental note to figure out who the mysterious benefactor was and repay him or her. The pool of people who knew what was happening today was small, so it shouldn't be too hard.

He filed it away as something to dwell on later.

"Did you grab Travis's jersey?" Wyatt had plans, with Travis' blessing, for his signed Muskegon Lumberjacks jersey.

Hudson grimaced. "Shit. I forgot. I need to pick up Rebecca and Liam in…" He glanced at his watch. "Twenty minutes."

"It's okay. You've done enough. I'll head out to the lake now and grab it."

"All right. I'll see you back here."

Wyatt headed to his truck and pulled out his cell phone. He tried Regan but got her voice mail. He left a message and told her he'd see her at the arena in a couple of hours and then headed out to the lake. It was warm out—unseasonably so for mid-February— and Wyatt cranked the tunes, enjoying the sunshine and the general state of happiness in his life. He didn't want to think about racing or Rob Tracy or anything else that could bring him down.

Today was about his pal Patrick, and he couldn't wait to see the look on the kid's face when he got to the arena.

Wyatt didn't bother to knock. Hell, he might not live here anymore, but it was still a home of sorts. The house was quiet, and he paused in the foyer. "Dad?" No one answered. He knew Darlene was still on her spa vacation, and with a frown, he headed upstairs. But his father's room was empty. The bed was rumpled, and a pair of blue boxers were on the floor. Wyatt scooped them up and tossed them into the laundry bin.

It wasn't like his father to leave things lying around, but he didn't think much of it. He poked his head into the bedrooms, noting that not one had changed since they'd lived here. Hell, his red, blue, and white bedding was still the same.

The kitchen showed signs of food prep. There were crumbs on the counter, and the milk had been left out. Wyatt put it back in the fridge and checked the rest of the main level, but still no John.

Huh.

He took a peek outside on the patio, but there were no footprints in the snow and again, no John Blackwell.

Wyatt headed down to the basement and heard music. It was faint, but it was coming from what used to be their games room, located down the hall from the main area that had been the hangout for the boys when they were teens.

He had a look around. Jesus, the furniture was still the same. A chuckle escaped as he strode past the purple-and-beige plaid sofa. He remembered making out with Melanie George right there on that sofa, when he was fifteen. She'd been a senior, closer to eighteen, and she'd been the first girl he'd had sex with. The entire episode had lasted maybe five minutes. He'd no sooner gotten his pants off and she'd been on him. For a young, horny guy, it was the stuff fantasies were made of, and he'd told her that he would get better. Last longer.

She'd kissed him. Let him touch her breasts again. And told him he definitely would.

Wyatt practiced a lot with Melanie that summer. Had her so many times he'd lost count. Right up until the night before she left for college and broke his tender heart.

Funny. He hadn't thought about her in years.

Wyatt tucked away the memories and opened the door to the games room. It was dim in here and looked like one of the bulbs in the track lighting was out. The pool table was gone, but the bar was still there. And sitting at it, with his back to Wyatt, was his father.

His thin shoulders were hunched forward, their bony ends emphasized by the threadbare blue T-shirt. The man still had a thick head of hair, and it glistened under the light as he turned his head. He was reading something. Or studying something.

And Johnny Cash played on. Folsom Prison Blues.

Wyatt cleared his throat, and his father froze, slowly turning in his chair until their eyes met. John's looked huge, in part because of the thick glasses perched on the edge of his nose.

For several long moments, neither one said a word. And then John patted the chair beside him. "Come see this." His voice was rough, as if he hadn't used his vocal cords in a while, and Wyatt found himself moving toward him.

Wyatt stopped just behind his father, his throat tightening

when he spied what it was his father was looking at. The large black scrapbook was something he hadn't seen in years. But he knew what was in there. Photos of him and his brothers. Of John and Angel.

It was a collection of images from a time that no longer existed. "She was so beautiful."

Wyatt took another step forward. The picture John gazed at was of his mother at the beach. Her long hair blew in the wind. Her eyes were wide and expressive, her smile so full, it took his breath away. She was obviously pregnant, with one young son digging in the dirt and a puppy nipping at his heels.

"That's you." John's finger shook as he pointed to the photo. "You were born about three weeks after I took this photo."

"That must be Hudson."

"Yes." John nodded, touching Hudson's face and then lingering on Angel.

"And whose puppy?"

John chuckled. "That's Diesel. Belonged to the people in the next cabin." He glanced up at Wyatt. "Do you remember them? They had that bird they'd bring as well."

The memory was a slow burn. It slid into his mind, leaving a trace of warmth. The bird was a cockatoo, and its filthy mouth was legendary.

He nodded. "Hudson and Nash spent hours teaching it curse words. I tried once and got caught." He frowned. "I think I got grounded for teaching the damn thing to say 'screw you.' Which is nothing compared to the things Hudson taught it."

"Hmmm." John seemed lost in thought.

Wyatt spied Travis's jersey on the wall. "I came to grab the Lumberjack. It's for this thing in town."

"Ah. Yes. The event you planned for the young Bergen boy."

Wyatt's jaw nearly fell on the floor.

"You looked surprised as hell, son."

Wyatt thought back to what Hudson had told him earlier. "You paid for the food."

"I did."

"How in hell did you find out?"

John Blackwell gave him a look that told Wyatt the old man still had game. "Just because my body is falling apart doesn't mean my faculties are in any way limited. I know what goes on in my house. I'm on top of these things."

"You just...knew. That's some kind of talent."

John shrugged. "I overheard your brother on the phone."

"This is my thing, Dad. You didn't have to do that." What he wanted to know was why?

"It's the least I can do for the family." John got off the stool. "I'll leave you to it."

Wyatt watched his father leave the room and then pulled one of the barstools over to the wall. He retrieved the jersey. It was the first one Travis had received from the junior hockey team that would eventually lead him to the NHL draft, where he was a first-round pick for the Detroit Red Wings.

He tossed the shirt onto the bar and got down from the stool, putting it back in place before gathering up the jersey. The scrapbook his father had been looking at was still open, and Wyatt found himself drawn to it. He knew what was in there. The book was something all the kids had searched through from time to time.

He flipped through the pages and couldn't help but smile at the antics three young boys got up to when they were happy, healthy, and loved. One photo in particular got to him. It was a family shot. All the boys looked uncomfortable in their Sunday best. If Wyatt remembered right, they'd been on their way to a family wedding. Wyatt was tugging at his collar. Hudson scratching his newly shorn head. Travis was staring at his undone laces.

But their parents... Well, Angel and John only had eyes for each other.

God. They'd really been in love.

Somehow, the notion shocked Wyatt. Though it shouldn't. Not really. Even as a young boy, he'd known his father was devastated at the loss of his wife. Agitated, he flipped the page over, remembering this as being the last item in the scrapbook.

He couldn't have been more wrong. There were dozens of

things he'd never seen before. Articles related to Hudson's career in the FBI, and Travis's rookie year for the Lumberjacks all the way up to the draft, the Detroit Red Wings, and the previous run for the Cup. There were also articles and photos of Wyatt in the winner's circle. Beside his car. On the track.

Slowly, he closed the book and turned off the light. He headed back upstairs, jersey in hand, and paused in the middle of the great room.

He was feeling a lot of things as he stood there, looking around a house he knew but didn't recognize. It didn't feel like home, and yet….

Wyatt decided not to dwell on any of the stuff going on inside him. He decided to actually live in the moment and go with it.

"Dad?" His voice echoed in the seemingly empty house.

"That you, Wyatt? You still here?" His father poked his head over the landing from upstairs.

*He looks so old.* The thought hit Wyatt hard, like a punch to the gut.

"You want to come to this thing?" He had no idea where that thought came from, but the longer he stood there staring up at his father, he was kind of happy he asked. The man's eyes brightened, and he stood a little straighter.

"You sure you want me to?" John sounded hesitant and hopeful, and something about the look on his face made Wyatt feel sad.

"Yeah. I can wait if you need to change."

John held his gaze for a few seconds and then slowly nodded. "Okay."

# CHAPTER TWENTY-FOUR

Regan stood in front of her closet for a good five minutes before she finally decided on what to wear. She had no idea what to expect, and all Wyatt had told her was that she needed to dress warm and casual. She chose a pair of old jeans that A) were comfortable as hell, and B) made her butt look amazing. At least that was what Wyatt had told her the last time she'd worn them. He'd rewarded her by ripping them off about ten minutes after she'd put them on.

Her cheeks grew pink at the thought, and she gave herself a mental shake, breaking out the new undies she'd purchased after getting her manicure and pedicure the day before. The matching bra and underwear were hot pink, with tiny little Hello Kittys adorning them. She couldn't resist. And even though Carly had looked at her as if she were crazy, she knew Wyatt would love them.

She pulled out a kelly-green turtleneck made of the softest cotton ever and checked her hair and makeup before slipping on black boots and a long wool coat. Bella wagged her tail, looking up expectantly.

"Sorry, girl. I'll take you for a walk later." She grabbed a new bone from the bin in the kitchen, and Bella ran off with her new treasure just as the doorbell rang.

The sound kick-started her heart, and it thumped fast and hard as she opened the door with a smile. "Right on time," she said, her words slowly dying as she found a young man standing there. He looked vaguely familiar, about twenty, with big blue eyes, a face that didn't look as if it could grow facial hair if it wanted to, and a smile that was infectious. Dressed all in black, he turned to the side, and she spied a classic-looking Cadillac big enough for eight.

"Miss Thorne?"

She nodded. "Yes?"

"I'm Dave Grady. I'm here to pick you up."

"Dave Grady," she murmured, pulling on her gloves. "Dixon's grandson?"

He nodded. "Yep. Seth is my dad."

"Did Wyatt send you?" She was confused because she'd been expecting him.

"He did."

"And where are we going?" She closed the door behind her and inhaled some fresh Michigan air. The sun was warm on her face, and she turned toward it.

The young man shook his head and motioned her forward. "I'm not supposed to say. I've been instructed to pick you up, and then we have one more stop before our final destination."

"Sounds quite mysterious."

"Right?" he said, opening the door for her. "It's kind of cool."

She spied Mr. Abercrombie on his front porch and made a point of waving to him before slipping inside the car. The roads weren't busy, and they sped through town, and in less than ten minutes pulled into the Bergens' driveway.

"I'll be right back," Dave said.

Regan watched from the backseat as he knocked on the door, which was promptly answered by Gwen. She was wearing a red-and-white sweater, jeans, and fluffy boots, and talked animatedly with Dave as she glanced at the car. She disappeared for a few moments, and then reappeared dressed in her winter coat, with a few bags she handed to Dave, her husband Brad a few steps behind.

They looked surprised to see Regan in the car, and she got a quick hug from both of them.

"What's going on?" Gwen asked, clearly puzzled.

"I have no idea. Something Wyatt cooked up." Regan arched an eyebrow. "Where's Patrick?"

"Wyatt came for him about an hour ago." Brad looked as confused as Regan. "He didn't say much other than that he needed Patrick and that we were to wait for our ride."

"Wyatt's always been a bit of shit." Gwen looked up and chuckled. "I mean that in a good way. But when he gets his mind set on something, you never know what to expect. I remember once, when he was about ten, he got it into his head that snakes were endangered or something like that. I don't know if it was because of some show he'd seen, or something they talked about in school. But Wyatt wasn't content with thinking that snakes were endangered. He decided to do something about it."

"God. I hate snakes." Regan shuddered.

"He convinced Travis to help him and to distract Mr. Gunnery from the pet store, and he stole all the snakes he had. Grabbed them and put them into a bucket."

Regan's eyes widened. "Oh my God. I remember when that happened. But they never found the snakes."

"No, they did not. But I sure as hell did. I found them a few weeks later down in their games room and nearly had a heart attack. I have no idea what he did with them, but they were gone the next day. He claimed he was saving them. I told him to save them somewhere else or his father would find out."

The three of them had a good laugh, and when the car came to a halt, Regan looked outside. "We're at the old arena. I didn't think the place was in use?"

Dave hopped out of the car and opened their door. His grin was so wide, it distorted his features a bit, and Regan looked around him as she got out. There were several taxis there, as well as a couple of vans all parked along the side of the building. And behind them, she spied what looked like two large coach buses.

Gwen and Brad joined her.

"Do we just go inside?" Regan asked Dave.

"Yeah. Wyatt said to make sure you head right in. Things are gonna start soon."

"Things," Gwen said cheekily, poking her husband in the shoulder. "I'm dying to see what the heck this is all about."

"Let's go." Regan took off, stomach more than a little nervous, filled with anticipation and a need to see Wyatt so bad that it should have made her take a step back. And yet she increased her pace until she was nearly running. She pushed open the doors and strode inside. The interior was much darker, and after the brilliant sunshine from outside, it took a bit for her eyes to adjust. When they did, they nearly popped out of her head.

Standing in front of her in a line that stretched nearly the width of the arena lobby was a group of men. Big men. Men in hockey equipment, with sticks and skates. Men wearing the Detroit Red Wing uniform on one side. On the other? The Crystal Lake Warriors. She spied several guys she knew, including Jarret.

And on the Red Wings side, Travis Blackwell.

"What the hell?" Brad came up short, his arm around his wife.

"I have no freaking clue," she replied, her voice breaking when she spied Wyatt walking out from the dressing room area, Patrick drowning in a hockey jersey at his side. Coming up behind them was none other than Cain Black, Crystal Lake's very own bona fide rock star. The three were chatting, and Regan's heart swelled when Wyatt glanced up and saw her.

He winked, and she didn't know what to do. She gave a small wave and held back, suddenly conscious of the moment. She could see through the glass out into the arena. There were a good number of folks out there, and the man standing not more than a few feet from her had arranged this all for a little boy he'd just met.

Wyatt came to a stop and put his arm around Patrick's shoulders. They stood in front of his parents, and Regan didn't dare look at them, because her throat was so damn tight and filled with emotion, she was afraid she'd burst into tears and spoil everything.

Wyatt shook Brad's hand and gave Gwen a quick hug. "The

other night, Patrick asked me to see if I could get tickets for you two to go and see a Red Wings game. He told me the Wings were your favorite team and that Travis was one of your favorite players." He paused. "Sorry. I did everything in my power to get tickets, but it just wasn't happening."

Several of the players laughed at that, and Patrick giggled, his cheeks flushed red, his eyes shiny with excitement.

"Turns out the guys had a day off and decided to come out here for some fun. It's not Joe Louis, but hey, it will have to do. They've brought their friends and family, and if you have a look out there, you'll see everyone who means anything to you guys." He looked down at Patrick. "Including Matthew, Joelle, Caleb, and Shannon."

If Patrick's eyes got any wider, they'd pop right out of his head. "From the hospital?" he whispered. "My friends? I thought Caleb had to be, like with his IV and those other machines."

Wyatt nodded. "He does, but we've made a special area that fits everything he needs so he could come watch."

"He gets cold, though."

"Yep. He does. He told me that when I went to see him a few days ago. I told him we wouldn't let him get cold."

Patrick stared up at Wyatt, and suddenly, his arms were around him, the little limbs small and frail against the big man who'd managed to bring nearly everyone in the room to tears.

Again. Regan's heart squeezed hard.

"He's a keeper," Gwen whispered in her ear.

She yanked her eyes away from Wyatt and Patrick, but Gwen wasn't looking at her. She was looking at her son, and for the first time in ages, it was hope that lit up her features.

Travis walked over on his skates and shook Patrick's hand. "My old jersey looks good on you, kiddo. What say we get this thing started? Would you like to drop the puck?"

Wyatt snuck over and dropped a kiss to Regan's forehead. He opened his mouth to speak, but Patrick's excited chatter got his attention.

"Go." Regan pushed at him. "We'll have time later."

His dark eyes made her tingle in places that were going to make it hard to sit still for the next few hours. Dave Grundy escorted them out to the arena, and she was surprised to see the intense modifications made to some of the seating. Mainly, the section behind the team benches.

The entire area had been leveled and then raised to a few feet above the ice. It was a luxurious lounge, with beds for the kids, sofas and bar tables for the adults, and it was able to accommodate any of the medical equipment needed. There were staff on hand, Regan had no idea how Wyatt had managed that, and she spied John Blackwell sitting in a Lazy Boy, a cold beer in one hand, a Detroit Red Wings hat tucked over his head.

"John," she said, bending close to give him a hug. "So nice to see you out. How are you feeling?"

"Never better," he said, taking a long pull from his beverage. "Although I would love to have a cigar."

"Yeah," she replied with a smile. "Not happening."

"That's what Wyatt said." John set down his drink. "This is something. What he did for this boy."

"It is," she said softly, eyes now on the ice where Cain Black had walked out. He stopped in the center, stood there with a guitar, and waited until the crowd's excited cheers died down. He began to strum his guitar and sang a version of the Star-Spangled Banner that brought tears to Regan's eyes. Seriously. What the hell was wrong with her? But his rendition was poignant and heart filled, and she was pretty sure she wasn't the only one in danger of becoming a blubbering idiot.

When he was done, Wyatt walked out with Patrick, and his parents beamed as he dropped the puck. The little guy looked so happy and healthy. If you weren't in the know, it would be hard to believe he had an inoperable, invasive tumor in his brain.

Regan decided now wasn't the time to think about such things. And for the next two hours, life was good. It was simple and fun and full of joy. It was Patrick giggling on his parent's lap, and John being in the same room as all of his boys. It was Regan watching the faces of those she loved. Of Wyatt's hand on her leg, and later rubbing the back of her neck. It was small-town community, and the genuine need to share. It was the delicious fries and burgers and sandwiches prepared and cooked by friends and family.

It was all that and more. And if Regan could bottle this feeling and keep it hidden for the days she needed a lift, she would. But life didn't work that way. Life was full of brilliant highs and bone-crushing lows. The true test was in the way one handled these things. And sometimes, the true test was in letting go.

"Hey," Wyatt said. "You okay?" The game had just ended, and he pulled her close.

*No.*

*Maybe.*

"I'm good."

She leaned into him and decided to forget about her doubts and fears. About the fact that she had no idea what they were doing or where they were going. Regan had no idea how long Wyatt would be in the picture, but she decided she'd be stupid not to take full advantage of him while she could.

And she planned on doing just that as soon as she got him home.

# CHAPTER TWENTY-FIVE

Wyatt had been in Crystal Lake for over six weeks, and with the beginning of March only days away, he knew he had some decisions to make. But at the moment, he didn't want to think about them. He wanted to settle back and watch the sleeping woman at his side for as long as he could. Which, when he thought about it, sounded pretty damn silly. And yet, here was, staring into a face that he'd grown to love.

Wait.

He sat up a bit. Love? Was that what he felt? Wyatt thought hard. He'd never been in love before. He'd been in lust many, many times, but what man hadn't? Sure, there might have been a few times he'd confused lust with love, but again, that was pretty much what every guy did at one point.

But this? What he felt when he looked at Regan? This was different. This went way the hell beyond the broad spectrum of lust. Whatever this was brought up something deep from inside him. Something heavy and hot. Something that made him want to beat his hands against his chest like a damn gorilla when he made her smile. Or moan when he was inside her. Or laugh when he said something clever.

Nothing please him more than when she was happy. Christ,

only the day before, he'd made a happy face in her latte. Him. Wyatt Blackwell. Barista at large.

Holy. Hell. How had he gotten here? Stuck between what he thought he felt and what he didn't know. This was definitely uncharted territory for him.

Wyatt sat up in bed. Regan was on her side, one hand under her cheek, the other settled just below her chin. Her long hair was a tangle of brown on her pillow, and the curve of her cheek was barely visible from several dark strands that lingered there.

Her mouth was open slightly, and he grinned, listening to her breathe, and, even though she vehemently denied it, her soft snores. Everything about this woman was adorable and strong and infuriating and passionate. She was the smartest, classiest lady he'd ever met. Everyone liked her. Hell, after the hockey game, it was all he could do to drag Travis and several of his teammates away from her.

She was independent, secure, kind, and compassionate. He had to wonder, what the hell was she doing with him? The sex. He chuckled and dropped a kiss to her nose. The sex was off the charts.

Wyatt loved this time of the morning. It was early, still dark outside, and the house was quiet. Bella, the little pervert, was asleep on her bed, and he had Regan all to himself. The clock on the bureau glowed, telling him she had about thirty minutes before the alarm sounded.

Hmm. Thirty minutes. A man could do a lot to a woman in that amount of time. If he knew what he was doing. Thing was? Wyatt knew exactly what he was doing.

With a wicked grin, he gently tugged down the blankets until he could see every delicious, creamy inch of her. The curve of her hip. The cute-as-hell tattoo just below her bikini line. Her full breasts with their dusky pink nipples. The small V between her legs.

The feeling in his chest got big again. It expanded, and he might have growled like an animal while he looked her. The thought in his brain was primitive. It was loud, and it wouldn't go away.

*Mine.*

"Yes," he murmured, moving lower on the bed. "You're mine, Doctor Thorne."

Gently, Wyatt moved her legs so that her most private area was exposed to him. The sight of her sex had his heart beating rapidly, and he could hear it in his ears, *thump, thump, thump.* The rhythm as old as time. Erotic in nature. Primal in sound.

*Mine. Mine. Mine.*

She was still asleep, her limbs pliable, and he separated her legs, moving closer to the prize, as that song in his head grew louder. His fingers caressed her skin, there in the crease of her leg, along her thigh and knee. And then back to the soft folds that seemed to swell beneath his touch.

She made a noise—a soft groan—and he glanced up. But other than her chest rising and falling a bit faster than before, she was still out.

Not for long, he thought, bending close. He inhaled that musky, sexy scent that was all Regan. The one that told him she was already aroused and ready for him. Gently, he spread her lips, his own breaths falling fast when he spied the telltale glisten of desire. Softly, he teased the entire area with his fingers, a light touch here, a soft massage there. Her clitoris was engorged, and she twitched when he gentled rubbed her, her legs more pliable, her offering more wanton.

By now, Wyatt was painfully erect, but he ignored his discomfort and lowered himself even more so that he had access to every single inch of her. He flicked his tongue across her clitoris and smiled when she jerked, then inserted one long finger inside her while closing his mouth over her.

The taste of her was enough to drive him insane. She was sweet and musky and so damn wet, he knew it wouldn't take long.

Wyatt suckled at her, fingers expertly working her over. Inside. Outside. He licked and thrust and used his tongue and teeth to drive her crazy. By this time, her hips gyrated—she'd found the rhythm he'd started—and they were in sync.

"Come for me, babe." His voice was a hoarse whisper, and

when he heard her answering groan and felt her tighten around his fingers, he knew she was close. He increased the pressure, curving his finger upward, seeking that sweet spot she loved, while his tongue worked her hard bud with long, intense strokes.

He smiled when her hands crept into his hair, and the triumph he felt when she came for him was indescribable. If he was a writer, he wouldn't have the words for how she made him feel. It was deep-seated male pride, wrapped in a hard need to please, surrounded by that now-familiar warmth that clung to his chest and made his heart beat even faster.

"Oh. God." Regan fell back against the pillow, her body alive with the aftershocks of her orgasm. "I can't… I thought I was dreaming." Her voice was husky, that sweet-as-hell, sleep-heavy huskiness he'd grown to love.

Wyatt checked the clock. Right on time.

"Buckle up, Doctor Thorne. We've still got fifteen minutes."

"Is that all?" She licked her lips, and he knew she was ready for more.

"Maybe fourteen."

She gyrated against him. "I think you've got this, Mr. Blackwell."

He grinned wickedly. "I know I do."

Wyatt slowly pulled himself up and, without hesitation, thrust inside her. He went all in and grabbed her hands, holding them down on either side of her head as he rose above her.

"Good morning," she gasped, eyes wide as she stared up at him, that delectable tongue of hers darting out to lick her lips.

Wyatt's strokes were long and slow and precise. Her forehead furrowed, and she bit her lip. "You need to go faster, Wyatt."

"Nope." He fought to control the urge to do just that. "Got another twelve minutes." Sweat broke out on his brow. His body was a knot of sensation. Hot. Wet. Silky. Tight. And then there was that beautiful friction only she could give him.

"Jesus," she said, flinging her head back against the pillow.

"I've heard that before." He tilted his hips a bit, looking for a better angle, and bingo…

"Oh." Her mouth opened, her back arched and her breasts

lifted, begging for his touch. He wasn't the kind of man to say no, so he dipped his head and suckled her breasts, quickening his pace a bit as his balls began to tighten.

"So good," he whispered. "So damn good." She tightened around him, eyes wild as she upped the stakes and forced him to go faster.

"I need this. Right now, Wyatt. Right. Now." She barely got her words out when she jerked against him and her head rolled back and forth.

Wyatt was done. He came so hard, he literally saw stars, and collapsed on top of Regan, trying his best to ease the burden of his weight. Their bodies were slick with sweat and sex, and when he was done, he rolled over and brought her with him, arms folding her into his chest.

"That was so good," she managed to say between jagged breaths.

Wyatt looked over her shoulder. "We've still got two minutes."

"Yeah. I don't think so. I just might die of pleasure if you do anything else to my body." She pushed against him. "And I can't die today. I'm too busy." She nipped at his ear. "Shower?"

"You bet."

Wyatt picked up Regan and strode into the shower. Maybe a woman could die of pleasure. He grinned as the hot spray beat down on both of them. He took her face into his hands and kissed her. Guess he was going to find out.

As it turned out, Regan did make it through one more orgasm. Mind you, it was intense, and her legs gave out so they both almost fell on their respective asses, but she made it through, and it was a happy woman who left for her office an hour later.

Wyatt's plans were to clean up the kitchen and head out to the cabin to finish the floors he'd started refinishing the week before. He wasn't the kind of guy to be idle, and the little cabin he never stayed in was starting to look really good. Once the floors were done, he'd return Rob Tracy's calls and figure that shit out.

That gave him a couple of days to figure the other shit out. The Regan stuff. The love stuff. He needed advice and called the one person he always looked to when things got confusing. His brother. He knew Hudson had reservations about him and Regan. He also knew the two of them didn't always agree, and that was okay. It was okay because Hudson had the uncanny knack of seeing the big picture, and right now, Wyatt could use a second set of eyes.

When Wyatt called, Hudson was on his way out the door, with Liam in tow. He would take his stepson to school and swing by for a coffee. Wyatt had about twenty minutes and quickly cleaned up the breakfast stuff. He fed Bella and had just topped up her water bowl when the doorbell rang.

The little dog went mad, prancing around on her three paws, and jumped up at the door, nearly tripping Wyatt when he tried to open it. He finally managed to move the dog out of the way, but it wasn't his brother standing there. It was his past staring at him.

"Stu." The owner of the team and the man who paid him to race nodded and walked past him into Regan's house.

Wyatt didn't have to ask him how he'd found out where he was. The man had more time and money than anyone he knew. He probably knew when Wyatt started sleeping here the day after it had happened.

Stu Randall was a big man from Texas who was born on a cattle ranch. He was used to hard work. Used to giving orders and getting what he wanted. He was a no-bullshit kind of man who Wyatt respected. If he'd come all the way to Michigan, it was for a good reason. And with it being close to the end of February, Wyatt was pretty sure he knew exactly what that reason was.

Stu wasted no time. He looked at Wyatt. "I need you back for Daytona."

Wyatt took a moment. He crossed the room to the kitchen and set down the dish he'd just filled with water, watching Bella as she scooted over for a drink. A month ago, he'd been itching to drive, itching to get back to his old life, back behind the wheel. But somewhere along the line, something had changed. He didn't need to prove anything to Rob. He needed to prove to himself that he was good to go.

He needed to prove to put his buddy's death behind him and

face his fears head-on. Just like he'd done all those years ago. He didn't a shrink to tell him that.

Hudson and Regan would understand. He'd make them understand. He'd fill Hudson in when he came by and then have a conversation with Regan.

"What about Rob?" Wyatt asked.

"You leave him to me."

Wyatt looked up at Stu and slowly nodded.

"Okay. I need a day to tie up some loose ends, and then I'll be back for a week to get ready for the qualifier."

Stu smiled. "That's what I was hoping to hear."

# CHAPTER TWENTY-SIX

Regan should have known things were going much too smoothly. In her world, when the good was more than twelve hours long, something always happened to knock you on the chin and remind you that life doesn't work that way. She'd gotten to work ten minutes early and had time to stop in at Coffee Corner and indulge in a mocha latte along the way. Her patients were either early or on time, and by three o'clock, she was actually ahead of schedule—something that rarely occurred in a doctor's office.

All that allowed her a few moments to sit down and go through her email, which she did while munching on a bag of stale potato chips she found in one of her desk drawers. She hadn't bothered with lunch because there was a large pot of stew waiting for her at home. Wyatt had decided to get creative the night before, and the beef stew he'd put in her crock pot (first time it had ever been used, but she didn't see the need to share that with him) had been delicious.

It didn't matter that she'd be eating beef stew for days. It was Wyatt's beef stew, and she'd eat it every day for the rest of her life with no complaints.

God, she thought, that was corny.

She scrolled through her email, opening ones marked urgent,

including one with test results for one of her elderly patients, George Darville. With a frown, she read the entire email twice before slumping back into her chair and tossing the now-empty bag of chips into the bin.George had come in a few weeks earlier complaining of pain in his abdomen. The results of the tests she'd ordered were in. Tumors on his liver and several more on his pancreas. It didn't look good.

"Shit," she muttered, twirling her seat around so she could look out the window. The view was pretty. Your typical Michigan winter wonderland. But she saw none of it because she was so pissed off. She hated cancer. She hated it with every fiber of her being.

A knock on the door had her turning around in her chair, and she spied Lynn standing there with an odd look on her face.

"My next patient in?" she asked, getting to her feet and clearing her mind.

"No. Actually, Diana Evans canceled. Turns out her daughter wasn't feeling so hot because she'd contracted chicken pox."

"Okay. Did you give her the proper procedure?"

Lynn nodded. "Sure did." It was a stupid question, because Lynn was awesome. "There's someone here to see you, and because you had the cancellation I didn't think you'd mind if he came back."

The thought of Wyatt immediately got her blood pumping, and she glanced away, picking at an invisible piece of lint on her dark navy suit, hoping her blush wasn't too obvious. "Oh sure, send Wyatt in."

"It's not Wyatt."

Regan jerked up her head, surprised.

"It's his brother Hudson."

Okay. That was a little strange. So was the way her stomach rolled. She felt queasy and moved back to her desk, taking her chair just as Hudson walked into her office.

"Hey, Regan. Sorry to bother you at work, but I took a chance you'd have a few minutes for me."

"No worries. Have a seat."

She waited until he took the chair across from her. "Is this about John?" Their father wasn't due for a visit until next week. His condition, while not improving, had been stable over the last few months.

"No. Actually." Hudson leaned forward, his expression grave. "It's about Wyatt."

"Wyatt?" Suddenly on edge, Regan grabbed a pen and her notebook. It was a reflex action, something she did when chatting with patients, but she held the pen as if it were a weapon and watched Hudson closely. "Is he okay? Did something happen?"

Where the hell was her phone? Had he tried to call and she hadn't heard? Had he messaged her?

"Don't panic. Nothing's happened." His gaze shifted, and a muscle worked in his jaw. She got it then. Hudson Blackwell was angry about something, and whatever that something was had to do with Wyatt.

"You say that, but I can tell something's bothering you. Or you're concerned, so why don't you tell me what it is?"

"All right. I'm going to be frank with you, Regan, because I think you and Wyatt might have a chance at something, and I don't want him to screw it up." He offered a weak smile. "I just had a long talk with him, about a lot of things. And he's not going to like that I'm here, but I think he might listen to you."

Hudson was starting to scare her. She didn't reply, she just waited for him to continue. He sat back in his chair as if contemplating the right way to say whatever it was he needed to say.

"It's easier if you just say it, Hudson. I promise."

He got up out of the chair and began to pace, his hands shoved into the pockets of his jeans. "Did Wyatt tell you why he's not racing?"

*Thud.* There went her stomach again, and she swallowed hard, trying to quell the nausea. She'd known all along things weren't what they seemed, but she'd been afraid to ask. Afraid to rock the boat and knock them overboard.

"No. But I know what's been reported in the press isn't true. He wasn't suffering from a concussion. At least not the kind that was alluded to. The kind that would keep him from racing. I know he was a little banged up after his last crash, but there were certainly no brain deficits to deal with."

"I wouldn't be so sure." Hudson muttered the words under his breath, but she caught them and sat a little straighter in her chair, more unnerved than ever.

"You know about the crash that took Diego's life."

She nodded. "Yes."

Hudson opened his mouth, but then closed it. She could see his fists through his pockets and knew the man was on edge. He wasn't just angry. He was upset and concerned.

"His boss, Rob Tracy, called me because Wyatt had walked out on a mandatory evaluation with a sports therapist or psychologist or whatever the hell you call them. This therapist recommended to Tracy that Wyatt be suspended from driving until he'd completed at least a full session. According to this guy, the crash triggered something in Wyatt. He admitted to nightmares and trouble sleeping. It's not just because of Diego. I know it's deeper than that."

Regan slowly nodded. "Because of what happened with his mother?"

"You know he was in the car with her when the accident happened, right?"

"Yes. He told me a little bit about it."

Hudson blew out a long breath. "It was a drunk driver. She was on the road that day, heading out to meet someone, and Wyatt just happened to be with her. I know she was alive after the initial hit. I know he crawled from the backseat, his little body broken ... I don't know how he did it. He'd sustained substantial injuries himself. My little brother held our dying mother until the ambulance arrived."

Hudson swore and ran his hands through his hair, still so affected after all these years. "Things were bad after that. Wyatt was in the hospital for a long time. Dad was...well, he was never the same, and he made things difficult for all of us."

Chest tight, she thought back to their conversation. Of how John had forced him to drive. And of how he'd found some sort of peace on the track.

"I'm worried about him. I don't think he should be driving. I don't think he has the focus he needs to compete at that level. He needs more time."

"Hudson, I'm not well-versed in psychology, even though it was part of my studies. I can't say for sure either way, but when he meets this sports psychologist again, this man might be able to shed some light on things."

"That's the problem. He's not meeting with this guy again. He's racing next weekend at Daytona."

"I…" Shocked, she could only stare at Hudson. "When? He never said anything to me." She thought of their morning. Everything about it had been amazing. Hell, if she heard birds singing all day, it would have been because her morning had been Disney perfect.

Hudson sighed. "The owner came to see him this morning. Stu Randall isn't as concerned about Wyatt's mental health. He wants to win this race, and he wants Wyatt behind the wheel."

Hudson stopped pacing. He walked to her desk and placed each of his hands there. She saw the worry close up. The anguish and uncertainty.

"You need to stop him."

"Me?" Regan shook her head. "I don't know what difference I can make." She made a noise and closed her eyes. "He's Wyatt. He'll always do what he wants to do."

"He's changed, Regan. Since he's been with you, he's changed." Hudson pushed away from the desk, and for a long time, there was only silence. It rang in her ears so heavily, it was loud.

"Maybe I'm wrong. Maybe Rob Tracy got it wrong too. But the thing that makes me nervous is the fact that for the last six weeks, he's been here. He hasn't been fighting to get back on that track. Now, I don't know what that says, but it sure as hell says something. I just… I've got a bad feeling about this, Regan. He can't drive at Daytona. You need to make him see that. I tried this morning, but he wouldn't listen. I think he might listen to you."

Regan slowly got to her feet, still holding on to that damn pen and paper.

"And if he doesn't? If he tells me to go to hell and mind my own business? What then? He'll feel like we ganged up on him. He'll feel betrayed."

"I'm willing to take that chance if it keeps him away from Daytona." He paused, his tone frank. "I guess the question is, are you?"

# CHAPTER TWENTY-SEVEN

Wyatt rolled into the Coach House around five o'clock, looking for Jarret. He'd been pissed off since Hudson had stopped by in the morning, and now Wyatt needed a beer and someone who was on his side. When Jarret had sent him a text message asking for a meet-up, he'd agreed right away.

His pal wasn't there, so he sat his butt down at the bar, and Tiny, the massive bartender, made his way over.

"What can I get you?"

"Draft."

The place was mostly empty, but he supposed this time of day, it was the norm. He accepted the cold mug from Tiny and took a good, long draw. His cell phone buzzed, and he pulled it from his pocket with a frown when he saw the caller ID. John Blackwell.

Christ. He didn't have it in him to get into it with John. Not tonight. Especially if Hudson had gone to their father and told him about Daytona. He was ready. He could do this. He didn't need some pussy shrink to tell him whether or not he could get behind the wheel.

He didn't need this crap. He still had to figure out how to tell Regan he was leaving. Had to figure out what that meant. More importantly, he needed to know where her head was at. He'd never been so nervous about a conversation as he was right now. He had to get it right. No way did he want a repeat of the shit show from this morning.

"Damn you, Hudson."

"What was that?" Tiny perked up.

"Nothing." He glanced up at the television. "Really? What the hell is that shit?"

Tiny gave him a *don't screw with me* look and shrugged. "I like *The Bachelor*. Sue me."

Jarret slid onto the stool beside him and ordered up a draft. "Hey, Tiny. Is this the episode from last night? I missed it."

Tiny grunted.

"Which one do you think will get the rose this week?"

Wyatt looked at his Jarret in surprise. "You're into this stuff too?"

His friend didn't skip a beat. "You're not?"

What the hell was the world coming to? When a man couldn't walk into his local watering hole and watch sports or racing or some of that Duck Dynasty shit. He shook his head and cradled his beer, seriously considering leaving before the two of them waved some voodoo wand at him and got him hooked on the show.

"What's up?" Jarret asked while he waited for Tiny to pour his draft.

"I'm headed to Daytona for the qualifier tomorrow. Gonna race the 500 next week."

"Shit, man. Congratulations!" Jarret slapped him on the shoulder. "When did this happen?"

"This morning."

"Right on. This is something to celebrate. Guess your concussion stuff is all fixed up?"

Guilt made Wyatt turn away, and he took another sip from his mug before answering. "Yeah. It's all squared away."

Jarret raised his glass and shouted to the group of men hanging at the end of the bar. "Hey. My boy here is headed to Daytona! Next round is on me." Whether it was the promise of free beer or that the men actually gave a damn whether he drove or not, they all raised their glasses and whooped it up.

Wyatt settled onto his seat. This was what he needed. Positivity. Not the negative bullshit his brother had thrown his way.

"Regan good with all of it?"

He looked at Jarret. "I haven't told her yet. I just found out this morning."

"I'm sure she'll be pumped. She knows it's your gig. She's not the type to hold a guy back."

"Yeah." Wyatt nodded. "I hope so."

"This means you'll be back in Florida for good?"

"For the immediate future. They'll be more races coming up, so I've got to get my head in the game if I want to do well this season. I'll need to be with the team, and that's our home base."

"And you're leaving tomorrow."

"Yep."

"So why the hell are you sitting in a bar with me when you could be with Regan?" Jarret winked, a wicked grin on his face. "Seems to me you'd have a lot to keep busy with tonight, making sure she won't forget you while you're gone."

"True." He looked at Jarret. "What's up with you?"

Jarret's grin widened. "What do you mean?"

Wyatt sat back on his stool. Something was definitely up. "I haven't seen you in days, and all of a sudden you want a beer, which is great. But I don't think you hauled my ass down here to watch *The Bachelor*."

Jarret fiddled with his beer mug. "Everything all right?" he asked, suddenly concerned.

"Yep." Jarret nodded. "I, ah…wanted to ask you something is all."

"Okay. But you have to open your mouth and actually speak to get it out."

"Don't be an asshole." Jarret pushed his beer away. "This is important."

"Then tell me." He watched his friend closely. The guy was nervous, and that wasn't like Jarret.

"I need you to block off some time later this summer. Say,

July."

"You need to be a bit more specific than that. There'll be races in July, so I need dates."

Jarret cleared his throat, and, shoot, was that sweat on his forehead? What the hell? "We were thinking the twenty-ninth. Maybe."

"I'll have a look and see and..." Wait. We? Wyatt was confused. "What the hell is going on, Jarret?"

"I'm off the market."

"What?"

"I'm off the market." Jarret's voice rose, his words coated with a tinge of irritation.

"I know what the hell being off the market means, but what are you telling me exactly?"

A slow grin crept over Jarret's face, and he shrugged. "I'm getting married."

Wyatt's mouth fell open. He honestly didn't know what to say to that. "Married."

"Yep." Jarret nodded. "Hitched. That's gonna be me."

"To who?"

Jarret looked at him as if he'd lost his freaking mind. "Are you kidding me? To Carly, for Christ sake. Who else?"

"Carly Davis."

"You know any other Carly?"

"How the hell did I miss that? I know she's been around lately, but I had no idea you guys had gotten so damn serious."

"Hey." Jarret winked. "When you know, you know. We're not kids anymore. I don't need to date someone for years to know if she's right for me or not. And trust me, that wasn't the issue."

"What was?"

"Keeping her interested long enough for her to get it and making sure she knew I was the one."

Wyatt slapped Jarret on the shoulder. "And how did you manage to get that done before she dumped your ass?"

"I kept her knee-deep in champagne and went downtown every chance I got."

"You're a pig."

Jarret chuckled. "A pig in shit and happy to be there."

Wyatt pondered his friend's words for a few moments. "How did you know?"

"Know?"

"That Carly was it for you? How did you know?"

"She's all I thought about. And it didn't matter that she was living on the West Coast. Or that it might be months before I saw her again. When I pictured myself in a few years, it was with Carly. When I think about kids, about my kids, it was always with Carly. I just knew. She gets me like no one else does."

"You sound like one of those romance novels Darlene reads."

"Hey, don't knock those things. Carly reads them like they're candy, and she always comes to bed ready to get busy, if you know what I'm saying."

"Like a trip downtown?"

"Exactly."

"You two knuckleheads sound like a bunch of pussies." Nash Booker appeared from nowhere and shook his head. "What's up with that?"

"Jarret's off the market." Wyatt held up his nearly empty glass. "I think we need another round, Tiny."

Nash grinned and shook Jarret's hand. "It's on the house, boys."

Wyatt stayed for one more drink, which he nursed and didn't finish on account he was driving and had no intention of staying longer than he had to. As it was, it was nearly six thirty when he left and headed to Regan's. No longer in his happy place, he was plagued by a darkness he couldn't explain. A feeling like things were about to change and maybe not in the way he anticipated or wanted.

It stayed with him the entire trip to her house, and after he parked his truck, Wyatt sat in the dark staring at the soft light that fell from her windows. He was anxious and on edge, and that was never a good thing. He was still looking at her place when someone knocked on his window and scared the crap out of him.

It was the neighbour, Mr. Abercrombie, and Wyatt lowered his window.

"Evening," he said. The old guy was bundled up against the cold, his long thin nose barely visible above the thick blue scarf wrapped around his neck and face.

"You shouldn't sit here with your truck running, son. It's not good for the environment."

That was the last thing he'd expected to hear come out of Abercrombie's mouth. "Sorry. I wasn't thinking." Wyatt cut the engine.

"None of my business, but you've been sitting there for a good fifteen minutes."

"Yeah. I didn't realize it was that long."

"You afraid to go in?"

Wyatt considered lying, giving the man an answer that would send him on his way. He was, after all, just an old nosy neighbour. Maybe it was the full moon that lit up the snow and cast a hazy glow over everything that got to him. Or maybe it was the need to be honest. Or it could simply be that he was tired of lying to himself.

"Sounds about right," Wyatt finally admitted.

"She's a tough one, that little girl. Tough enough to take on the likes of you."

He looked at Abercrombie with a frown. "The likes of me? You don't even know me."

The old man tugged down his scarf and sighed. "Oh, but I do, son. I know you because you're just like I was when I was a young lad. Taking chances. Living life like there's no tomorrow. Riding a wave that'll take you far above the crowd because it makes you feel good. Makes you forget. You feel like you're invincible, like nothing can touch you."

Abercrombie paused, a faraway look on his face. "It took a lot for me to learn the most important lesson in life that there is."

This had to be the strangest conversation Wyatt had ever had. But he couldn't help himself. "What's that?"

"Riding a wave like that isn't good for the soul. Not when you're riding it alone. The saddest thing, the most pathetic thing, is to come to the end of it alone. To stare back at a life lived selfishly. It's not fun to choke on regret. Not fun at all."

Mr. Abercrombie cleared his throat. "Anyway. What do I know. I just thought you should turn off your truck."

He turned and headed for his home, the small bungalow across from Regan's, leaving Wyatt staring after him with a head full of questions. The main one being, what the hell had just happened?

# CHAPTER TWENTY-EIGHT

The door opened, and Regan's stomach tumbled for what had to be, the hundredth time in the last few hours. Bella immediately began her happy dance and galloped over to greet Wyatt as if he were the most important thing in her life.

Regan got it.

She busied herself in the kitchen and pasted a smile to her face. Her skin felt plastic, and her nerves were shot. She had no idea if she'd overstepped and things were about to go south. Or if she'd somehow managed to bring a sort of clarity to the situation.

She knew things weren't wonderful between Wyatt and his father, but they seemed so good lately. And she knew Wyatt loved Darlene, so maybe if...

Maybe if what? This was dumb. So dumb. What the hell had she been thinking? But that right there was the problem. She hadn't been thinking. She'd been flailing around, trying to come up with a way to convince Wyatt to stay.

She wasn't good at this sort of thing.

John and Darlene sat at the island, which Wyatt discovered after he hung up his jacket and took exactly two steps into the house. He froze. Got that weird look on his face. The one that told Regan he had no idea what was happening, and he was not exactly happy about it.

"Hey," he said, when he recovered his senses. He looked at Regan, a questioning look on his face.

"I thought, um, since we had so much stew left that it would be nice if John and Darlene joined us for dinner."

"Really. Dinner."

"Yes. Dinner."

Wyatt stopped a few inches from her, his expression now closed off. She couldn't read him, and that made her nervous.

"If I'd know we were having company, I would have stopped and picked up some wine."

"Don't be silly," Darlene said. "We're fine." Her voice was bright—too bright—and Regan cringed.

Wyatt gave Regan another look that made her uncomfortable and headed for the bathroom. "I'm just going to wash up."

He disappeared down the hallway, and she exhaled, tucking back a long piece of hair with shaking fingers.

"You don't look so good, dear."

She glanced up at Darlene. She felt awful. Using them like this. Knowing things might end badly for all persons involved. Knowing she just might be on the verge of losing everything she wanted. Hell, she didn't even have a plan. Not really.

"I'm okay. No worries. Maybe we should sit at the table?"

She got busy grabbing plates and cutlery, while Darlene helped John over. He seemed shaky to her, short of breath, and that was a worry. But it was something she couldn't think about at the moment.

Wyatt joined her in the kitchen. "Kind of weird. You inviting them for dinner...*tonight*."

She shrugged and tried to keep her voice light. "I just thought it would be nice."

"Bullshit." His voice was low, dangerously so, but she heard the anger there. "Nice and Blackwell family gatherings don't exactly go hand in hand."

"Why not?" she asked, kind of surprised to hear the words come out of her mouth. But once they were out there, she didn't back down. If this was going to hit the fan, it might as well hit now instead of dragging on.

"Excuse me?"

She folded her arms. "Why are things always so hard for you and John? Why the distance? Why the anger and resentment?" She paused, watching him closely. "Why the blame?"

He looked over her shoulder at his father and Darlene. "You want to do this now? With them here?"

*No.*

"Yes, Wyatt. I guess I do. Considering you're off to Daytona tomorrow, I'd like to do this now."

His eyes narrowed dangerously, and he took a step back. He was angry. No denying that. His hands fisted at his sides, and he shook his head. "Unbelievable. When I see Hudson, I'm going to kick his ass all the way to fucking Daytona and back."

"Not if I kick yours first."

That comment had his mouth hanging open for a good five seconds. "Where the hell is this coming from? Why are you pissed that I'm headed back to Daytona? It's not like you didn't know it would happen. It's what I do. It's who I am."

Their voices rose, and she glanced over her shoulder, stomach churning yet again when she found both Darlene and John watching them. Shit. This was so not how she saw things going down. But they were already on the road, and there was no turning back now.

"Why won't you see that sports psychologist?"

"Oh, I see you and Hudson had a thorough heart-to-heart."

"Can you answer the question?"

"I'm not sure." He straightened, giving up his death grip on the counter. "Give me a minute." He moved past her and didn't stop until he stood at the table, his gaze on John and Darlene. "Did Hudson fill you in on what went down with my boss? Is that why you're here?"

Darlene shook her head. "I don't…" She turned to John, but he only had eyes for his son. She obviously had no clue.

"What are you running from, Wyatt?" John's voice wavered a

bit as he gazed at his son.

Regan swallowed the lump of fear in her throat and moved to Wyatt's side. She tried to touch him, but he moved out of the way and glared at them all.

"Maybe we should just forget about all this." Regret made her nauseous, and she wanted nothing more than to rewind the clock and make a better decision than bringing his father into the mix.

She'd reacted blindly in a way that wasn't the norm for her. And now she was going to pay.

"No." Wyatt moved closer to the table. "I think it's time to get this shit out in the open. I'm not a scared little kid anymore, John. I'm not going to let you walk all over me. I'm not going to take the blame for something I had no control over. Not anymore."

John exhaled and closed his eyes. "No. You shouldn't. I'm sorry I made you feel that way."

"Sorry?" Wyatt made a sound of disgust. "You're sorry? That's all you've got?" He looked up at the ceiling. "Unbelievable."

Again, an uncomfortable silence fell over them, broken only by Bella's agitated panting. The small dog had picked up on the angry vibes in the room and wasn't too happy about it. She stood in the corner watching all of them, her small tail wagging as she tried to catch her breath.

"Sorry is only a beginning, Wyatt.""

In the space of a few seconds, the mood went from anger to something else entirely. The two men stared at each other as if they were the only ones in the room.

"Maybe we should go." Regan looked at Darlene, but John shook his head.

"No. Please stay. These things are never more real than when witnessed by those we love and care about. When your mother died, a part of me went with her, and it's something I've never managed to get back. She made me a better man, and I…" John sighed heavily. "I didn't deserve her. God knew that, and he took her from me."

"God didn't take her away, old man. A drunk driver did."

"No." John looked away. "It might have been a car that took

her from us, but it was my fault she was on the road that day. My fault she was on her way to that motel just off the interstate."

"What the hell are you talking about?" Wyatt's expression was thunderous.

"A woman I'd been involved with made arrangements to meet her there. Angel was on her way to the motel when that bastard crossed the center line and hit the both of you."

Regan saw the shock on Darlene's face, but it was nothing compared to the look in Wyatt's eyes. His face was white, his lips pulled back in a snarl.

"You had an affair."

"I did."

"And she found out about it."

"I don't know what she was told. I only knew she was going to meet her. I pray she didn't find out about…" He stumbled over his words and whispered. "About the affair."

Wyatt shoved his hands into the pockets of his jeans and stood there, glaring at his father, not bothering to hide his dislike, disappointment, and anger. He took a few steps until he was inches from John, forcing the older man to look up.

"Do you remember what you said to me that first time you took me to the graveyard?" His voice shook, and tears sprang up in the corners of Regan's eyes.

"It was months after she was buried. I didn't make the funeral because I was still in the hospital. And the first time I was able to go and pay my respects to my mother, you said…" Wyatt looked away, his gaze on the window and the darkness beyond.

"You told me it was my fault she was six feet under." His voice broke, and Regan's heart shattered along with it.

"I was nine years old. I held her hand while she took her last breath. I listened to her talk about how much she loved all of us. Hudson. Travis. Me." He turned back to John. "You. After she died, as young as I was, I was grateful she wasn't alone. Grateful that I was there with her to comfort her in those last moments. Do you want to know what her last words were, old man?"

John was silent and made no effort to wipe away the tears that flowed freely down his face.

"She told me to take care of you because this would break you. Said you were a strong man when it came to most things, but this, her dying, was something that would bring you down." Angrily, Wyatt swiped at his face. "And I tried. Even after that day by the graveyard, I tried. But you didn't want my help, or Hudson's. Hell, I think you forgot Travis even existed. Not a great way to honor my mom's legacy, but I guess I wasn't strong enough."

John's gaze fell. "I was the weak one, and it's a hard thing to admit, one that's taken me years to do so. You boys deserved a lot more than I could ever give you, and there isn't a day goes by that I don't wish I'd been the one in that car."

"John." Darlene stood. "Please don't talk like that." She glanced at Regan. "I think we should go."

Regan nodded and whispered, "I'm sorry." She grabbed their coats, aware that Wyatt had retreated to the kitchen, hidden in the shadows with his back to them. There were no more words, and after she closed the door behind Darlene and John, Regan stood in the foyer, cold and shivering and so miserable, she didn't know what to do.

She was more confused than ever, and watching Wyatt hurt and in pain made her sick to her stomach.

Slowly, she made her way to the dining room table and tidied up the dishes, stacking them neatly on the island. Wyatt still stared out her kitchen window, and she paused, unsure how to proceed and scared that she'd lost him forever.

"Why would you invite him here?" Wyatt sounded cold. Bitter. Not at all like the man she'd come to love.

She walked into the kitchen and stood behind him, wanting to touch and to hold, but so very afraid to do so.

"I don't know. I'm sorry," she managed to say before bursting into to tears. "I just…We're all worried about you. We care about you."

*I love you.*

She spoke quickly, trying to get her words out. Trying to make him understand. "I didn't know what to do. How to help. I just need to know that you're okay. If you tell met that, I'll believe you."

Wyatt turned to her, his face hard. "I've got to tell you, Regan, that was the wrong way to go." He ran his hands through his hair and shook his head. "I can't believe he fucked around on my mother. He's the reason she died. She was upset and not watching the road and..." He swore and looked away.

Regan reached for him, but he moved away, breaking her heart as he did so.

"I have to go. I need to get ready to fly out tomorrow."

Shaking, Regan wrapped her arms around her body, trying to find what little bit of warmth she could. "I know you're angry."

"I'm beyond angry." His dark eyes told her that and so much more. "Way the hell beyond angry."

"I understand."

Wyatt cut her off and pushed past her. "You don't. If you did, you never would have called him here." He stopped in his tracks. "Neither you or Hudson took the time to ask why I want to race at Daytona. What it means to me. Why I do it."

She swallowed thickly and managed to speak. "Why?"

"Because I have to."

He grabbed his coat and closed the door behind him, leaving Regan alone. She sank to the floor and cradled Bella in her lap. She had no tears. She had nothing.

She looked around her empty home. *Nothing.*

# CHAPTER TWENTY-NINE

Race day was always electric no matter where you were. But something about Daytona was special. The crowd's energy was contagious, and Wyatt fed on it, pacing nervously in the pit. Up until a few years ago, he'd spent a good amount of time puking his guts out, and though it had been a while since he'd done that, it just might happen again.

Rob Tracy nodded to him—the guy was still giving him one word answers and pissed as hell that Stud Randall had gone over his head. He pointed to his watch. "Ten minutes."

Wyatt found a quiet corner and tried to clear his head. It was hard. He was miserable as hell without Regan. Still pissed, but miserable. They hadn't talked all week. Him because he was stubborn as hell. Regan, well, she was probably unsure and feeling badly for the way things were left.

He needed to focus and put that shit behind him. At least for now.

Wyatt rolled his shoulders, willing away the butterflies that had decided to take over his stomach, when he noticed a couple of the mechanics staring behind him as if they were looking at a piece of candy. It couldn't be Marissa Hadley. He'd had it out with her as soon as he'd come back home. She'd wanted to pick up where they left off, but he wasn't interested.

At about that point, the hair on the back of his neck stood on end, and he slowly turned around. If someone had told him his heart could fall out of his chest and land on the ground with a big old *thud*, he would have told them they were crazy. He would have given them the finger and told them that kind of stuff only happened in one of those sappy Hollywood movies. It wasn't real. Wasn't possible.

Except it was.

He watched Regan walk toward him, his heart flopping around on the floor like a fish out of water, and when she stopped in front of him, he knew he wouldn't be able to talk, so he didn't even try.

She was dressed simply in jeans, a plain white T-shirt, white runners, and hair loose and floating in the wind. An all-access pass hung around her neck, a pair of silver aviators attached to them.

He managed to clear his throat. "This is a surprise."

"A good one, I hope."

He took a moment because he didn't want to sound like a damn pussy. "It is."

Wyatt could have apologized for leaving the way he did. For blaming her for his issues with her father. He could have said a whole bunch of things, but he didn't. He cupped her head and bent forward, his mouth grazing hers intimately before he kissed her. It was the kind of kiss that spoke volumes. The kind of kiss that had the mechanics and all the other men standing nearby hooting and hollering and whistling like a bunch of teenagers.

His chest tight, he finally let her go and pulled her close. "I needed this." He was shocked at how much. "How did you make this happen without me knowing?"

"A girl has to keep a few secrets." She bit her lower lip, and a small frown marred her perfect skin. "I'm so sorry, Wyatt. For before. For that last night."

"Hey. It's behind us. You're here, and that's all that matters."

"And you're sure everything is good with you? Promise me."

He hesitated. "Hey, I'm good. I am. I just need to be faster than the guy beside me. Better. That's all. That's all it's ever been."

Regan nodded. "Okay."

"Believe me?"

"I do."

He swooped in for one last kiss, and rested his forehead against hers. He hadn't been lying. He needed her more than she knew.

"Blackwell, we need to move."

He nodded and stepped back. "I have to go."

"Wait." Regan reached into her pocket and withdrew a small slip of paper. She pressed it into his hand and kissed him one last time.

"What's this?"

"It's me. Your future."

"I like the sound of that," he murmured.

She smiled, a slow, tremulous smile that made him want to grab her again and never let her go.

"Blackwell." Rob Tracy motioned to him. "Get your ass over here, or I swear to God, I'll put Gilroy in the seat and you can kiss the 500 good-bye."

"I have to go."

"Good luck," Regan said. "I'll see you after the race."

He nodded, and then Rob escorted her out of the pit area. Wyatt shook out his limbs and loosened up as best he could. He made a point of shaking every man's hand that touched his car and then slipped inside. Once the safety harness was in place and he was secure, he made sure his in-car communication was working and then had a look at the piece of paper Regan had given him.

*That which you look for is not behind you. It is in front of you if you are brave enough to grab it.*

He turned it over, and then it hit him. Chinese night at her parents. It was from his fortune cookie. The one she'd pilfered from him.

"All set, Blackwell."

He stuck the paper in the cuff of his race suit and nodded. "I'm ready." He gave the thumbs-up and let the engine roar. It competed with the roar of the crowd and echoed in his head. He took a moment and pushed all of it aside. He glanced up and spied the tattered old picture he always took with him on race day.

It was a photo of his mother on the dock, so young and beautiful. So alive. He tapped the picture twice.

"I've got this."

He cleared his mind and focused. It was all about the race. All about winning. That's all there was.

\*\*\*

Racing was a funny thing. On one hand, the spectacle was big and grand. It was exciting, life and death, passion and living all rolled into one ball of dirty exhaust, screaming tires, and roaring engines.

For so many years, being inside a car, pushing himself and the machine to its limit—that made life worth living for Wyatt. That, and the chance at every turn to beat the man who'd killed his mother. He could never explain it to anyone, maybe because he could barely understand it himself.

Racing had made him meet his fear head-on. And today, with Regan watching, he would win. He unclenched his hands and then gripped the steering wheel. It was time.

The race ran fast and aggressive. By the time he entered the last ten laps, Wyatt was feeling the effects of it. His shoulders were tight, and his neck killed. His hands were starting to cramp, so tight was his grip on the steering wheel, and his jaw ached from clenching his teeth so damn tight.

He was currently sitting second and needed to make a move to take the number one spot. He just had to be smart about it. Wyatt cleared his mind and waited for his chance. It came with two laps to go. The car in front of him took the turn a little too wide, and Wyatt gunned his engine. The speeds were upwards of 160 mph, and he held tight, going for the inside so he could pass.

But the bastard swerved, and…

Shit. He saw Diego. His mother.

"What the hell?" Wyatt shook his head violently, correcting the wheel just in time to avoid a crash. His heart sped up, and he gritted his teeth. He was going to do this. He needed to do this.

*That which you look for is not behind you. It is in front of you if you are brave enough to grab it.*

"Fuck this shit," he snarled.

He pressed his foot down harder on the accelerator, and at the last moment said a silent *fuck you* as he sailed past the first-place car and took the lead.

It was a thrilling moment for those in attendance, one many would talk about for years to come. Wyatt Blackwell's triumphant return to racing and his spectacular, nail-biting win that guaranteed him a pole spot in the Daytona 500.

When he finally managed to pull himself away from the reporters covering the race, and the rabid fans who were literally tearing at the barricades to get to him, he headed for his trailer, hoping that was where he'd find Regan.

He opened the door and found her inside, but instead of the happy face he'd expected, she was quiet, pale, and wouldn't meet his gaze.

"Congratulations," she said softly. "I hear you'll be racing next weekend."

"Hey." Concerned, he took a step closer but stopped when she took one back. "What the hell, Regan? I thought you'd be happy. I needed this win. I wanted this win."

She nodded. "I know." And when she finally met his gaze, he was taken aback at the look in her eyes. At the sadness and...was that fear?

"And I'm glad for you if that's what you want but..."

"But what?"

"On that second-to-last turn..." Tears filled her eyes, and she wiped at them angrily. "I thought you were going to crash. I thought..." She shook her head and looked away. "It was so close. Oh my God, it was so close."

He took a moment, his body shaking from the adrenaline drop. "I didn't. I didn't crash. I beat him."

"This time. God, I had no idea. It was so fast, the cars, the laps." She nodded behind him. "Those people out there, they come to watch you race. Come to watch you defy the odds and take those turns at incredible speeds, and the whole time..." She lost her voice for a moment. "The whole time, they're waiting for something to happen. Waiting for something more than just a car speeding around a track."

He was silent, watching her and hating that he didn't know what to say.

"The woman beside me." She shuddered. "When you took that turn and hesitated, and it looked like you might crash…she poked her husband and ordered him to get his phone out and video. You know, just in case you crashed because they had such a good view of the turn." She shook her head. "I wanted to punch her in the throat, and I think I would have, except her husband moved in front of me to video the turn."

"Regan."

"No. Please. Let me say this before I lose my nerve."

He nodded. "Okay."

"I love you." She smiled then, a half smile that tore at his heart. Her mouth quivered, and she exhaled a long, shaky breath.

"I don't know how or why. You showed up in my ER last fall, and I haven't been able to stop thinking about you."

"Even when you hated me." His attempt at humor fell flat.

"I never hated you, Wyatt. I envied your lust for life. Your need to do everything at two hundred miles an hour. There was never anything halfway with you, and I wanted that. *I still want that.* But…"

"I hate that word."

She attempted a smile and gave up. "But I can't live this life. I don't see how anything could work between us." She sniffled. "Last week, I watched the crash that killed your friend. I saw interviews with his wife and his young child. It was awful. I deal with death all the time. Little boys who will never experience love. Boys who will never go on a date and know what it's like to kiss a girl in the rain because they have cancer and won't live to see their tenth birthday. I hate it, but I understand it."

Her voice broke, and Wyatt reached for her. He held her close, even though he knew she was already drifting away from him.

"I can handle that kind of death, Wyatt. What I can't handle is one that's wasted. This life you live isn't for me, and I'm sad that I can't share it with you."

He froze and took a step back. "What are you saying?"

"I've never wanted to be that girl, Wyatt. The kind would give a man an ultimatum, but I find myself doing just that. I'm sorry. I can't be a part of this life. Not the way you're living it. I just can't."

Anger flared inside him. It was hot and full, and it took everything in him not to put his fist through the wall.

"That's it? You come and watch one race and we're done?"

She reached for him and pressed her mouth against his. But there was nothing in him to give back.

"I love you," she whispered against his lips. "And if you ever decide that you don't need this, this racing and death-defying stuff, you know where to find me."

With that, Regan moved away and left him alone in the trailer. Outside, the crowds were still electric. The campers and tailgaters were partying it up but good. He knew he could go out there and be with hundreds, hell, thousands of admirers. People who were more than happy to talk about the race and his win and the Daytona 500 next week.

Wyatt wasn't sure how long he stood alone in his trailer, but eventually, his legs cramped, and he took off his racing gear. He hopped in the shower and let the hot spray wash over him.

He stood under it until the water went cold.

# CHAPTER THIRTY

Regan spent the week trying not to think about Wyatt or the race or anything to do with NASCAR. She hated her empty bed, and by Friday, she was getting sick of Bella's mournful stare.

"I miss him too," she said, grabbing herself a glass of wine.

The doorbell rang, and she padded over to answer it, surprised to see Carly standing there, and more than a little pissed at her friend as well.

"Wine is on the counter."

Carly helped herself and sat on the floor, placing her wineglass on the coffee table as she looked up at Regan.

"You look like shit," Carly said.

"And you're getting married."

Carly swore. "Dammit. How in hell do you know? I told Jarret not to tell anyone until I'd had a chance to talk to my folks."

"Well, I'm sure they know by now since everyone in town does."

"Well, my parents don't, because they're out of town." Carly sipped her wine. "I'm going to kill Jarret. Who told you?"

"Who else?"

"Abercrombie. Geez, does that guy not have anything better to do with his time than gossip?"

Regan sighed. "He lives alone. Gossip is all he has. Actually, he's been checking in on me every day. Seems to think I'm heartbroken or something."

"You are."

"I am."

Carly balanced the wineglass in her hands, swirling the deep red liquid around. "Are you sure it's over between you and Wyatt?"

"I know I can't live with a man who plays Russian roulette with his life. The way he drives, Carly, it's like the hounds of hell are on his heels. I can't do it. All those people find it thrilling and breathtaking. I just was scared the entire time."

"Well, none of those folks were watching the man they love driving two hundred miles an hour or however fast they go. I mean, it's crazy. They don't think about it the same way you do. For them, it's a way to pass the afternoon. It's a social thing."

"I guess." Regan wasn't about to share the other stuff. The dark stuff that clouded Wyatt's life and touched everything that he did.

"Anyway," Carly continued. "I'm sad for you but hopeful you guys will figure it out. Maybe you just need to attend a few more races."

"Maybe," she murmured. "Enough about that." She leaned forward. "You need to tell me everything. How did Jarret propose?"

Carly squealed. "Oh my God. You won't believe how he did it. It was so cheesy and dumb, and yet I loved every single minute of it."

Intrigued, Regan was more than happy to forget about the crap week she'd had and listen to something good.

"Tell me." Bella hopped onto the sofa, and Regan gently kneaded the dog's shoulders as Carly launched into her story.

"Well, you know what a promposal is, right?"

"A what?"

"Promposal! All the kids do it now. It's an elaborate way to ask someone to prom."

"Oh. Well, I don't feel so bad since I've been out of high school for years."

"Anyway, so Jarret flew out to the West Coast to see me last weekend, and we went to see this play I'd been telling him about. It was at this small community center near where I live and it's about these two gay guys who each think the other is straight, and it's all confusing and funny, and they end up together and—"

"Carly. Promposal. Or whatever it is he did."

"Right." Carly giggled. "At the end of the play when the cast came out to do their final bow, they each had a large piece of cardboard with writing on it. Each one told of some silly story from our past and how Jarret fell in love with me. They sang the words, Regan. Everyone sang the words, and then Jarret stood up and asked me to marry him, the two main leads on either side of him, one holding a yes sign, the other holding a yes sign." She laughed.

"You had no choice."

"I had no choice. I had to say yes." She paused. "We're planning something fairly quick. I don't want to wait. So we're thinking July, and I want you to be my maid of honor."

"Of course." She hugged her friend. "I'm so happy for you."

Her cell rang, and she slid off the sofa. "Let me get this, and I'll grab another bottle of wine." She knew by the ringtone it was Gwen Bergen.

Regan grabbed the phone and pressed the talk button as she searched in the cupboard for another bottle of red.

"Regan?"

She froze and slowly set down the bottle. "Gwen? What's wrong?"

"It's Patrick. We've had to rush him to the hospital." Her voice broke. "Regan, he had a seizure, and we… I don't know. It doesn't look good."

"Where are you? Children's Hospital or here in town?"

"Here. We're here."

"I'm coming. I'll be there as soon as I can."

"Thank you. I didn't know who to call. Brad's out of town. He won't be home for a couple of hours."

"I'm coming, Gwen. Hold tight."

Regan set down her phone. "I'm sorry, Carly. I have to go. We'll have to do this another night."

"Sure, honey. You go and do whatever it is you have to do. I'm fine. I need to hunt down Jarret and kick his ass anyway."

Regan topped up Bella's food and water and made a note to call her mother later if she was going to be at the hospital all night. She wasn't exactly dressed for the hospital, but then she wasn't going there in a professional capacity. Her pink sweatshirt and baggy sweats would have to do. She slipped on her coat and headed to the hospital.

She made it there in record time and immediately went to ICU, nodding to the nurse as she made her way to Patrick's bedside. Her heart squeezed, painfully so, at the sight of him. He was so little and pale and sweet, and there were so many machines and tubes. He was intubated, and Regan hugged Gwen tightly, her eyes on her colleague, Doctor Hanson.

After a while, Gwen let go and sank to the chair beside her son. Regan tapped her shoulder and whispered, "I'm just going to have a word with the doctor. I'll be right back."

She followed Doctor Hanson out to the lounge, and he wasted no time.

"It's not good. We're running some tests, but it looks as if the infection surrounding the lining of his brain didn't respond well to the medications prescribed. I've been in touch with his oncologist at Children's Hospital, and we've started a new drug protocol. In addition, unfortunately, there is tumor growth. He's suffered several seizures and is currently in a coma."

Regan's heart sank.

"I'll keep you up to date, Doctor Thorne, but the family is going to have to prepare themselves for the possibility their son might not leave this hospital."

"Thank you." She turned and walked back to the bedside, sinking to the floor beside Gwen's chair.

"It's bad, Regan," Gwen whispered. "Really bad. I can feel it. He seemed okay, you know?" She smiled through her tears. "He talked to Wyatt yesterday, and they made plans to play Xbox when he's back. Brad's out of town, so he's been sleeping with me, and I thought he was off. I should have brought him in last night."

"Don't second-guess yourself. You can't do that, Gwen. Patrick's a sick boy, but he's also a fighter. If anyone can come through this, he can."

Gwen looked down at her, and Regan's heart crumpled, crushed beneath the sadness in the woman's eyes.

"Have you ever seen someone this sick come back to you?"

Regan slowly shook her head. "It doesn't mean it can't happen."

The two women fell into silence, each lost in thoughts, thinking of things that could have been and might not be.

"Brad will be home soon." Gwen broke the silence as they watched the nurse come in and chart Patrick's vitals. "I think Wyatt should know. I think Patrick would want that."

Throat tight, Regan nodded. "Do you want me to call him?"

"Could you do that?"

"Of course."

Regan left the room and found some privacy in a storage closet located at the end of the hallway. It was nearly eleven at night, and she had no idea if she could even get hold of him, but she calmed herself and called his number. He answered on the first ring.

"Regan."

"Hey," she replied, her throat scratchy.

"What's wrong?"

She squeezed her eyes shut and counted to three.

"Regan? You're freaking me out."

"Sorry. I… Wyatt, it's Patrick. He's in the hospital, and things don't look good for him."

"That can't be. I talked to him yesterday. Told him I'd see him next week. We had plans." She could feel his hurt and anger through the phone.

"It's a number of things, but there's concern over tumor growth, and right now, he's in a coma."

Wyatt swore, and she winced at the sound of something crashing. "Look, I know you have your big race on Sunday and need to prepare, so please try not to dwell on it. Gwen just thought you should know what the situation is, and if there's any change,

I'll let you know."

Silence greeted her words.

"Wyatt?"

"Yeah."

"Please drive safely, okay? Can you do that for me?"

"I gotta go, Regan. Thanks for calling."

She stared at the phone, a little shocked at his abrupt dismissal, and more than a little hurt. She knew Wyatt was upset, and the clinical part of her brain told her to forget about it and move on. People handled stress and disappointment and pain in different ways.

It didn't make it any easier to deal with.

Regan hung her head in her hands and cried. She cried for Patrick. For Gwen and Brad. For Wyatt and all the Blackwell boys. She cried for John and Angel. For Darlene, whose love might have been enough to keep that family glued together, but ultimately wasn't returned by the man who held her heart.

She cried for herself, for the love and the life she would never have.

And then she got up, found a basin, and rinsed her face before heading back out to the ICU and the little boy who'd managed to steal her heart.

# CHAPTER THIRTY-ONE

Wyatt wasn't the kind of man to ask for many favors, but he had no problem asking Stu Randall to borrow his private plane. After he got off the phone with Regan, he'd driven out to Stu's mansion and, over the protestations of his staff, insisted they wake up their boss.

Maybe it was the fact that Stu was half-asleep, or maybe it was because he wanted him the hell out of his house. Whichever it was, Wyatt managed to convince the man to call up his pilot and get things in order so Wyatt could fly home to Michigan immediately.

"This boy, is he going to die?" Stu's own family had a tragic history not many people knew about. His brother, Angus, had been in a farming accident on their ranch. The boy had been fifteen. He'd sustained massive head trauma and had existed in a vegetative state for years. The only reason Wyatt knew this was because one night over a bottle of bourbon, Stu had shared the story.

"Not today," Wyatt replied.

"He must mean a lot to you."

"He does."

"Okay, then."

They didn't talk about the race on Sunday or anything to do

with NASCAR. Wyatt hopped in his truck and headed to the airport, hoping like hell the pilot would be there and ready by the time he made it.

In the end, he had to wait a few hours for a flight plan to be filed and for another pilot to be located. Stu's regular guy had been at a family function and was in no shape to get behind the controls of a plane. By the time he landed at a small commercial airport about thirty minutes from Crystal Lake, the sun was just painting the edge of the night sky in streaks of orange and yellow.

It was cold and crisp and a bit of a shock after being in Florida for the past few weeks. Hudson met him on the tarmac, and he climbed into his brother's truck.

"I appreciate the lift."

"No problem. I was sorry to hear Gwen's son was back in the hospital. We're all pulling for him."

They sped out of the airport. "You talk to Regan at all?"

"She's the one who called."

"Gotta be tough, her job. On one hand, you need to be strong for your patients and their families, but when you have that personal connection, it makes it that much harder."

Wyatt didn't answer. He couldn't shake the echo of her voice in his head. Of knowing she was in pain and hurt and scared for this boy who meant so much to her, while he was in Florida, waiting on a race.

He felt like an absolute shit.

Hudson dropped him at the hospital with the promise to call if Patrick's condition changed. Wyatt hurried inside and headed straight for the ICU. He knew exactly where it was. Hell, he'd spent a lot of time in there after the accident.

He spied Brad at first, talking quietly with a doctor Wyatt didn't know. The nurse behind the desk looked surprised to see him, probably because he wasn't family, but he breezed past her and paid no mind.

He found the room right away. It was the first one just past the nurse's desk. Wyatt put on his game face and walked into the room. Regan wasn't there, but Gwen was beside the bed. When she saw him, she burst into tears, and he didn't stop walking until he was able to gather her into his arms.

He held her long enough for her tears to dry up and for Brad to find his way back. "You gonna be okay?" he asked gently, helping Gwen back to her seat.

"I'm trying to be strong, Wyatt. I'm so sorry you have to see me like a blubbering idiot."

"Don't worry about me. I'm good."

She smiled up a him, her red-rimmed eyes crinkled. "He's going to be so happy you came back." She looked at the bed. "When he wakes up, he'll be so happy."

Brad joined his wife, and Wyatt took a step back, coming up against something soft and warm. He turned around, eyes taking in an overlarge pink sweatshirt, baggy track pants, and the sweetest face he'd ever known.

Her eyes were wide with shock, and her mouth was open. Wide open. But there was nothing coming out.

Wyatt didn't hesitate. He picked her up into his arms and pressed his face against her soft warm neck. She was trembling, and he held her until she stopped.

"You came back," she whispered.

"I did."

She paused. "For how long?"

"As long as it takes."

The four of them spent the next twelve hours with Patrick. They told stories and laughed. A lot. They cried, and they held each other up. Wyatt knew what Gwen and Brad were feeling. Helpless. He knew what that was like because he'd lived it. It was a hard thing to know you might lose someone you love more than anything. And it was hard to be there with them and watch them suffer.

And so they took turns.

By Saturday night, everyone seemed defeated. Wyatt borrowed Regan's keys and headed out for a coffee run and food from Coffee Corner. Angie outdid herself and presented him with enough food to feed the entire ICU staff.

"You just tell them to look after that little boy and make sure he gets well." By the time he got back to the hospital, it was closing in on nine, with snow starting to fall and a cold wind from the north to carry it. His cell rang, but when he saw Rob Tracy's name, he pocketed the phone and grabbed the food.

His body was tired, yet his mind was wired. It was a strange combination, but he tried to forget about it and headed back up to ICU. He set down a coffee at the nurses station, but Claudia wasn't there.

It was then that he saw all the activity near Patrick's room, and he had a moment when he thought he might lose it. Claudia rushed out of the room and headed in the opposite direction, and with dread sitting hard in his gut, he walked to room.

At first, he couldn't see because of all the staff. Gwen and Brad were beside the bed, but the doctor obstructed his view of the bed. Where the hell was Regan?

He stepped inside, unsure and just as scared as he'd been, alone in that car with his mother. One of the nurses stepped back, and he ducked to the side to stay out of her way. And it was then that he saw a pair of dark eyes looking at him. A small boy who was finally awake.

He looked scared, but that wasn't surprising considering the doctor was removing his breathing tube. After that, things were a bit of a blur. He knew Regan was beside him. Her hand had somehow found his. He knew that Patrick was going to be okay. At least for the time being.

It seemed like it was hours later that they were able to sort things out. The change of meds had started to work, and the infection was under control. As for the tumor itself, a CT scan was ordered and the doctor was shocked to see that the tumor was smaller. Not by much, but enough that they were hopeful the seizures would stop.

It was midnight before the four of them were left alone with Patrick. He kept trying to speak, but his throat was sore from the tube. After a while, it was better, and he was able to tell one hell of a story.

He told them that he'd traveled in the night sky. That he could see into his hospital room and saw his parents, Regan, and Wyatt. He wanted to talk to them, but he couldn't. His throat hurt, and his eyes were heavy.

Patrick said he got tired of flying in the night sky and asked his friend why they were up there. He was cold and wanted to go home. His friend told him he could go home, but he had to fight a little longer. So they kept flying.

"What do you mean, fight?" Gwen smoothed back his hair.

"I don't know, Mom. She said I had to fight. She kept saying that, keep fighting. And then when I was so cold and didn't want to fight or fly anymore, she said it was time to go home. She was so pretty."

Gwen kissed her son on the forehead. "She was your angel, sweetie."

"No." He frowned and shook her his head. "That was her name."

"What?" Wyatt took a step toward the bed.

"The pretty lady who flew with me. She had long blonde hair and a pretty smile. She smelled like summer, like the grass in the backyard when Daddy cuts it. She's not an angel. That's her name."

\*\*\*

It was later, much later, when Wyatt tried to process Patrick's words. The kid was finally asleep, and his exhausted parents had been given beds as well. Wyatt was waiting for Regan. She was having one last conversation with Patrick's doctor.

She looked as tired as he felt. No wonder. It was nearly three in the morning. He watched as she shook the doctor's hand and headed toward him. Her steps got slower, more hesitant the closer she got, and he could tell something was bothering her.

"What is it?" he asked, reaching for her.

"Where am I taking you? Are you flying back to Florida?"

"No." He pulled her close so he could whisper into her ear. "You're taking me home, and home is wherever you are."

"Are you sure?"

He knew what she was asking.

"I've never been more sure about anything in my life. I'm not going to lie. I love racing. I love everything about it. But if racing means I can't have you in my life, then I'm good giving it up."

She started to shake her head. "You say that now, Wyatt, but you'll resent me."

"No," he said slowly, as realization hit. "No. I won't. I don't have anything to prove anymore. It's time for me to look ahead and find that future. Thing is?" He nuzzled her cheek. "You're in it."

"I like the sound of that."

He kissed her. "I was hoping you would"

"But what about, your father and...all of that?"

"I don't know." And that was his honest answer. "You're the only thing I'm sure about at this point. I love you."

She dropped her hand into his, and the two of them strolled out of the hospital, looking forward to whatever life was going to throw their way. They had each other, and as long as he had Regan in his corner, he knew he could face anything.

Even his past.

# EPILOGUE

"You never told me about prom." Wyatt leaned on his elbow in bed and gazed down at the woman who'd stolen his heart. His world. His life. She *owned* him. And he was okay with that.

Regan stared up at him and hesitated.

"It's not important."

But it was. He could see that. "Tell me," he said gently. "I know I was an asshole. I was a dumb boy who wanted to get laid, and you weren't the girl for that."

She sat up, pulling on the sheets to hide her nudity. "Why would you say that? Was I that unattractive?"

"What? No. You were always a beautiful girl."

Regan made a face. "I was chubby and wore glasses."

He kissed her nose. "You were still cute as hell."

"Really?" Regan played with the edge of the sheet. "And that's why you asked me to prom?"

Okay. They were getting into some tricky territory here. "Totally."

"You're lying."

He was, but he didn't want her to know that.

"You asked me to prom because you lost a bet to Sean McAdams."

Dumbfounded, he stared at her, mouth open. "How did you know that?"

"He told me prom night. At about the same time I walked in on you with Lana Parsons." She looked away. "Everyone knew except me, and that was hard." She glanced back at Wyatt. "I would have you know, with you, I would have had sex that night. In fact, I planned on it. Thought about it for days."

"I had no idea."

"No. I guess you didn't."

"Babe, I'm so sorry."

She shrugged. "It's not your fault that my juvenile fantasies weren't exactly on the same page as yours. I should have known. God, I should have known."

Silence fell between them, and Wyatt inched closer to Regan. He thought back to that night. To her tearstained face. The mud on her dress. The tear in that same dress.

"What happened, Regan?"

Her lower lip trembled, and she exhaled slowly. "I decided that I wanted to be like everyone else. That I was going to have alcohol and sex." She looked at him and shrugged. "So, I did. I had too much to drink, and I went out to the boathouse with Damien Allero, and I had sex. It was awful because I didn't like him all that much. It hurt, and I was ashamed, and as soon as it was over I ran. I fell down, ripped my dress, and of course, you were the first person I saw right after it happened."

"Shit. Regan, I…"

"No." She shook her head and leaned toward him. "The past is gone, Wyatt. It's over and there's no use dwelling on it. As cliché as that sounds, it's the truth. That night made me strong. As shitty as it was, I was stronger, because I realized that I would never give myself to a boy or a man unless I wanted to. I was never going to settle."

He pulled her in close and rested his chin on the top of her head. "I love you," he whispered. "And I'm sorry."

"I know. But there is something you can do to make it better."

He smiled. "Yeah?"

She nodded. "You know that thing where you…"

"Yeah." His hands pulled the covers back, and he pressed her into the pillow. She gasped when his mouth closed over her nipple.

"And then you…"

His hand was between her legs. "Yep."

Wyatt had his entire life to make things better for the woman he loved. The other stuff? The family stuff? His father? He'd deal with that later. Right now, it was all Regan.

"And then…" She barely got the words out before he slid two fingers deep inside.

"Yeah." He nuzzled her neck.

"God, Wyatt," she breathed the words.

"I got this, babe."

And he did.

## -THE END-

Made in the USA
Middletown, DE
24 July 2019